TROUBLE IN THE GLEN

also by MAURICE WALSH

The Key above the Door
While Rivers Run
The Small Dark Man
Blackcock's Feather
A Strange Woman's Daughter
The Road to Nowhere
And No Quarter
Danger under the Moon
The Hill is Mine
The Man in Brown
The Spanish Lady
Castle Gillian
Green Rushes
Thomasheen James
Son of a Tinker and other tales
The Honest Fisherman and other tales
Son of Apple
Sons of the Swordmaker
The Smart Fellow

also available from Balnain Books by Maurice Walsh,
The Key above the Door and *The Small Dark Man*

TROUBLE IN THE GLEN

Maurice Walsh

BALNAIN

first published by W & R Chambers Ltd in 1950

This edition published in 1994 by
Balnain Books
Druim House
Lochloy Road
Nairn IV12 5LF
Scotland

Printed and bound by The Cromwell Press, Melksham

Cataloguing in Publication Data:
A catalogue record for this book is available from the British Library

ISBN 1 872557 31 7

FOREWORD

When Maurice Walsh produced *The Spanish Lady* in 1943, a novel of wartime murder and romance in the West Highlands, he said that as far as romantic stories were concerned it 'was the last squeeze of the bag'.

But later he produced *Castle Gillian* (1948), which has a horse-racing setting in Ireland, and the under-rated *Trouble in the Glen* in 1950 set in the Scottish Highlands.

This book should be absorbed as a period read, but many of its themes are topical today, the wealthy overseas incomer who purchases an estate in ancient clan lands, his failure to understand the character of the local people, the sometimes all-powerful role of the estate factor, the persistent memory of a Gaelic golden age lasting from the dim centuries until the years immediately following the Second World War, and the life-style and fate of the travelling people, the tinkers, depicted here as still clinging to their old way of life, a pattern which is dwindling fast — and perhaps for ever — in our own age.

This plot of a love affair between the beautiful daughter of the owner and visiting ex-R.A.F. hero and friend of the glen-folk, who takes their side in a dispute with the laird, might seem to have the trappings of melodrama, but like so many of Maurice Walsh's novels it has often surprising complexities and deeps to it. Like so much of his work, it revels in the beauties of the Highland landscape.

He was originally going to call the book 'Marianna in the Glen', but his publishers, Chambers, persuaded him to change the title. Maurice Walsh wrote twenty books, a play, poetry and many articles. Six of his full length books are set in Scotland and *Trouble in the Glen* is the last of his Scottish novels. As well as being successful in Scotland, Ireland and elsewhere in Britain, it also did well in the United States and was translated into Danish.

It was made into a film with Orson Welles and Margaret Lockwood in leading roles, and with Moultrie R. Kelsall and John Laurie in strong cameo parts, all well-known cinema names in their day, but Maurice (rightly) thought it was an inadequate portrayal of his book. He had refused to take part in the planning or production stages of the film because he was sickened over the financial wrangling with the film companies that had taken place when one of his short stories, *The Quiet Man* (from a book of short stories called *Green Rushes)* was filmed and which has now become a cult film.

Maurice Walsh had a fascination for tinkers and they figure in some of his books and particularly in *The Road to Nowhere,* but in *Trouble in the Glen* he makes the point that tinkers fought in the Second World War against evil creeds and they, too, deserve their chosen way of life.

It is worth reflecting on the fact that as tinkers do not belong to settled communities their names are not on war memorials.

Maurice Walsh also had a liking for Spain and Spanish speech (although he never visited there) and the heroines of two of his books have a Spanish ancestry pedigree, as with Iosabel Mengues in *Trouble in the Glen* and Ann Mendoza in *The Spanish Lady*.

The theme of roots is strong in *Trouble in the Glen*: the incoming laird has a Menzies ancestor, and resembles R.B. Cunninghame Graham, the Scots hidalgo, the hero Gawain Micklethwaite has ancestors who came north from England with Queen Margaret and became Scottish, Oliver Dukes, the factor/secretary who also seeks Iosabel's favours, is irredeemably an outsider. The glen folk are nearly all of Norse or Gaelic stock in a way which is fast disappearing nowadays and the incomers from military or specialised backgrounds sensitively adapt and become part of the community.

As with so many of his plots Maurice Walsh drew on real places, in part, for his locations. The house of Luke Carnoch, Gawain's friend, is called Blinkbonny and takes its name from Dufftown, in Moray, parental home of Maurice's wife, Caroline Begg, nicknamed Toshon because that was how she pronounced one of her names, Thomson, when a child. But it is impossible to be dogmatic about the root-origins of some of the hills and glens. There are clear hints of the Western Highlands, and the land dispute centres on the laird closing a road to a town called Greyport and which may be Oban. Maurice was there several times, both sailing, and with his seminal friend, writer Neil Gunn. Some of the terrain could fit Helmsdale or Dunbeath, on the eastern fringe of Sutherland and Caithness — Neil

Gunn territory. Knockindhu might well be Dufftown and Glen Shinnoch, Glen Livet, in Moray.

Like so many of his novels, there is a strong cultural and educational element, carefully woven into the narrative and which comes over so easily to the reader. He may not have intended to write deliberately like that, but his style has that instructional effect. Have a look at the conversation between Iosabel Mengues and the ill child-woman, Alsuin, when they discuss heroes and heroines from literature and mythology, or when he makes Gawain reflect on the meaning of the word *corran*, a shearing hook, and a name for a curved point of land, a nugget which may have stuck in Maurice's mind from sailing past Oban or up Loch Linnhe when on holiday or with Neil and Daisy Gunn. The narrative is peppered with such musings. Time has caught up with some of the plot: corncrakes are no longer so readily heard; but the issues are profound, the characters vibrant, the story-line captivates and the setting is the glorious scenery of the Highlands, depicted with much love, knowledge and skill. It is good to see it re-issued and one hopes for more.

Rennie McOwan
Stirling, February 1994

Chapter I
KNIGHT-AT-ARMS AND HIS QUEEN

I

THE TALL, lean veteran of twenty-nine—but he looked older—leant on the red garden gate, and looked through a screen of young fruit trees at the white, flat-fronted, slate-roofed cottage forty yards away at the end of a concrete path. Red and yellow tulips flamed along both sides of the path.

"One, two, four—yes—seven—no eight—apple trees, and two cherries," murmured the veteran. *"They've grown some. Let me see! Three Bramley Seedlings gone a bit to wood, a Lane, a James Grieve, that spire is a Charles Ross, and two too-delicate Orange Pippins; and the cherries are Morello, I think—'cos the blackbirds leave 'em alone, sometimes. You got a hell of a fine memory, Gawain!"*

The Bramleys were gorgeously pink-and-white in full bloom, the dessert trees just burgeoning, but the cherry trees had already cast their blossom. The lengthening lace shadows of afternoon slept on the grass, and the grass had a brown sole to show that it recently had had its first after-winter cut. Bees were planing busily amongst the blossoms, and making lazy sounds.

A lank, long-jointed individual, probably male, was using an edging-shears along the margin of a tulip bed, but without enthusiasm, and as he snip-snipped he was murmuring grumblingly to himself:

"Dom' the grass whatever! It is tougher nor a pig's ear—"

"No toiler of the soil, yon! Why don't he take his jacket off?" said the man at the gate who had called himself Gawain.

The lank man straightened nine or ten kinks in his backbone, and turned slowly. His long-jawed face was of that sallow pallor that refuses to tan; his eyes were the mildest blue; and a wisp of sandy moustache drooped listlessly over a melancholy mouth. But he had a long, interrogative nose, and one sandy eyebrow quirked antically,

"I'm no' dreamin'—or am I?" he said mildly. "It was a voice I kent long ago."

The visitor pointed a stern finger.

"If that grass got a last cut in October, someone would not be cursing the order o' nature this fine Spring day."

"Ay so, indeed! But how was a man to know that Spring would come again?"

"A man couldn't, of course—not these times," agreed the other. "Would this be Blinkbonny Cottage by any chance?"

The lank man dropped his edging tool carelessly, stepped sheer-legged over the tulip bed, and came down the path, slow-striding and loose-kneed.

"Blinkbonny it is," he said, "and I mind seeing your face somewhere—a nightmare I had. Wait you! Don't tell me. By Hector! It isn't—it is: Sir Gawain Micklethwaite, Bart., Wing-Commander-be-chance from foreign parts. Man-oh-man!"

"Mr Luke Carnoch, I presume?" said the other. "War-lord in Glen Easan, aren't you?"

"That's the Major's fun. Give us your hand."

These two had known each other for twenty years, and had not met for four. The two hands, big and bony, clasped and held over the garden gate, and the two tall, angular men looked at each other unsmilingly. But they were not gloomy men. Luke Carnoch cloaked a lively mind behind a melancholic exterior, and Gawain Micklethwaite had come out from under the shadow of three terrible years.

"How are you all—how's good-wife Kate?" the visitor enquired.

"I'm bearin' wi' her—just about!"

"And Davy Keegan?"

"The Major! Fine—fine! But his new leg's no dom' use to him."

Gawain Micklethwaite hesitated, and then spoke slowly. "And our little majesty?"

Luke Carnoch did not smile, nor did his eyes light up. He said evenly:

"She is no worse, I will say that."

"You have said enough," said Gawain gravely.

"Ay! but summer is coming." Luke gestured a hand. "She'll be in her sunroom day after to-morrow—if this weather holds."

The hand-gesture directed attention to a green-painted, wheel-less omnibus set close against the gable-end of the cottage, its many windows curtained brightly in flowered chintz.

"Manalive!" said Luke suddenly. "I'm no' holding you outside the gate. Come away up! They're lookin' for you."

"Wait! There's Kate." Gawain's hands came down firmly on the top bar of the gate, and gripped.

A youngish, tall woman—they were all tall in this place —had come through an open white door at the head of three sandstone steps. She was wearing a long white linen coat over a man's flannel trousers, and franciscan sandals on slender stockingless feet. She stood a moment, head-high at gaze, threw a hand up, leaped the three steps, and came swinging down the path: a fine figure of a woman, with a near-ugly face and red hair: an adequate, wise woman, and acquainted with life. Before her marriage to Luke Carnoch she had been District Nurse.

Her husband sidled out of her way, and her rich Glasgow brogue caressed Gawain.

"Gawain my darlin'! is it your ain self?"

Is it the same self? wondered Gawain.

Her freckle-backed hands came down on his on the gate; and her strong-boned face stilled as she looked into his eyes. So they stood and looked at each other, and everything was still about them. The blossoming trees made no stir, the laced shadows on the grass were asleep, and the pine trees, down the slope behind the house, paused in their sighing. Then a white cloudlet, high up, moved across the sun, and a sadness—not a gloom—came on the day. And the woman spoke almost in a whisper.

"It was bad while it lasted, Gawain?"

"Bad enough," said Gawain quietly. He could not hide from this experienced woman the malaise of mind that had weighed on him after that terrible campaign in the Jungle, the malaise that had kept him away from Scotland until the cloud lifted.

"But you are all right now, my dear—almost?" she said softly.

He moved his hands, caught hers firmly, and gave them back to her.

"No almost about it, and keep your hands to yourself, you red-headed devil!"

"That's the way to talk to her," commended her husband.

Gawain moved a hand to unlatch the gate but she stopped him.

"Wait! I was afraid one time a woman had nobbled you in a reduced condition. No?"

"No. She married an Australian that one."

"Fine! There was a woman in my mind for you, but I'm not sure any longer."

"Tell her shut her big mouth," advised Luke, moving off towards his edging tool.

Kate Carnoch's hand moved towards the latch, but Gawain stopped her in turn.

"Wait you! Our little Alsuin, she's none better, I hear?"

"She's none the worse either," she told him in a quiet voice. "You'll see for yourself."

"And her father?"

"Davy was quiet for a long time, but once he gets used to his leg and puts a fly on the water he'll be all right." She moved a hand and her eyes watched him. "But where is he going to fish?"

"Fish in them thaar waters, ma'am," Gawain said.

"Another man's fish now—or don't you know?"

"Fish belong nowhere—"

"There's a new laird in the glen, my lad—and he knows not Joseph."

"Our own Scots glen—never!" His arm swept wide. "Never!"

Behind Blinkbonny half-a-dozen little fields—two of them sown—sloped down to a belt of larch in new green, backed by a bulk of deciduous trees just burgeoning. A strong wall, topped by barbed wire, ran away right and left on the near margin of the larch belt. To the left of the cottage the wooded slope broke down into a wide notch, and through that notch, not half-a-mile below, the green seawater of narrow Loch Easan sparkled under the westering sun; and beyond the loch, a steep ridge, red-gold in the bloom of the whin, rose into the sheer craggy uplift of Stob Glas grey and green against the fragile Spring sky. Blinkbonny! Luke Carnoch's house was well named.

The evening thrushes were not yet singing, the rooks were far afield, and, through the afternoon stillness, from far away, came the pulsing sigh of running water. That was where the Aanglas River came cascading down from the upper glen. It was, indeed, fishing country.

The three sandstone steps were hollowed in the middle, in proof of the many footsteps that had mounted them through many generations. At the head of them the open white door led directly into the living-room. It was a long, low room, brightly curtained, and with geraniums in the open windows; and it was cool and shadowed because the afternoon sun had circled away from it. Kate Carnoch leant a shoulder on the jamb, and spoke softly.

"A soger-man hame from the wars, your honour."

"Let me have a look-and-a-half at the black devil!" said a voice of many inflections.

Gawain Micklethwaite brushed by Kate's shoulder, and a big, loosely-built man was on his feet out of an armed windsor chair. His right leg made half a stride, his left trailed and came forward with an automatic jerk; and the big man balanced himself with his hands as if on a narrow plank.

"Oh hell!" he said disgustedly.

He was Norse-Gaelic, with a round, unlined, youthful face, grey eyes, and an uptoss of fair hair. His face lacked colour, but he was not a sick man. Gawain strode at him, caught him at the lapels, and thrust him forcefully but carefully back into the windsor chair.

"I can handle you at last," said Gawain.

His big brown hand ruffled the toss of light hair, and David Keegan caught and held it. The two men looked steadily at each other, and Gawain's eyes did not flicker once.

"'S'all right, Davy!" he said. "It is me myself, all of me."

"Thank the Lord!" said his friend. "Where do we begin?"

"In the wee sma' hours," Gawain said. "At the moment I have an important audience." He lifted his voice. "Where does the queen hold her court?"

A low, happy tinkle of laughter answered him through a half-open door at the back of the room.

"God is good!" said Gawain deeply. His black eyes lit under his black brows, and he ran his big hands down his hollowed cheeks in a cleansing motion.

The floor was cork-matted, and he moved silently across, tapped with one finger, and softly pressed open the door into a room full of light.

Blinkbonny was a bigger house than it looked from the

front, for it was of generous double-width. This sunny room opening from the day-room had a door in the left wall leading to a bedroom, and in the gable-end a french window giving to the bus sun-parlour. The light came through a low, wide window in the back wall. The casement was open, and delicately-blue curtains moved leisurely in a soft draw of air. Through that wide window one could look down at green Loch Easan wimpling in the sun, and across at the gold-and-grey bulk of towering Stob Glas etched sharply in light and shade.

The whole tone of the room was blue-and-cream, and there was very little white anywhere, for white is strangely depressing within-doors. In the middle of the floor, away from all walls, a wide, plain, brass bedstead winked in the sun. And in that acre of bed, under a blue silken spread, lay little Alsuin Keegan, queen to this knight-at-arms, Gawain. She was eleven years of age, and her back had been in a plaster cast for six months.

She was a brown little lass, as had been her mother who was with God, and she did not look to be at all ill. Her brown hair had a lustre, and so had her brown eyes, and there was a freckle or two across the bridge of her child's nose, and delicate colour on the childish curve of her cheeks. But the general impression she gave was of a great and equable gravity: the gravity that only a child can have—or a queen—or one already within the Shadow.

Her arms, in open cream sleeves, were outside the coverlet, and her hands, delicately shaped and not emaciated, were full of a strange vitality as she moved a reading-board aside over a scatter of books.

She made a little controlled gesture of welcome. "Sir Gawain," she said, and her voice was softer and deeper than silver.

He pushed the door to behind him, stood up straight and tall, and his right hand made a slow gesture that shaped itself into a saltire cross.

"At your service, ma'am!"

As he stood there he did look like a knight-at-arms out of his mail: tall and supple, cool-eyed and bronzed, and his black hair, like a close-fitting casque, cut straight across above a black bar of brow; and, surely, those broad hands were for the swinging of a two-handed sword. Those hands had never swung any sword, but they had flung a fighting plane like a falchion.

Little Alsuin drew in her breath with a soft sigh of contentment, and the look of eager welcome in her eyes moved this man who had hoped that nothing would ever move him again; for he had been mentally sick in an unclean and deadly world, and was afraid of emotion.

He went forward now, took one small hand in his brown paw and bent to it. Her other hand came over his, and she smoothed a cool palm over his hard knuckles. Yes, her hands were cool, but, as he held them, a small thread of temperature came to the surface.

His heart hollowed and filled again. Was this girl-child that he loved on her own lonely road? Was some hellish evil, deep down, gnawing away at the life force? Was their little kingdom of make-believe going the way of all kingdoms?

In her very earliest years they had set up their own little kingdom of make-believe, in which she was Queen without a King, and he her faithful Knight-at-arms. It was a lively kingdom, too, and mixed in its origins, for she had been brought up in the Celtic mythology of King Arthur and the Gaelic one of Cuchulain and Finn. To her that kingdom was as real as the day, and she was wont to send out her own champion amongst the Knights of the Round Table or the Knights of the Red Branch, to return victoriously with the very flavour of Romance about him. That flavour was about him now, and he must hide the aridity that life had become.

He wondered if the little one felt his thoughts through her sense of touch. She was smoothing the back of his hand, and her big serious brown eyes were intent on him. Her voice was softly sober.

"It is all right, Gawain! It is all right, my dear!"

He tried to keep the hurt out of his voice.

"Yes, ma'am! It's all right, of course. It's all right."

The pith had gone out of his knees, and he sat down on the bedside chair, and abandoned his hand to her. And she had not forgotten her old habit of patting with her palm, and softly pulling at his fingers as she talked. And all the time that hellish, thin thread of temperature came through. She gestured aside with her chin.

"It was lovely to get your fine letters," she said. "I have them all there."

On the undershell of her bedside table was a neat packet of letters tied in blue ribbon. Gawain had written them over two years, very carefully and painstakingly, translating ugly war into presentable knightly adventure.

"You had great—great—adventures, Gawain, and sometimes in your letters I could feel the heat, and—yes—much fierceness, and the yellow magician with the queer name frightened me one time. Wasn't that silly?"

"No, ma'am! I was frightened too," Gawain told her.

"And no woman at all." She opened her eyes wide at him. "In all your stories there was no princess—no princess at all, Gawain dear?"

"Not where I was looking, your Majesty."

She tugged playfully at a finger. "But, indeed, you are not good at looking. It is myself must find a princess for you."

"And I'll chop her head clean off," he warned her. "A queen is good enough for me."

"But no! You will not know until the right time." She paused and became serious now, pressing his hand between hers. "Listen, Gawain! I am needing you badly. For three months now I am needing you."

"If you do not need me I am no use any more," he said gravely.

"I do need you. There is a trouble on the glen, and this house is not happy. Look!" She gave her chin-gesture towards the window. "You can see the road—my road."

The road he had come by from the bus-stop at Ardaneigh curved round the house and went on into the gap leading to the sea. He could see a hundred yards of it down a short slope of grass, and then it disappeared between bushy banks. It was an oiled, well-made road, a brown streak across the green, but ragged grass and yellow dandelions had encroached on the margin of it.

Alsuin spoke sadly, and her eyes darkened with the pain of childhood meeting sorrow.

"That was my road, Gawain—and all the people."

"As they rode down to Camelot," he murmured.

"But I could look and see—and make stories to myself. It was a lovely road, Gawain—and now it is dead-and-empty. Did you know?"

"A little, but you will tell me." David Keegan had mentioned in a letter that there was some trouble in the glen, but he had not told how it had hurt this little sick maid. Her voice hurried now.

"I used to see all the little lambs, and hear them ba-a—and the sheep-mothers—and the wise sheepdogs running—and the cattle black and dun—and the people of the crofts, and the men going down to the harbour for the fishing—and I knowing every one of them. And at the turn, just there by the bush, they would be looking up and waving a hand to me—not once did they forget—and I used to wave back to them. But oh me! there's no one to do it now." She paused and went on sadly. "And there was the bus—the red bus—twice a day, and it saying toot-toot to me. And now, there is nothing, for three months nothing—only a big—big car hurrying by like a long hound, and saying nothing. Isn't that all wrong, Gawain dear—isn't it now?"

"Wrong, indeed, my little one," he said heavily. *Wrong as hell, my lassie! but what can I do about it?*

"Look now, Gawain!" went on the eager, sad little voice. "Isn't it wrong for people to come into the glen and be no part of the glen?"

"Cut off?"

"No, not that—"

"Beleaguered?"

She chuckled then. "That was one of our long words. But no!—not beleaguered either! A man turning his back—shutting the South Gate, and making everyone go the long-long way round to the sea."

"A tyrant has come into our glen?" Gawain said.

She shook his big hand. "A tyrant! I am not sure. At the beginning he was nice—everyone said."

"That is how tyrants begin—"

"But it was Lukey that began it. Something he said that was not taken back in time. And then all Ardaneigh got angry, and my dad got angry, and everyone got angry—everyone but Lukey, who was so sorry, but has his pride too. I do not like anger, Gawain—it hurts inside me."

"It is not a good thing, anger," said Gawain, who knew.

She put his hand carefully away, folded her own delicate hands below her round chin, and was queenly and wise.

"Anger is bad always. It eats in and in, if it is let—and then one is all lonesome. Look! The Big House behind the gate is lonesome all the time. I know, for sometimes I hear a lady singing to herself in the woods."

Hell and it hot! "A lady singing to herself might not be lonesome?" Gawain said.

"Her songs are proud and lonesome."

Gawain thought this was his cue. "I see! She is held—a captive, you would say?"

"But no! for she drives out alone in her big car. Dark she is—dark and red—and she never waves to me—"

"The devil melt her!" said Gawain warmly.

"That is my dad's voice. You talk too much, sir! Listen! Trouble in the glen I will not have, and I am putting a Task on you—"

"I am on my holiday, ma'am," protested Gawain, meekly enough.

She gave him an imperious brown eye. "You are, but I am not asking much of you—not for a beginning. You will make yourself invisible like you did in that place—Burma—and go looking round and round, and finding out things for me. I don't want much at all, darling Gawain!" she said persuasively. "The road open again, and friendliness, and peace. Peace, Gawain dear!"

Peace! You are wanting too much, my darling. Peace! There is this peace and that peace, but desolation is the only lasting one. He bent over Alsuin's hand. "Have your way, ma'am! I will put on my invisible cloak, and sally out for to behold—"

The inner door was pushed open, and Kate Carnoch came in trundling a dumb-waiter laden with tea-things. Gawain rose to his feet. The evening ritual of Tea was about to begin. Though he had no least inkling of it, he had lightly undertaken a Task that was to lead him far.

Chapter II
THE TROUBLE IN GLEN EASAN

I

KATE CARNOCH hung a full kettle high on the kitchen crook, and built the peats up under it.

"The Bart. will be tired, Lukey," she said. "Send him to bed early! But why am I wasting breath?"

"A habit we have!" Lukey told her. "Would there be a bit of a lemon anywhere?"

"I saw you looking, and you're no' blind. There's three,

and I'll be needing one the morn. Good night to ye!"

The three men sat in the kitchen at the back of the house, so that their voices might not disturb Alsuin, two rooms away. The kitchen was a low, wide cavern of a place, lit by a peat fire that had not gone out day or night for fifty years. The only light came from that fire of peats and bog-pine; and the warm wavering glow gave a sense of intimate cosiness that was old and self-satisfied.

The window was curtainless, and the black-out blinds had been removed, so that the four panes of glass stood out against the iridescent, pale-blue light of the gloaming. Beyond that ghostly glow, far below, the faint phosphorescent gleam of Loch Easan could be seen in the notch of the black woods.

Gawain sat back in a home-made armchair, and could feel the hardness of a springless seat through a flock cushion. This was like old times—not so old, but at the other side of terrible years—with his slippered feet on the warm bricks, and the hunched shadow of himself and his chair alive on the ceiling and against the dresser of old delf on the back wall. On his right, David Keegan reclined in a long chair that creaked as he moved, a pipe between his teeth, and his artificial leg no longer alive with a discomfort that had toes all its own. Lukey Carnoch was busy at a table below an open cupboard, where glasses clinked and a bottle gluck-glucked. He spoke carefully.

"We could be for the first one cold, I'm thinkin'. It is a quart the Major coaxed off Dinny Sullavan up-by at the pub. We told him you were on the home road."

"Every day for a week we told him," the Major put in.

"Try that, Bart.!" Lukey invited. "Small for its age—half-and-half, and plenty o' water."

Gawain felt carefully for the glass. He knew the ritual. They would have one good drink now, and a bigger later on, and a full jorum of punch before going to bed. And there would be a spate of talk, if these two got their heads; and he would try to get the talk going in a certain direction. He sampled his malt whisky twice, first daintily and then deeply, put his glass cautiously on the floor at his side, and felt for his cigarette case.

"It is some sort of whisky I would say," he said judicially.

David Keegan cleared an appreciative throat. "Only two better, but not in this place."

"We ken—we ken!" said Lukey. "I tried the two, and they have their taste."

Lukey sat low on a straw hassock at the fire corner, and rammed cut plug into an almost black meerschaum. He smoked only in the evenings and in his own kitchen, and had miraculously preserved that meerschaum, amber mouthpiece intact, for all of ten years.

No one talked for a while. David Keegan, at ease, smoked and sipped whisky; Gawain, his head over the back of his chair, sent smoke rings curling to the ceiling; Lukey lit his pipe with a blazing splinter of bog-pine, and built up the peat sods with a crooked-thighed, long tongs. There was no sound but the soft sibilance of the fire flames. And then, from Lukey's meadow close by, came the earliest sound of summer, the rasp of a corncrake in the gloaming.

"Ay so!" Lukey lifted a head. "There she goes! Our wee lassie was wondering which would be first—crake or cuck-oo."

Gawain thought he would come in here. He said:

"The young lady you call our lassie was wondering more than that."

"Not that I heard."

"But you should know, Mr Carnoch, sir! She was wondering who was the biggest dam' blunderin' blunderbuss in Glen Easan."

"Dom'! She never put tongue to them words!" protested Mr Carnoch, poking a peat sod into sparks.

"Translated into your own brand of language," Gawain told him. "Someone, but not nameless, got that road out there closed on her—her own road down to Camelot—and she will not have it—"

Lukey sat up and shed something of his melancholy. "Man! did she put one of her Tasks on you?"

"You go and boil your head, Lukey!" Gawain told him warmly. "I'm not pulling any chestnuts out of the fire for you—"

"Dambut! that's mutiny," exploded Lukey. "You're a disciplined man, and orders are orders. They're no' my orders."

"Oh hell! Wait—wait! Will someone tell me why that road is closed at all?" He picked up his glass and cupped it in his big hands. "Go on! I'm listening." He took a small sip. "You begin, Dave!"

Dave threw his head back, and laughed, and his artificial leg twitched spasmodically.

"It is no' that laughin' matter, Major," said Lukey weightily.

"Nothing is spoiled by a taste of laughter," said the Major. "It is so easy to loose anger." Forthwith he loosed a little himself. "Blast all lawabidingness! and blast wooden legs! If the damnonsensical thing that happened happened in a place I know, no road would be closed—or the man that closed it would know all about it."

"We move cannier this side," Lukey said. "But, mind you, I'm no' that sure of lawabidingness any more. Some of the lads up at Ardaneigh, hame from war, will stand just so much and no more, and it takes me all my time to moderate them. Do you know: the river is poached a' to hell—"

"The dom' scoundrels!" mimicked Gawain solemnly. "Was that fresh salmon we had for supper?"

"A gift horse in the mouth, my man!" upbraided Lukey. "What's a bit fish out of the sea anyway? But the grouse is another matter, and I'm feart they'll be picked off, and they no more than cheepers. Ay! and, come September, the darin' ones will be sweepin' the hills for the laird's stags. An' then, some wild lads, ower bold, will be caught by the new head-stalker, an' that'll be a jailin' matter—unless they sink the deevil in a moss-hag. That's the sort o' trouble we do not want. That's the sort o' trouble our lassie doesna want—and you are her knight-at-arms—my canty man!" Lukey finished his drink at a gulp, laid his glass down, and went through the exasperating motion of washing his hands.

But Gawain would not show exasperation. He sipped his whisky, lit a fresh cigarette, and spoke slowly.

"I was only asking for a leetle information, you know?"

Dave Keegan resettled his shoulders comfortably, and lifted a finger.

"You knew this estate of Glen Easan pretty thoroughly, Mick?"

"As well as yourself."

"There have been a few changes, and we'll take another look over the lie of the land."

"Off you go!"

Keegan moved a hand. "You know! Half-a-mile up the slope from here the main road comes through the township of Ardaneigh, and slants down to the Loch, three miles below. That's where the old jetty is, now silted over. And from down there another road comes back by the loch-side to the new pier below the Tigh Mhor, and that's only half-a-mile from where you're sitting—"

"But there's Alsuin's road out there?"

"Precisely! The connecting link, running direct from the township to the new pier—just one curving mile. It was made by an old laird of Glen Easan."

"No—it wasna!" Lukey said quickly. "It was dug and soled by the clan under the old system."

"Yes, but once it entered the demesne of the Tigh Mhor, it became a private road, and was gated and gate-lodged accordingly."

"But everyone used it, and the South Gate was never shut," Gawain said.

"It was shut just one day in the year," Keegan corrected him. "That is the legal requirement to counter a right of way."

Gawain nodded. "Yes, that is quite customary in Scotland where a road runs through private policies."

"Exactly. And do you know of any reason why such a road cannot be shut all the year round?"

"Several—"

"But none in law. That road out there has been closed for three months now."

"And, again, I am asking you why?"

"Just a moment! You know what the closed road means to Ardaneigh—to the whole hinterland of crofters?"

"I can guess."

"Faith, you can! For the sea-road is the only road to market, and the only market: Greyport, eighty miles away. Cattle, sheep, pigs, poultry, corn, spuds, eggs and homespuns, all must go by sea to Greyport, and all consumer goods must come back the same way. That road out there was a busy and a friendly mile, and, now that it is closed, the crofters, to get to the pier, have to go three miles down and three miles back again. Two sides of a triangle longer than the third—and the cause of many a bloody war!"

"And we are back where we started," Gawain said. "Why was the road closed?"

Dave sighted his pipe-stem at Lukey.

"The culprit in the first instance—Mr Luke Carnoch!"

"Not forgetting that Foreign Prince—" began Lukey.

"No!" snapped Keegan firmly. "You'll not blame any

Foreign Prince. If I were he I'd ha' cut your bloody gizzard out."

"He dom' near did," said Lukey.

"Supposing you tell me," suggested Gawain patiently.

"We are coming at it, and the night is young," said the Irishman. "I like to hear myself talkin', but I would need another small lubricant out of the bottle."

"It has to last us three nights," protested Lukey, rising to his feet with alacrity.

They had their drinks, and, again, Lukey sat on his hassock, built fresh peats round the fire, and sighed deeply and resignedly.

"Ayeh me! I'll have to listen to this once more, over and over again. But 'tis no harm to ask a friend hame from war to take off a coupla hunder' per cent for exaggeration."

III

David Keegan resettled his shoulders comfortably, and looked up at the ceiling where the firelight gleamed ruddily and shadows wavered.

"I'll have to go back a bit, but not far," he began leisurely. "Two-three years ago a thing happened in Glen Easan that has happened often all over the Highlands: the last of a hundred lairds sold his estate, lock-stock-and-barrel, and a foreign man bought it. The name of that foreign man is Mengues, which is a sept name of Clan Menzies, and he wears the tartan of white and red, and for a badge has chosen the Larch, that his forbears brought to Scotland two hundred years ago."

"A foreign man, quoth you?" Gawain said.

"His name is Sanin Cejador y Mengues. His grandfather, plain Sandy Menzies, went out, a young man, to Chile—or Peru. I get them two places mixed—the long thin one it is!"

"Chile—no! Peru—Hell! I don't know either."

"It might be Ecuador! Anyway, Sandy Menzies went out to that coast, and made money as money is made, and married a woman of the place claiming pure hidalgo blood, which is always pure even if with a brushful of Aztec—"

"Inca, darn it?"

"Inca or Indian, but pure Spanish all the same. And Sandy had a son, who made some more money, and married likewise. And that son's son, with all the money there is, came home to Scotland a couple or so years ago. He's the new laird of Glen Easan."

"Let foreign man stand, blast him!" said Gawain.

"But *home* to Scotland, mark you! for a drop of Scots blood is aye dominant. He claimed that he was a sept of Clan Menzies, with a chief's blood in his veins, and he acted accordingly. Maybe his nostalgic old grandfather had given him golden-age notions of clans and clan-chiefs; or he might have read Rudyard Kipling on the rights, duties and privileges of a transplanted squirearchy amongst Sussex peasants; or, maybe, he had ruled peon serfs in a patriarchal sort of way; but no one at all could have told him what had befallen a kindly industrial baron who had tried to impose a new culture on an old Western Isle. Anyhow, whatever, here he was in the Tigh Mhor, a kindly, paternal chief, with money *galore* and a will to spend it. And no one hindered him. For why should they? Wasn't he doing good, and rubbing no one the wrong way—yet."

"A patronising sort of cuss?" suggested Gawain.

Lukey stirred on his hassock. "I wouldna say that—no I wouldna!" he said musingly. "He was proud by nature—ye ken? After the manner born, and, man, I liked him fine—and he did a lot of good."

"Even a Highlandman will stand a share of pride if there's a bit good to show for it," said Keegan quirkily. "And there was. Laird Mengues asphalted that road out there; he got a regular bus service running through to the harbour, and added a cubit's length to the pier; he slated black houses, and put a new roof on the school, and had plans ready for a parish hall; he put in the electric light for anyone that wanted it, and dam' few did; he brought in a decent tup or two, and a polled Angus bull to improve the scrub stock; and he raised no rents—"

"He couldna do that," Lukey put in.

"In some cases he could, but he didn't. And then, Mr Carnoch, you threw your spanner in the works—"

"Dom' the spanner!" protested Lukey. "Just a few hot words under great provocation. Mind that! the very greatest provocation."

"They were fighting words, you ould devil, and I'll let Mick here be the judge."

"So will I—he's a friend o' mine," said Lukey hopefully.

"You'll be surprised," Keegan said. "Listen, Mick! It happened three months ago, early on the fishing season. The

Tigh Mhor was full of visitors—it usually was—it is now.
The new laird is hospitably minded, with aristocratic leanings, and he likes his guests out of the top drawer. He gets 'em, too, for folk out of the top drawer are notably hungry and thirsty these times. And he had one real, buck-aristocrat for the first of the salmon fishing: an Aryan Prince, scion of Aryan Princes away back to the time of the great gawd Buddh, autocrat to a couple o' million of some lesser breed without the law. Let him be nameless, but he was the genuine article, of the very highest caste—even if he was a shade off-colour. And he wanted to catch a salmon in the approved way—"

"He couldn't fish worth a dom'!" Lukey said.

"But he was willing for to learn, and he tried his damndest. And that being so, no ordinary ghillie would do to handle him. No, sir! He was delivered into the hands of the Head-Steward, one Mr Lukey Carnoch, who was supposed to know fishing, approved or otherwise, as he never knew his prayers. And there you have him."

"Look, Mister Bart.!" said Lukey appealingly. "I did my best by the Prince laddie—an' I'm no' sayin' he was a bad lad at all. I took him out on the water in a bit skiff, where he couldn't snarl in the bushes or break a barb-and-tip on the stones, and I gave him the rudiments of layin' a fly on the water in a decorous way. Hour after hour I wrought wi' him, and then a miracle—a bluidy miracle—happened. There was the fly—a big eight-o *Mar Lodge*—trailin' deep, and the line loose, and the Prince beginnin' to reel in, when dambut! a fish in a thoosand hooked himself. I'm tellin' you! hooked himself as solid as the gates o' hell. And sich a fish! I saw him—ten times I saw him in the next half-hour! I was as near to him as you. A cock fish, clean run as a new shillin', an' if he was not thirty pounds—"

"Half that, and he's still a good fish," Gawain said.

"Thirty pun' and no' an ounce less! Hadn't I the gaff within an inch o' his navel. Goad! I endanger my 'mortal soul when I think o't." And Lukey, in chagrin, gulped his glass empty.

"You see, Mick? Not a scrap of penitence! And note that our Prince wrastled that whale for half-an-hour—and that's a good long time for a novice. And behold! there was our good friend, Carnoch, sometimes praying and more times cussin', and all the time bellowing instructions, 'Let him run, my bonnie prince—give him more line, your darlin' majesty—keep your point up, your high royalness—gently now, gently, your holy reverence! Lord in glory, dinna give him the butt for a whilie yet! Holy Goad! take in the slack an' we have him, my princely gent—!'"

"Allowin' for a small ex-aggeration, I'm denyin' nothing," Lukey admitted. "My advice was judeecial, I will say that, and, moreover, most of the time, I was playing that bonny fish with the skiff—back an' fore, and up and down, and round and round till I had a megrim in my head—"

"Surely! and at the end of half-an-hour you had your fish at the boat-side, and your gaff ready. And then?"

"Look, Bart.!" Lukey's hands appealed, and his voice was anguished. "The fish was spent, and the white showin'; but seein' the boat close at hand it did the usual thing, gave a bit of a splutter and a final run, but with no power to it. 'Ease him off, Misther Prince!' says I like that, 'an' we have him next time—the best fish in ten seasons.' But what did he do the—! Na! I'm not sayin' it again. 'Come to heel!' says he. 'Come to heel, you—!' A foreign word that sounded bad. And he up and gave one almighty lift an' tug an' heave to tear a mountain up by the roots. Och—och—och—!"

"Och—och, and ochone, indeed!" said Keegan. "For there was the great fish gone, an eight-o *Mar Lodge* in his gob, and three yards of trace trailing after."

"Ay! he was well hookit," said Lukey.

"And then, my dear Sir Gawain Micklethwaite, Bart., a certain irate Highlander, famed for his courtesy, spake the unforgivable words. You'd never guess?"

"Not Lukey—he wouldn't!"

"He did. The serf Carnoch said to an Aryan Prince: 'You lost him now, you big black pugger!'"

"Them's the very words," said Lukey, "and not a word more."

Gawain sat up. His mouth opened, and shut again with a click. There was awe in his voice.

"My God, Dave! He never said that?"

"The very words: 'You big black pugger!'"

"He was no' that white, whatever," palliated Lukey.

"There you are!" said Dave. "He simply cannot see the enormity of his words. To call a Prince of the highest caste a black so-and-so is the final offence. A black! a *hubshi*! a nigger! Blood only can wipe that out."

Gawain pointed a violent finger at Lukey. "How is the scoundrel alive?"

"Because he kept hold of the gaff, and smashed the butt

of the rod an inch from his head. And then our gamecock Prince hopped the unspeakable Carnoch, and the two went down on the gun'le, and over into the water—"

"I saved him from droonin', whatever," said Lukey.

"Like hell you did! The Prince played water polo in Edinburgh, and you can't swim twenty yards. You got a good grip of him, and he hauled you to shore willy-nilly, and you popped his head under more than once."

"Was I wrong to cool the temper in him?" said Lukey indignantly.

"Wrong but judicious, old boy! You cooled him all right. They emptied two gallons of water out of him. It was February weather, and the cold should have killed him, but the ragin' heat of insult and indignation would melt ice; he lived to tear a passion to rags; and a certain dastardly culprit got the order of the boot then and there. It could be that Sanin Cejador y Mengues—"

"Hold it!" interrupted Lukey. "The laird was not at home that day. It was that factor-secretary, Dukes, put me off—"

"And the laird backed him up—naturally. As I was saying, it could be that Sanin Cejador y Mengues was raging, too, at the reflected slur on his pure hidalgo blood, for, if there be anything in ethnology, some great-great-grandmother of his was of a virtue not uneasy with an Inca buck. But how do I know? All I know is that Lukey got his—ordered off the policies, ordered off the whole estate, ordered to vacate this house—"

"I'm still here, I am," Lukey said, "and you'll be noting the same, Bart.—and a dom' nice friend you are!"

Gawain ignored him. "You spoke of blood, Dave! Was the grieved party mollified by the dismissal of a mere underling?"

"Evidently not. He came looking for Lukey, but Lukey was not here at Blinkbonny. Lukey was up at Ardaneigh trying to pacify the boys, and there the Prince sought him. You see, all the ghillies, keepers, watchers, stalkers were recruited off the estate, and when they heard what had happened king-peg Carnoch they walked straight out. They had a meeting that night at Dinny Sullavan's, and Lukey was preaching what he calls moderation to deaf ears. Into that angry pack, many of them back from war, an angry Prince propelled himself, not to be cowed by any bunch of menials of the sweeper caste." Dave's voice coaxed Lukey. "What happened then, Lukey?"

"Nothin'," said Lukey shortly. "Nothing at all! The

young man came to his senses—that's all!"

"There you are, Mick! Lukey won't talk. No one will. A Highland characteristic since the days of Prince Chairlie, but of no meaning any more. But whatever happened, the Aryan Prince disappeared—"

"In the usual moss-hag?"

"I assumed so. But I kept an ear lifting, and heard a careless tongue make remark of a fishing boat that went out with the morning tide—and there was no fishing. And about a week afterwards I read an item in the social column of the *Irish Times*. Yes! It said that Prince So-and-so of So-and-so was staying in the Shelbourne Hotel after a brief fishing holiday in Scotland. Brief is right. He hasn't come back for more. And that's all."

Gawain lit a cigarette, and blew smoke towards his friend. "No, it isn't all," he said. "What did Mengues do next?"

"Do not blame Mengues too much. He came to manhood where peonage was still possible, and, maybe, saw things as he would see them in Chile—or Peru—or it might be Ecuador. He stood by his factor's dismissal of the fellow, Carnoch, and, through the same Dukes, sent an ultimatum to his rebellious myrmidons: *Come back at once, or stay out for good!* And they practically told him: *If Lukey is out we're out, and you can go to hell or South America.* He did neither. He is a man of some character, and stayed put."

"And he had a bite too?"

"He had, but there was nothing desperately vital that he could do—or, perhaps, wanted to do. As you know, the crofters, including Lukey, have security of tenure under an old Land Act. But he turned his back on them, abandoned all his pet schemes, and put the running of the estate into this Dukes' hands—lost all interest, as it were."

"Dukes is his factor?"

"Not quite. The real factor—agent I would call it—is a firm of solicitors in Greyport, and Dukes is a son of the senior partner. But he took control when he got the chance, and the first thing he did, the laird willing, was to shut the South Gate and close that road out there. And that's how things stand at the moment."

David Keegan sat up and reached his empty glass to Lukey.

"Will it be punch this time?" enquired Lukey on his feet.

"Next time. I'm tired of talking, and it is your turn now."

“Dom’ the word!” said Lukey.

IV

Glasses clinked at the cupboard where Lukey was whistling softly to himself. Gawain got to his feet, groped in the corner, put a knot of bog-pine on the fire, and, head down, watched the flames leap smokily. He was wondering what Lukey was going to say. These two friends of his were leading him on, and he would give them no help. Then Lukey stopped whistling and spoke ruminatively.

“That’s how things stand, is it? No, no! Things like yon do not stand still. They keep staggerin’ on, this way an’ that, but aye towards more trouble; and more trouble we do not want. Not in Glen Easan, where there’s room for us all: laird and crofter—and friendly men coming in among us. Ye would agree wi’ me there, I’d say?”

Keegan had finished talking for the time, and Gawain would not be drawn. Lukey, at the cupboard, whistled some more, and clinked a glass with a fingernail.

“Ay indeed!” he said remotely. “And we doin’ our best to keep things from our little lassie! But could we? Her road was closed, and that was plain to be seen, and she knew there was trouble, an’ that troubled her. Ay, did it! Iosa Chreesta! to keep trouble from her I’d burn the Tigh Mhor to the ground—but what good would that do?” He chuckled there. “And then, ye ken, a month ago, the wee lass brightened up wonderful. That was when she heard her knight-at-arms was on the way. ‘I have a Task for him,’ says she—”

Gawain sat down solidly. “What the blue blazes are you doing with that whisky?”

“Makin’ sure I’m gettin’ my share,” Lukey said. “Here she comes!”

Gawain felt for his glass, and took one mouthful. It was a round and pleasant whisky, and was already twisting little maggots of wisdom in his brain. Lukey sat on his hassock, and carefully scraped out his meerschaum. He addressed himself to the Major.

“Man dear, Major! do you mind the gran’ fairy stories the queen used be gettin’ from her knight across the water? She used be readin’ bits o’ them to me for a reward, and I was often wonderin’ if there was anything at all behind them?"

"Dam' a thing," said the Major, looking at the fire through his half-empty glass.

"Man, you'd never know!" half-mused Lukey. "And, anyway, a body, no' named, will be expected to make up another story in the bygoin'—"

"Founded on fact, you would say?" added the Major.

"Will you two bohunks go to Hades?" suggested Gawain. He would take the war to them. "In a fortnight I'll be out of here."

"A fortnight?"

"Just. And I'm not going to waste it talking nonsense and drinking malt whisky. I am here to see Alsuin—"

"Well then! Well then!" said Lukey brightly.

"And in a fortnight I'll be gone," said Gawain firmly, "and I'll not stop until I am five thousand miles away. Got that?"

"You'll be missed," said Lukey quietly.

"Thank you, Luke! And thank you for the whisky too. There's wisdom in it." He grinned. "Would you like some?"

"Whatever you say," said Lukey cautiously.

"I'll say it. This Sanin—what do you call him?"

"Sanin Cejador y Mengues," Keegan told him.

"Is he married?"

"A widower."

"A pity. Any family? A son?"

"No son." Keegan hesitated strangely, and then said: "There is one daughter, I believe."

"Ay! just the a'e daughter," said Lukey carelessly. "What's this her name is?"

"Iosabel, isn't it?" said Keegan.

"No! Ay! that's it," said Lukey.

"Is she the lady who sings in the wood?" Gawain asked.

"Gosh!" cried Lukey in surprise, and added: "She could be."

"I have often noticed," said Gawain sententiously, "that a stubborn man can be got at through his women-folk. A young woman given to sylvan melody will be as sentimental as a dying duck. Did you never try your wiles on her, Mr Carnoch?"

"Goad be here! that one!"

"What's wrong with her?"

"She's prood—"

"You don't like her?"

"Like her! Like her! Why, man—" His voice had

warmed, and then he stopped short.

"Well?"

"She'd cut my gizzard out, she would," said Lukey tonelessly.

"Hope I'll be there," Gawain said. "But you try your wiles on her, brother."

Gawain tossed off his drink and reached his glass to Lukey. "Make it punch this time, Mr Spider Carnoch. I'm for my bed."

But no one went to bed, for an hour yet.

Chapter III
PROUD MAISIE IS IN THE WOOD

I

GAWAIN MICKLETHWAITE thought he would go out for a stroll this fine morning. A stroll—and no more—across a field or two, while smoking a before-breakfast cigarette. And, moreover, his head needed the morning air to clear and cool it. That second punch last night was, probably, a mistake, but, after all, what was one quart of good whisky amongst three growed-up men? Pounding one's ear in a down pillow was never a cure for a thick head. Get out into the air, and souse the thick member in running water: that was as good a cure as any hair of any dog—if no better.

Gawain opened the red gate and stepped out on the brown road, instinctively glancing left and right for traffic. There was not a wheel-track or a hoof-mark or a sheep-dropping on that brown road between its ragged-green edges. And who was he to work a miracle? There were no miracles any more, he told himself, as he lit a cigarette, inhaled deeply, and watched the match burn down to his fingertips in the still morning air.

He spread his feet wide, thrust his hands deep into his trousers pockets, and looked up the slope. The road, fenced by low dry-walls, curved up among stone-fenced fields, and the fields were green as green under a translucent veil of gossamer that glowed like pearl in the shade, and sparkled like diamond where the sun struck. Half-a-mile up, along the breast of the hill, were the croft houses of the township of Ardaneigh: twenty, maybe forty, grey houses in a straggling line, and many others scattered amongst the stone-fenced fields: some of them blue-slated, but most of them thatched, and all of them squat and deep-planted. This early in the morning no one moved about the gable-ends, but, here and there, a plume of peat smoke, delicately blue, rose straight up and faded in the still air. On the hearths, down below, porridge skillets would be bub-bubbling over peat fires.

Away behind the houses the slope rose in easy ridges, dappled with the yellow-green of young bracken and the orange-gold of the whin, and curved over into a brown crown, beyond which, miles and miles away, lifted up, purple-blue and aloof, the saddleback of Corran Aiternach. And above the Corran stood the morning sun with one bar of pink below it, and a film of pink above.

Seven o'clock in the morning, and warm for that early hour—or was that only the heat in Gawain's head? No, this was that short spell of salubrity that sometimes comes before summer is ready. There might be ground-frost next week, and Lukey Carnoch cursing himself out of bed at dawn to water his potato shaws. But the air this morning was washed and clear and young and fresh, not like the air in the Jungle that was always old and stale, and perfumed to hide decay.

This, indeed, is the place where peace should be and not trouble. Peace and a new civilising force. No, not civilising! Civitas *a city—that is the wrong word, and has in it the spores of decadence. Who was it that contemptuously said there was no trace of civilisation in the Highlands away back in the seventeenth century? There was something better, and now it is dying—dying in this glen too; and Gawain Micklethwaite can do nothing about it. . . .*

That was Gawain thinking as he drifted down the road. He could not go far in this direction, today, but not so many years ago this was the way he regularly went for a morning dip in Cobh Echlan. He had no thought of a dip this morning. What was the old saying: "*April and May, keep away from the say!"* And, anyway, he couldn't get down to the cove, and, besides, he would not start anything that he couldn't finish.

But, still, he kept drifting along, hands in pockets, head down, smoke curling about his ears. If he looked up he could see the back of the house now, with its four windows blank in the morning, for the sun would not be shining on them yet awhile. One of the four, the far one, would be little Alsuin's, open at the top, but, surely, she would still be asleep at this hour.

The road dipped and curved before him, and the banks, grown with bramble, lifted and steepened. This would be about the spot where the little lady would get her first or last glimpse of wayfarers—all the friendly people waving hands to her. He turned then and looked up; and there was her blank window, and it *was* open at the top. He could not see into the room with any clearness, but, against a cream and blue background, he caught a yellow gleam that he recognised as the brass rail at the head of her bed. If she were awake she could see him, and would expect a morning salute. Better make sure! He lifted right hand above his head and wagged it cheerfully.

By the powers! She was awake and watching. That was the white of her arm signalling back in that live way she had. The poor little mite! Lying awake and still and watching! Lying awake how long? Watching the dawn come in, watching the light seep through the woods and over the water, watching the brightness of Stob Glas facing the sun, waiting for the sun to come round to her side of the house, waiting for a friend to wave to her from her lonely road? And patient as death is patient.

Gawain felt a small knot in his throat. He lifted his hand again, made a saltire cross in the air, turned, and moved out of sight into the dip of the road. For a moment he had thought of mounting the short slope of grass and talking to her through the window. But, no! Alsuin would not want that. He knew what Alsuin wanted done this morning. And he did not know how, in heaven or hell, to do it for her.

He went slowly round the easy curve, and there was the closed South Gate of the Tigh Mhor obdurately facing him. It was a double-winged gate, ten feet high, with a concave top, and blunt spikes projecting through a solid bar. No flimsy obstacle this. It was meant to keep people outside, or hold people securely within. And Gawain was outside.

Hands still in pockets, he leant shoulder against close-set, perpendicular steel bars, and looked through. Inside, and to the left, was a one-storeyed gate-lodge with a chimney on each gable-end. The door was shut and the two windows blinded, but from the far chimney a plume of smoke drifted blue against the bright green of a larch. A broad drive, arched over by smooth-trunked beeches, ran away, line-straight, for some two hundred yards, and then dipped out of sight. Beyond the dip, under the arch of polished green foliage, Gawain caught a glimpse of the sparkling, salty green of Loch Easan.

This is a place I knew of old, thought Gawain, *and now it is closed against me—the domain of a foolish tyrant and a woman that sings in the wood—blast her! And a certain little one wants this gate open, so that friendly men shall move under her eyes—down to Camelot. Alas, the day!*

He straightened, grasped two bars, and shook at them powerful-handed. *Open sesame!* But that gate did not open; it did not even rattle a protest, but seemed to stiffen obstinately against his hands. He stepped back and looked up.

You dumb brute! I could show you a trick learned in war—and bedam! but I will.

The hard thing he did then looked easy. He stepped further back, flexed his knees like a stiffly-taut bow, and took the air. A toe-tip found the cross-bar at the middle of the gate, and thrust him upwards; his hands reached towards a couple of blunt spikes; and he pivoted over in one smooth movement, dropping ten feet, and yielding to the shock until his fingertips touched the ground.

That for you! he said, straightened up, and faced round to the lodge. The lodge gave no sign.

Gawain gave it plenty of time, for he would not play sneak for any lodge-keeper. Then he lit a fresh cigarette, again thrust his hands into pockets, and in an easy slouch strolled along, dead in the middle of the drive. The morning sun, shining aslant through the beeches, made a laced pattern on the brown road, and Gawain's own shadow drifted across the lace in front of him.

He had vaulted that gate merely to show that he could; and here he was, now, in forbidden territory. What would he do next? He knew that too. He would stroll down and look at Cobh Echlan, and, maybe, give his hot head a douche in salt water. That was all, and not a thing more—even if he had to make up a bit story to please Alsuin.

But would he get as far as the Cobh? Probably not! For here came one that might dispute the way. A big, brawny fellow had come hurriedly up over the dip in the drive, striding along close to one margin after the manner of hireling men. If he had any authority he might tell a trespasser to *get to hell out of here*. And Gawain would hate to be rudely ordered off a place that had once been free to him.

Take it easy, my lad, he advised himself. *Just stroll along in the middle of the road as if completely at home in a friendly domain.*

He saw that the man coming was in working overalls, and evidently a mechanic, a smudge of oil on one cheek, and his hands greasy.

What the mechanic saw was a tall, lean, brown-faced man—and arrogant as hell—in a black high-necked polo jersey, grey flannel slacks, and with rope-soled sandals on bare feet—and his black helmet of hair should ha' been cut weeks ago. *No one but a bluidy gent would go round like that!*

"Good mornin', sir!" said the man, lifting a finger, and going by without stopping.

"A fine morning," said Gawain agreeably, and went on pacing.

But behind him he heard the footsteps slacken and stop, and a voice lifted.

"Beg your pardon, sir!"

Here it comes! thought Gawain, and swung round boldly. His craggy face was more intolerant than ever, and it made the mechanic hesitate before speaking. But he said:

"Might I trouble you, sir, to do me an obligement?" That was a Scots voice, but not Highland.

"Why not?" said Gawain. *Of course! The Tigh Mhor has visitors, and I am one of them out for a morning stroll.*

What the mechanic thought was: *Another o' they gents, pride an' bawbees stiffenin' his backbone—out to waylay Miss Iosabel by accident—as it might be. Ah well! he might serve my turn.* Aloud he said:

"Miss Iosabel—Miss Mengues, sir! You'd oblige by giving a message from Thompson—the shover, sir?"

Gawain moved a hand. "Miss Mengues—she is to be found?"

Dam' well you know! "She is out riding, sir. Her car will be ready for noon, and she wants to know. I'll be back at it in ten minutes after a bite o' breakfast."

"Go thou and bite," Gawain said. "If the damosel be

encountered—which God forfend—the word shall go forth."

Another bluidy foreigner, by dam'! "Thank you, sir!" The man Thompson lifted a finger, and went striding away rapidly.

Gawain went striding too, but leisurely, and smiling a little. *Miss Mengues—Isabel—no, Iosabel! That might be Highland, or it might be Spanish! The lady that sang? And out ariding? But no one was singing this morning! It takes a good man—or maid—to lift voice of a morning. I couldn't myself—not this morning, and damn punch!*

He came to the dip in the drive, and there he paused, boldly at mid-road, to look over a scene that he well remembered. The road he stood on went straight on down the slope, and at the end of it he got a glimpse, through the thinning trees, of the green waters of Loch Easan. The pier was down there. But another road, just as wide, branched off on the left, went between open ornamental gates, and curved deeply across a wide lawn to the front of the Tigh Mhor. That Big House stood high on a balustraded terrace, and towered to six storeys: a big house, a wide house, and yet too tall for its width. Scots baronial of the glen's grey stone, with tall narrow windows, steep roofs, pointed turrets, and massive chimneys. A solid tall house, but not beautiful, yet the grey solidity of it toned with the grey bulk of Stob Glas across the water.

Hello! someone has been making improvements. That'll be a sun-porch, I suppose.

The front of the house, left of the porch, from wall to balustrade, was covered in with glass, and the morning sun shone through it to show cream walls at the back and open windows. No one moved in there yet; not even a gardener worked on the lawn, where clumps of rhododendron cast long shadows. Gawain had the whole place to himself.

II

Gawain had not the whole place to himself. A thud of hooves on packed gravel, and he turned quickly. There was a third way through the woods. It was a track, not a road, coming down amongst humplochs of young bracken, and debouching on the other side of the drive. That track led to Cobh Echlan, and he had helped to make it. When the old laird had opened his private cove to free bathing, Gawain had engineered that track, and a squad of volunteers from Blinkbonny and Ardaneigh had cut it through waist-high undergrowth. It was wide enough for two to walk abreast, and the branches of overhanging trees had been lopped so that a horseman could ride through. A horsewoman was using it this morning.

She was riding a chestnut of the polo-pony type, riding easily, American style, almost standing on long stirrups, and her back arched forward a little. She had come round a hillock of bracken, and her eyes were at once set on Gawain. And Gawain's eyes were set on her.

This is the proud one. Was it Lukey said that? My certies! The most intolerant scrap of enzyme I have ever seen.

If the young horsewoman had any thought in her mind it might be: *Who is this truculent, arrogant, black-avised fellow holding the middle of the road?*

Was it the shape of her face that made her look so intolerant: broad and, somehow, foreign-looking, with fine black brows down-slanted, strongly-moulded cheek-bones, and a nose, not hooked, but flattened a fraction of a degree over the short upper lip and full sullen mouth? It was that slightly flattened nose and full mouth wherein the intolerance lay. Real intolerance is never thin-lipped.

Her face was not made-up this early in the morning, and it had a fine clean pallor touched with cream. And, foreign though she looked, there was nothing foreign about her eyes, which were only so big and not black; they were the colour of a sloe that is not quite ripe, and they had a directness that showed her Scots blood.

A brilliantly-scarlet kerchief loosely held down her black hair, which was not crinkly, but strong and inclined to wave. She wore a white roll-collared pullover, fawn doeskin breeches, scarlet riding boots, and, yes! scarlet long gauntlets. On her feet she would be reasonably tall, and she might be an inch too wide in the shoulder, and a curve too full in the bust.

A nicely-sexed young woman, and she has her looks! thought Gawain. *Once on a time I'd ha' kissed that mouth and taken a chance!*

She did not check or urge her pony's easy pacing. Her way to the Big House led a yard in front of Gawain, and she came out on the drive, looked through and beyond him, and rode straight on.

Begod! She'd ha' ridden ower me if I was in her road. And would she bid any man the top o' the mornin' in the young o' the day?

Gawain was forgetting his own duty of courtesy on a fine morning. But she had come out of his own track, no longer free to him, and she had ridden by as if he were invisible. His mouth twitched. Maybe he was wearing his invisible cloak after all. *Fine! Let her gang!*

Suddenly she changed her mind. She did not look over her shoulder, but a knee twitched, a red gauntlet moved, saddle-leathers creaked, and the pony was round facing him. She looked more intolerant than ever.

I'm for it! thought Gawain. And she said:

"Who the devil do you think you are staring at?" Her voice was deep for youth, and it had a flowing cadence not unfamiliar to Gawain.

It was a fair question. He had been staring at her underbrowed, and he did not know how arrogant had been that stare. A tall, black-browed fellow, whom she did not know, waiting for her at mid-road, and staring insolently at her in her own grounds—and not even saluting her with a friendly word on a fine morning. He was not a visitor, she knew. Then who was he, and what was he doing here?

Gawain threw up his left forearm to his chin, and lifted a cautious head, as if he were looking at an adversary over the rim of a shield.

He spoke almost in a whisper. "But a moment ago I was invisible."

And she said, her voice lifting a little:

"Who the blue blazes are you?" Her Irish governess had had the Irish habit of using cuss words with abandon.

"She sees not the blazes—I mean blazon—on my shield?" Gawain said. "Hold it! Keep the lid on! There is a message from yonder varlet." He glanced over his shoulder. The mechanic Thompson was standing in front of the gatelodge gazing their way. "He would have you know that a headless carriage awaits your pleasure at the hour of noon."

Her brows did not once twitch or frown, and the immobility of her face was the immobility of an old race. She said calmly:

"You are insolent—or a fool."

"Insolent I hope not!—but foolish alas!"

She moved a scarlet hand. "You are not a visitor at the Tigh?" She used the Gaelic guttural that is more than *g* and not quite *gh*.

"Not at that Tigh," Gawain told her. "In that tall house dwells one who is lonely in all his company—and a damosel who sings in the woods. Art thou that one? Or ride thou like that Woman who hath no Mercy? Indeed, you have the looks and the shape, riches greater than beauty, but beauty you have too, and beauty is aye sad and often merciless. You are sad, and your mouth is sullen, and pride is always sullen. The Tigh I sojourn in has an open door, and friendliness within—and, alas! a little sadness too. It is your turn now!"

She had not sought to interrupt him. He had spoken, looking over his forearm, his carved face wholly grave, and his voice rolling resonantly; and his words had a meaning that was only half-hidden. And those black eyes under their black brows had some queer holding quality.

There was a thrush singing somewhere, and the trees were hushed, and this was no longer the middle of the twentieth century. This was an old, old wood in an old land of an old culture, but life was young and surgent, and this strange madman touched her where she lived. But she touched Gawain in turn, for, at the back of his mind, he realised that her mouth was not really sullen but was part of a strange, foreign comeliness to make it alive and desirable.

Don't be a dam' fool, me lad! thought Gawain.

Then she surprised him. She flattened a scarlet hand at him and said:

"Put down your shield! You are foolish, of course—but not insolent, I think. Who are you? What is your name?"

"Ho-ho! possessing my name you would hold power. But your name I know. You are hight Iosabel."

He had aroused her curiosity now. She said:

"Whoever you are, you are a trespasser?"

"Go to! who is the trespasser?"

She found herself using his medium. "Now you are insolent, for I know your meaning, and I also know your myth of the secret name." She pointed a finger at him. "But today your name is trespasser. You will give me your other name, or you will come with me now to the Tigh, and my father will take your name. Come!"

Her knee twitched, and the pony's head turned away. Gawain threw a hand up.

"It is a road I might take with you, but I obey only one queen at a time. Go in peace!"

He turned on his heel, strode across the road and into the mouth of the track to Cobh Echlan. There was a clatter of hooves, and the pony's head was by his shoulder.

Good job she hasn't a switch, said Gawain.

One broad hand caught the pony's head by bridle and snaffle ring, and the pony went back on its haunches. The young woman swayed lithely in the saddle, tightened her reins, and gave her mount both heels. The pony reared, but that powerful hand brought it down again, and forcefully backed it out on the drive. The lady tipped and swayed, and felt maddeningly helpless.

"Let that pony go, you brute!" she cried at him.

"Begone!" he blared up at her. "Begone! Or I will take you down off your fine horse, and close your mouth with the kisses four. Go thou!"

He almost lifted the pony, stepped away, and brought a hard palm smack on the round croup. And the pony went cavorting from there.

Then Gawain turned and marched off down the path to Cobh Echlan.

Iosabel, daughter of Sanin Cejador y Mengues, like a slip of steel in the saddle, checked her mount, but only for a moment. She was possessed wholly by a sense of outrage—a fine honest sense of outrage that was as Highland as it was Spanish. She and her pony were no match for that nameless madman—him and his kisses four—but blast him! she must not let him get away with such insolence. And the first thing to do was to find out something about him.

On a tight rein she gave her pony both heels, and it went bucketing down the drive towards the South Gate. Thompson, her chauffeur, was bucketing along too, flag of battle on the breeze. *Begoad! he would take it out o' that dom' foreigner, gent or no gent.*

The lady pulled in her mount with a slither of hooves, her back arching like a bow, and Thompson got out from under.

"Did you see that—fellow, Sam?"

"I saw the—I saw him, Miss Iosabel."

"Where did he come from?"

"The Big House, would it be—?"

"No, it isn't. Yes, you thought it was—I got your message. But where did he come from?"

"He was walkin' the middle o' the road as if he owned it."

"He thinks he does."

Thompson gestured suddenly with a greasy fist. "By dom'! Your pardon, Miss Iosabel! The only other place about here is Lukey Carnoch's."

"Lukey's!" She sat up. Personally she had nothing against Luke Carnoch. Luke was all right, but he and her father!—and she was loyal to her father—

"Major Keegan, Miss—"

"I know Major Keegan. This devil has two sound legs."

"What I mean, Miss, the Major, I hear tell, was expectin' a soldier friend yestreen—frae the East I think it was."

"And tanned as leather. You know his name?"

"N-o-o, Miss!" He had heard the name, but wasn't sure; and, anyway, when he came to think of it, he wouldn't want to get any friend of the Major's—or Lukey's—into trouble.

"All right, Thompson!" She pointed a scarlet hand. "Could he have got over that gate?"

"A tough job, Miss!" said Thompson with some feeling. He turned head to look at the tall gate—and to hide a grin. His mother was lodge-keeper, and kept a tight hold of the gate-key to hold her innocent slob of a son—as she called him—from night rambling; but twice a week the same son climbed over the gate, to the detriment of his pants, for a bit of diversion at Dinny Sullavan's pub.

"If he got his bear's paws on top!" half-mused Iosabel Mengues, remembering the powerful hand that had lifted the pony under her.

"Sure enough, Miss!" Thompson agreed. "Is there anything you'd want me—"

"No, Sam! Get the car going—I'll attend to this."

She turned her pony around and rode off, not bucketing this time, but soberly pacing, and her thoughts busy.

A soldier from the East, a friend of Major Keegan's and staying at Luke Carnoch's? Very probably! And he was of the Highlands, that was clear. And here, in her father's demesne, he had made fun of her, using archaic language to puzzle a foreign interloper—damn him And yet! there was a meaning in his words, and—yes—a hint of a warning too. He would know of the trouble in the glen, but he would know only one side of it. . . She had no part in that trouble—it was folly—but there had been rank insubordination—and she was loyal to her own. And she would not be made fun of . . . in her own grounds! . . . A fresh thought made her throw up her head, and then she chuckled. But this was fine! This had lifted her out of the doldrums on a Spring morning! This was better than playing round with that herd of tame visitors! This was a new game worth playing. . . . But she would have to move very carefully. . . .

She came to the dip of the road, and, without hesitation, turned her pony into the track leading to Cobh Echlan. She was ravening for her breakfast, but breakfast could wait, and this interesting shield-striker might not.

And as she ambled along the path so nicely graded among bracken mounds, a high, clear, anguished yell came up to her from the Cobh.

He has fallen in, gracias a Dios! she said, and gave knees to her pony.

III

Meantime, Gawain had got down to the cove through the thinning trees and over a final ridge.

Cobh Echlan was the very head of Loch Easan. It was nearly circular in shape, and looked to be land-locked. Away on the right the crystal waters of the Aanglas came cascading down from the glen, and the soughing pulse of them reached Gawain's ears. On his left, a low promontory, mostly solid rock where red valerian got a scanty hold, ran far out to narrows that he could not see, but he knew how the tides raced in and out through that throat not a hundred yards wide. Beyond a half-mile of water the flank of Stob Glas, golden in whin, rose to the bare uplift glinting greyly in the sun. A narrow band of pearly mist bridged a corrie high up, and another, above the blunt stob, was fading out in the blue abyss.

Gawain knew this cove of old. He looked around him. *More improvements!* he thought. *Like giving a child a cake and taking it from him in a pet!*

A big, roomy bathing house had been built at the back of a concrete platform jutting out from the flank of the ridge. Wide, easy concrete steps led down to the shallows, and at one end a long diving-plank projected out over deep water.

He sidled down over a bank of shingle to the sickle of brown sand margining the shore. The sand was dry, and ran and crunched under his rope soles. The tide was barely moving. A small ripple lipped in, drew back, met another ripple, and made little wrinkles of commotion that cast shimmering reflections on the sunlit bottom. The ripple, the shimmer, the lovely translucent faint-green of the water were enticing.

A neap tide almost full, but how cold?

He kicked off his sandals, and dipped forward an inquisitive toe. The shock and tingle went up his leg, thudded within his breast, and made his breath flutter. But the water was not really cold here, over the sand that had absorbed a week's sun.

Gawain drew his flannel pants up at the groin, slipped in ankle-deep, and moved shuffle-foot along the shore towards the steps leading up to the platform. The water, washing over his insteps, had a pleasant tingle now, and he wanted to go in deeper.

I could do worse, and, if I put my head under, the water will sizzle. We used to go in here without togs in the old days—and the prood lady is awa' hame a flea in her lug. He hummed the old Scot's ballad:

> *"Prood Maisie is in the wood,*
> *Walking so early,*
> *Sweet Robin sits on the bush*
> *Singing so rarely,*
> *'Tell me, thou bonny bird,*
> *When shall I marry me?'*
> *'When six braw gentlemen*
> *Kirkward shall carry thee.'"*

He mounted the steps to the platform, and his feet left wet marks on the cool concrete. The bathing house at the back had two windows closely blinded, and a green door with a Yale lock; the use of it would be confined to the privileged. A teak bench ran along the front below the windows, and there Gawain sat him down. The sun was warm on his outstretched feet, and he moved his toes like a pleased boy. After a time a hand moved up to the neck of his polo jersey.

April and May, keep away from the say! he murmured. *But a'e plunge, and a fellow would be ready for his breakfast.* The last words were muffled in wool.

Standing naked on the coir matting at the end of the diving-plank he was a fine, long, lathy, sinewy shape of a man; but his colour was startling, and showed how nearly naked he had gone in the Jungle. From mid-calf down his skin was delicately white; to high on his thighs it was brown as a nut; his lean buttocks were again white, his back brown, his long neck red-brown, and his hands were teak below walnut forearms. Skewbald is the word.

The air was cool on his naked back, and he had no desire now for the chill of the water. But hesitation would not help. He drew in a long breath, brought his arms forward, and fell in neatly.

His black helmet bobbed up within a second. He shook it furiously, and loosed a bellow with all his might. That was the bellow that Iosabel Mengues had heard—and he had fallen in, sure enough. A good yell does help after a cold plunge.

To counteract the numbing sting he went up the loch in a trudge, turned over on his back, kicked the water furiously aboil, went off in another sprint, and then slanted inshore in a leisurely breast stroke. His breath was coming fast now, and his coursing blood subdued the chill. He kept swimming easily till he saw the bottom under his eyes. The water here over the warmed sand was delicious, and he back-pedalled, thrust his legs forward, and sat on the bottom, the water just above his navel. He smoothed the water down off his arms, ran fingers back through his hair, and glanced casually down the shore towards the bathing platform. His mouth opened, but no sound came.

Jumpin' Moses! She's up for the second round!

He caught only one glimpse of the figure that dodged and disappeared round the end of the bathing house, but there was no mistaking that white pullover, the scarlet kerchief, the red hands and feet.

She has me at a disadvantage, said Gawain, *or has she? I hope to Saint Bothan, my patron, she is not handy with a piece of rock!*

He crab-crawled into deeper water, and breast-stroked back, head well up and eyes watchful. Opposite the spot where he had left his sandals he trod water, and lifted up his voice.

"Home, tinker! I'm coming out."

The woods gave no sign or sound, and Gawain grinned smugly. She was evading the naked issue.

He came to land boldly then, brushed the sand off his feet, and slipped them in his sandals. He slapped some water off, sprinted fifty yards up the shore and back, and mounted to the platform by the flank where the path joined it. There he sat down on the bench near his clothes, and let the sun pour into him. His headache was gone, and there was a nice and well-known emptiness about his middle. Just one after-swim cigarette, and he would do justice to Kate Carnoch's breakfast.

His cigarette case and matches were in the hip-pocket of his flannel pants. He reached a hand towards where he had tossed them, and paused. His eyes batted, his hand remained poised, and there was dismayed awe in his whisper:

Bothan, you ingrate! You never would?

He picked up his shirt hastily, and put it aside. He laid his brief trunks on top, and then his black polo jersey. And that was all. He blinked his eyes, but there was no blinking the fact. His flannel trousers were missing. They were not on the bench, or under it, or on the platform, or afloat on the loch. They were not there. They were gone.

Gawain sat down on what was left of his clothes, as if to make sure of them, and contemplated the obvious. A fine smug feeling he had a minute ago, contemplating a proud and proper lady beating a modest retreat! Proud and proper! But with an antic streak—an imp hidden away for a suitable occasion! And the occasion had arisen—and here he was! He lifted a humble hand.

I concede that second round, he said, *and I ain't ready for a third—not today—not in my shirt-tails.*

He chuckled then, for he had an antic quirk too, and he could see his long, skewbald legs propelling him along the drive, shirt-tails fluttering. He could see himself vaulting over that cursed gate; and, sure as shootin', the shirt-tails would catch on a spike, and he would dangle a shame in the face of the day.

He threw back his head and laughed at himself. But he stopped suddenly, and dismay crept into his face. Murder! how was he to transliterate this, yes, catastrophe, into a knightly adventure for that queen of his? Pants and shirt-tails and skewbald legs into the panoply of chivalry! It couldn't be done—or could it? It might, if he took it as the dolour that always befell the knight at the beginning of the Task. As it was, this story had a beginning, but no end. Did he want an end?

His mouth shut like the proverbial trap, and his brows came down over intent black eyes. He put his hands between closed knees, and contemplated the concrete between his lean feet. He had been given an invitation as pressing as most, and had been thrown a challenge as direct as any; and it was a knight's duty to answer both—to call the bluff of this antic imp in the shameless manner in which it had been made. After a time he rose to his feet and reached for his shirt.

Dam' fool! he addressed himself bitterly. *You'll land on your ear this time.*

Chapter IV
THE LION IS NOT BEARDED

I

A NUMBER of people—half-a-score at least—were having breakfast in the sun-porch at the Tigh Mhor. The warmth of the morning was tempered by the freshness of the air flowing in through the open casements. The original flags of the terrace had been sheathed in plastic to resemble brown parquetry, and there was a plentiful scattering of hide-rugs. The porch was usually reserved for afternoon tea and evening drinks, and there were many small glass-topped tables. It was this early spell of fine weather that had induced the guests half-out-of-doors from the rather gloomy breakfast-room.

Breakfast, as in most country houses, was a movable feast. Guests drifted in, helped themselves from hot-plates, and chose a table at random. And there was not much talk. Most of the guests were up for the trout fishing on the hill lochs, and anglers do most of their talking at night—over the decanters—and are rather grouchy in the mornings.

Sanin Cejador y Mengues was there. He had been up early, was not a night-drinker, but also he was not an English-breakfast man. He was sitting on the sill of an open window, drinking black coffee, and talking business to a large young-man-in-homespuns wolfing kidneys and bacon.

Daughter Iosabel was there too. She had been up even earlier, and had now changed into a short-sleeved morning frock of light green; and she looked cool and feminine and patrician, and almost demure, her slim arms a lovely cream, and her throat finely rounded. And breakfast was a meal to her. She had had wheat-flakes and cream, and was now lifting covers off hot-plates, helping herself to bacon, eggs, kidney, some liver, and hot, buttered toast. She had a mildly speculative look, and was inclined to smile—like a cat with a canary inside.

She moved across to a table where a young man toyed with toast and marmalade, said, "Mornin', Sammy!" and bit into a wedge of toast before she sat down. The young man looked at her plate, and groaned.

"What a disgustin' spectacle!"

"Make yourself useful, Sammy Veller!" she ordered. "Some cawfee, like a lad—plenty of sugar and mostly cream!"

"My lawd!" deplored Sammy on his feet. His name was Anthony Villiers, which might reasonably be colloquialised into Tony Weller, but to his friends he was inevitably Sammy Veller spelled with a wee, who came out of an old book called Pickwick by a certain Charles Dickens. He was all of six feet, with a noticeable waist-line and a genial, more-or-less vacant face that in suffering too much sun had become red-peeled instead of tanned.

It was then that someone near a window said "Whoops!" loudly, and thrust a torso over the sill. Polite English usage is short in real expletives, and this "whoops" conveyed astonishment to the point of consternation, amazement and almost alarm.

Others of the breakfasters were at the windows now. Iosabel Mengues rose from her chair, had one look, and sat down again as if someone had snatched the legs from her.

Jesu! this would happen.

She might have known! It was the sort of predictable thing that that madman would do. The fool! Why did he not look in the first bush round the corner? And what would her proper father think of his proper daughter—convent-reared? But wait! No one saw her. *He* couldn't. His black poll was to her all the time.

She nearly choked herself on a scrap of kidney, and pushed her plate away. She strangled.

"Sammy, you hound! where's that coffee?"

Sammy splashed coffee in his hurry to see what caused the craning of necks. There were some surprised exclamations, and a cackle of laughter, but not real mirth. The surprise was too much. And there was some dismay too, as one or two wondered how near was the nearest lunatic asylum.

By the way heads slowly turned some portent or monstrosity was coming steadily across the gravel and up the steps to the side-door.

And then the side-door opened. It did not burst open to explode any monstrosity; it opened unhurriedly to admit a tall man, who shut the door behind him, pulled himself up stiffly, and stared dominantly down the room from under black brows.

No one at all thought of laughing. Open-mouthed they stared back—all but the lady Iosabel, who sat with her back turned. She thought better of that almost at once, for someone might notice—and wonder. She turned aside on her chair, an arm over the back, and looked; and a hand went over her mouth.

Gosh! I want to laugh. What astonishing legs! But my aunt in glory! if Dad finds out I lifted a man's bags bathing in the nude—! No! he never saw me!

The tall man had a damp, black helmet of hair and a brown block of stone for face; his torso was seemly enough clad in a black polo jersey, but below that was what might be a kilt, but looked uncommonly like a particularly brief shirt; and below that, astonishing parti-coloured legs rose starkly out of squashed rope sandals. The legs were shapely and sinewy, but even the finest legs look ludicrously inadequate below a short shirt. Yet, no one even smiled. That dominant face held them.

But Gawain Micklethwaite was not feeling in the least dominant. His eyes went over the company and came back to one particular person. *There you are, seemly daughter of pride! Hiding your kissable mouth! Inclined to laugh at me are you? Which side of your mouth? Not too sure are you? And your eyes betray you. Why the hell don't someone make a move?*

Someone did. A chair slid, and the big young man in homespuns, who had been talking to laird Mengues, was on his feet.

"I'll deal with this, sir," he said, and strode down the porch. He did not stride fast. The deliberation of his approach, the thrust of his long head, the way he held his hands away from his sides showed his intention more definitely than any hurried movement.

Gawain would insist that, outside the occasions of war, he was a man of peace and an avoider of trouble. All champions of all time have insisted on the same. He had come up to this Big House to wield a knightly blade and prick—if he could—a doughty player in a devil-may-care game. This was not likely any more. This big fellow, with a jaw like a paving-stone, would throw him down the steps, and the devil-may-care game would end ignominiously.

I knew I couldn't pull it off, he regretted. His poise never changed, but a spark lit in him. *Right, brother! Let's pull down the pillars of Gaza—and see how Delilah likes it!*

And there a coffee-cup crashed on the floor, and Anthony Villiers—*alias* Sammy Veller—leaped and yelped.

"Mick—Micklethwaite, on a new stunt, begad!" he cried, and there was enthusiasm in his voice. He went charging down the room, slipped on a rug, recovered complicatedly, thrust the big fellow aside with, "Go to hell, Nolly!" and leaped affectionately at Gawain.

Phew! Gawain released a long breath. Not for the first time was he glad to see his late Flight-Lieutenant Tony Villiers alive and coming. Fine! he could go along from here, using old Sammy for all he was worth, and ignoring the big fellow.

"Sammy, you old hog!" That is how he greeted Sammy.

Sammy was pumping his hand and chuckling, and the chuckles would break into uproarious laughter in a moment.

"Good old Mick! Fearless fellow! Back to the Jungle, practising nudism by inches—thirty-six of them at one go!" He drew back to look down at the shameless legs. "Oh lor'!" He was already bellowing when Gawain gripped his shoulder in a bone-breaking hand, and made his teeth thutter.

"Sammy you ass, shut up! Shut up, blast you! I am your commanding officer."

"But don't ask me to peel my legs—you've seen 'em."

"Shut up, will you!" Gawain didn't take time to explain to Sammy. Sammy was all right. "Listen! I must have another pair of bags, and you're elected. Do you hear?"

"Not the ones I have on? All right—all right! Let's go where I can be insubordinate—"

A cool and very deep voice spoke behind him.

"Your friend, Lieutenant Villiers?"

Sammy turned quickly and played his part.

"Sure, Mr Mengues! My commanding officer, Wing-Commander Sir Gawain Micklethwaite—I was telling you about him. Mr Mengues, Mick!"

So this is Sanin Cejador y Mengues! said Gawain. *And a hidalgo of the purest razorene! No! ray serene stands. An aristocrat out of the top drawer!—*

Mengues had breeding beyond a doubt. He was a very tall man, very lean and upright, and wearing his kilt of red-and-white checks as if to the manner born. His face was as colourless as tanned fawn leather, and was graved with lines of thought and character about the eyes and mouth. His eyes were northern-grey, not Latin-black, but his cheekbones showed some ancestry that was very old and very proud. A closely-trimmed, pointed, grizzled beard outlined an adequate chin. He gave an impression of quiet gravity that was almost aloofness.

Cunninghame Graham alive in the flesh, bejove! thought Gawain, *and he may have modelled himself on that great Scots-Hidalgo. He couldn't do better. But this man doesn't care for anything any more, and I think that is what is wrong with him.*

II

Away up the room Iosabel Mengues handled a fork. A minute ago she had been hungry as a hawk, but now the congealing mess on her plate looked disgusting, and she pushed it away, and nibbled a corner of toast. That ass, Sammy, had spilled her coffee all over the floor, and she wanted to wash the dry taste of dismay down her long neck. Fate was hanging over her imminently. Dad would find out—he was sure to find out—and he would never understand the—the indecent impulse that had moved her—that always would, curse her!

And then people were laughing all round her, and voices were lifted in surmise and half-decorous ribaldry. Iosabel turned quickly. Sammy Veller and the nude-legged tough had disappeared, and her father was walking slowly towards her table. *Oh, Saints in glory!* But her father was not looking at her, and he was smiling in his own grave way. He lifted finger, voices quieted, and he spoke with a formality that was a little foreign.

"My friends, that gentleman is Wing-Commander Sir Gawain Micklethwaite, D.S.O. He is Lieutenant Villiers' senior officer." The smile flickered again. "While bathing in Cobh Echlan someone—a tinker woman he said—" (*Blast his eyes!* said Iosabel)—"removed his trousers." He frowned now.

The big man in homespuns spoke up. "I don't see how any of that tribe could break in, but I'll look into it, sir."

"Thank you, Oliver!" The laird finished his explanation. "Sir Gawain came here to borrow some—ah—nether garments from his friend." He was frowning again.

You dear old ramrod! thought his daughter. *How could a noble knight burst in here in his naked shanks? and you wearing your red-and-white with no shanks to speak of. His were all right—if off colour.*

Her father walked to her table, and her eyes fluttered. "Iosabel, my dear, you will invite this gentleman to breakfast. I want an opportunity to question him further about this—ah—indecent trick."

"Certainly, Father," she said brightly. But she was not feeling bright. The fat was still in the fire, and she had let herself in for something. A wing-commander, a D.S.O., a knight! Sir Gawain Micklethwaite! what a name—and what a madman, all the same! He must have seen her! A tinker woman! just pricking at her! She smiled then. *Fair enough! I am a bit of a tinker.*

In a long, narrow, wainscotted room on the second floor two men were locked in strenuous endeavour. One of them was gasping laughter, and trying to pluck the shirt-tails off the other.

"I stood you on your head before now, my lad," said Gawain, tripped Sammy face-down on the carpet, heaved him up again, twirled him dizzily, and heaved him on the flat of his back on to the freshly-made bed.

"Pax—pax! Lor', oh lor'!" Sammy chuckled, and kicked his legs. "Beardin' old Mengues on piebald props!"

"Skewbald! you ignorant cuss. Where are those bags?"

"That wardrobe. Try the corduroys—they shrunk a couple o' inches on me. And speakin' o' pants, that tinker woman—"

"Go to hell!" said Gawain.

"I want to shake her hand for a pleasant mornin'."

Gawain was fumbling in the wardrobe. "Jeerusalem! Yaller-dog corduroys! But beggars can't be choosers—"

"Hey! them pants are not alms," cried Sammy. "I want them back."

"In due course. Forty inches in the waist about—and

they did not shrink, fatty. This bit of red rope off your dressing-gown—thank you! How did you get into a decent house, Samivel?"

Samivel, lying comfortably on his back, lifted a long leg. "Old Mengues likes select company—and good breedin'—"

"How did you get in, Sammy?"

"There was a Villiers, Duke of Buckingham, wasn't there? I know I come of rubber, but Mengues comes of guano—or something. It was the daughter invited me." He sat up. "Boy! you haven't met Iosabel?"

Haven't I, hell? He evaded the query. "Who was the long-jawed fellow, out to swat me?"

"He would too. Nolly Dukes."

"Nolly?"

"Short for Oliver. He's the secretary wallah—he knows every dam' thing. He's got a bit of a crush on the dark Iosabel, blast his eyes!"

"Jealous, Sammy?"

"No. She frightens me. I hang on to Dandy Dinmont—"

"Your terrier dog?"

"No. She's a wench—and dumb as a louse."

"Deep calling unto deep! What's wrong with the Iosabel one?"

"Nothing, brother, nothing! A dam' fine filly! not a scrap o' vice in her. Oh no! A blooded princess of vile degree, and next minute she'll put a prank across you to break a leg."

Are you telling me? said Gawain to himself.

"Take another hitch in that cord," Sammy advised. "Gosh! you got no greater intestine. You look fine now—pass in any company if you got yourself a new dial! Hey!" his voice was startled. "Where do you hang out?"

"First house outside the South Gate."

Sammy's voice was suspicious. "Got a spare pants—you never had?"

"No—I don't think so."

"Oh lawd! Begad we must find that tinker."

"We'll find her," said Gawain quietly.

Sammy was on his feet. "Come on! I'll set Iosabel on you. Bejove! You and she have the same hellish paces. Do you mind that night on Akyab—?"

"Shut up! I've an important engagement, and you'll slip me out a side-door. Come away!"

But Gawain did not slip away that easily. Iosabel Mengues was waiting for them down in the big hall, that would be gloomy but for the morning sun coming through high-set windows. She looked delicately patrician in her green dress, and had the aloofly serious air of her father.

You whited sepulchre! Gawain said to himself.

Sammy knew her too. "This is Iosabel Mengues, Mick," he said. "Bell, meet—"

"Sir Gawain Micklethwaite," said the lady.

Gawain inclined his head without bending his backbone, and he was as grave as she was. She turned to Sammy, and her voice was brisk.

"Dandy is on the lawn with a bag of clubs. Get out!"

"You couldn't stop me," Sammy said, already on the move. "Hey, you tike! I warned Mick about you—but don't you turn your back to him, any time, anywhere. Begod! you two should play poker."

She ignored Sammy. She said in a new voice touched with a foreign formality, "My father, Wing-Commander, has asked me to invite you to breakfast. You will accept?"

"Breakfast!" said Gawain remotely. "I had a meal so named—yes—a year ago."

"That is how I feel too," she said and smiled, and the transformation nearly did for Gawain's serious mien. But he said:

"Señorita, I would remind you that you are inviting me to break bread with you?" And she replied just as seriously:

"Señor, you and I may forget eaten bread with the last bite."

"Hunger breaks a man," said Gawain.

That was how these two came to have breakfast together at one of the glass-topped tables. And her appetite had come back. She heaped plates for them, and poured fresh coffee, and ordered in fresh toast, and they maintained a busy silence for ten minutes. All the guests had left the sun-porch; the laird and his secretary had gone round the corner to the Estate Office; the two had the place to themselves. And though they did not talk, they were busy in their own minds.

Gawain swallowed a final scrap of toast, emptied his cup, and, without thinking, put a hand to his hip-pocket.

Damn! that cigarette case is in a bush somewhere.

She noticed the gesture, and faint and lovely colour came to her cheeks. She rose to her feet, went quickly through an open window into the house, and returned with a pack of Virginia cigarettes and a lighter. She lit his cigarette and her own, and placed the packet close to his elbow. It was a brand that he could not afford.

They had eaten the last bite, but replete Gawain had no desire to break the truce. For some reason of her own she had a different idea. She said in her smooth formal way:

"There was one bearing a shield ordered to come here to this Tigh and meet my father. He is here, and he has met my father."

"It was so arranged?" Gawain queried.

"It was so arranged."

"Cross your heart?"

"No! I'm a dam' liar—but you are here."

"I am here," said Gawain, "and will someone look at the elegant pair o' pants I hornswoggled."

Iosabel's chuckle stopped abruptly.

The side-door from the steps had opened, and her father came in followed by Oliver Dukes. She pushed a plate aside and leant forward.

"Are you sticking to your tinker girl?" she asked in a low voice.

"She was a dam' nice tinker girl," said Gawain equably.

Iosabel said surprisingly: "Shut up, blast you!" and put a hand over her mouth.

Mengues walked unhurriedly up the long porch, gestured Gawain to remain seated, and sat down himself. He was smoking a long thin cheroot, and his lean face was composed in its characteristic immobility. Dukes leaned on the sill of a window close by.

"My secretary, Mr Dukes," Mengues introduced with a quiet gesture.

"Our acquaintance might have been closer," said Gawain. There was a little choked sound across the table, as if someone had swallowed a small cough.

Dukes replied promptly, "My intention was obvious, Wing-Commander." He had a curiously light voice for such a big man, and he was big, with high square shoulders and unusually long arms. His face was long-jawed and narrow, his eyes a peculiar red-brown, and his hair that deep-red that looks black at a distance.

So this is our Mr Dukes! thought Gawain. *Lukey blames him, and Sammy don't like him—and he has a crush on the daughter of the house! Ruthless sort of beggar I would say*. It was evident that Gawain was prejudiced right from the beginning.

Mengues put his cheroot carefully on a plate, and came to the point at once.

"This—ah—not-very-nice trick was played on you within my demesne, Wing-Commander, and I feel some responsibility. You said a tinker woman in a red shawl—?"

Damn! that was a blunder, said Gawain to himself. Aloud, he seemed to evade the issue. "Are the tinkers—Parlan MacFie and his tail—camping at Corran Hook this season?" He would not get his ancient friend Parlan into trouble for any sprig of a tomboy.

Mengues looked up interrogatively at his secretary.

"They are not," that man answered firmly. "I threw them out after three days."

"That clan of tinkers has been camping at Corran every Spring for three centuries," said Gawain mildly.

"High time they were ejected then—they were ruining the run of fish," said Dukes. "That wastrel crew should have been dispersed, absolutely, years ago."

"So thought a couple of Stuart kings in their time, but some of the broken clans still roam Scotland," Gawain said. He leant back in his chair, and inhaled cigarette smoke, and no one would know from his face and voice that a thread of indignant temper was mounting in him. He was here in the house of the stranger, and he would keep his head, but there was a thing or two that he would like to say. He addressed himself to Mengues.

"It is possible, Mr Mengues, that Scotland has again reached the state in which tinkers are made. Make enough of them and they may repossess the glens. That broken clan of the MacFie is older and more native than the—Micklethwaites."

"Or the Mengues, you would say?"

"Or the Menzies—you wear their white and red."

"It is my clan," said the other quietly.

Iosabel leant forward, and her voice was smooth. "We claim an older race, too, Wing-Commander—older and prouder—and more debased now than your broken clans."

"And who debased it?"

Mengues answered that gravely. "Who, indeed? The conqueror, the incomer—the conquistador."

Gawain sat up and fixed stern eyes on him.

"Remember that, sir, and remember that it is not wise to

make an enemy of the MacFies."

"Do I take that for a warning?"

"Just that, sir."

"Just nonsense!" said Dukes, a sneer in his voice. "These vagrants daren't bite, and if they try, the law is quite adequate to deal with them." He shrugged. "In fact I got one of them a month in jail, and he is there at the moment."

"They are used to that," said Gawain, who would not be roused. He turned to Mengues, and kept the brusqueness hidden. "As regards that nether garment, I caught but the barest glimpse of a vanishing figure. I took it for a woman, and assumed the tinker. That is all I can say."

That was a definite dismissal of the subject, but Mengues was not finished.

"Did the article contain anything of value?" he enquired.

A battered cigarette case, a box of matches, a few coins maybe. He turned a fleeting eye on the lady, and looked up at the glass roof. "Let me see! nothing of any value, but it stood for a thing or two: an invisible cloak, a shield, a casque, a greaves—a challenge to break a lance."

"You are being whimsical, Wing-Commander," said Mengues coolly, and looked gravely at his daughter. "Iosabel, my dear, you were out riding early—"

Phew! a man of parts, and even his daughter can't fool him, said Gawain.

"—Did you observe any young female in a red shawl?"

"Not to notice, Father," Iosabel said composedly, "but evidently she was there, and a graceless hussy too!"

Mengues sighed faintly. "I shall have some enquiries made," he said, and abandoned the subject.

There was a pause then, and Gawain was thinking. *An adequate man, Sanin Cejador y Mengues! I am in his bailiwick, and I got in by climbing a gate. What about it?*

Sanin Cejador was an adequate man, and he had his own method. He rose to his feet and said:

"If you are staying in the vicinity, Wing-Commander, I would be honoured—"

Gawain was on his feet too, a hand lifted.

"I am staying at Blinkbonny, Mr Mengues, with my friend Luke Carnoch."

Mengues never fluttered an eyelid. "Luke Carnoch, yes! You will be quite comfortable there."

"Off-and-on for twenty years, Mr Mengues."

"Just so. The South Gate is locked at present, and I will arrange to let you through when you are ready—there is no hurry."

He lifted a finger, turned on his heel, and walked, kilt swinging, up the length of the porch.

"That is my father, Sir Gawain," said Iosabel softly. "Have a cigarette?"

Gawain decided that Mengues had definitely dismissed him, and was waiting. He bowed stiffly.

"Thanks for the meal, Miss Mengues, and forgive my unwarrantable intrusion." The antic imp grinned at her in spite of himself. "I wouldn't have missed any of it for twa bawbees—but keep you your lance in rest."

He ignored Dukes, and went long-striding after Mengues.

Iosabel was chagrined. She would have liked a little more sparring, and it was hellish rude of him to leave so abruptly. Oliver Dukes, sitting on the sill, fingered his long chin. There was something here that puzzled him.

"Look here, Iosa!" he said. "Did you meet that fellow anywhere?"

"Go to blazes, Nolly!" said Iosa, and she too went up the porch, but more slowly.

IV

Gawain and Mengues walked down the drive side by side, two tall, quiet men who, for that time, had nothing more to say to each other.

This man, Sanin Cejador y Mengues, was a man by any standard, but he was not the man that Gawain had imagined. He was not the blatant tyrant of any little fields. He had poise, and dignity, and courtesy; but, somehow, he was not getatable because he was no longer interested in anything—not even in Glen Easan and the trouble within it. It was as if he held himself in abeyance, had turned his back on his duties, rested on his privileges, and given the reins of mere routine to his secretary, Oliver Dukes. To get at him something must happen to urge him out of his indifference; and what that thing might be was, at the moment, altogether outside Gawain's imagination.

And dammit! I haven't even decided to take a hand. In ten days I'll be out of here.

There was Dukes now! Oliver Dukes. He was the man

 to get at—or was he? Gawain decided at once that he was not. Dukes was not profitable. Gawain sensed a streak in him that was not biologically sound. Once or twice in his life Gawain had met men not unlike him: big men, with that queer colouring and the same light voice, and all lacking in the one essential human quality of ruth.

To hell with him! Give him his head, and throw him out on his ear. There is no other way.

Not once did Gawain think of getting at a certain lady. She was unpredictable, and, moreover, woman was no longer in his cosmos. But she had lifted his cheap flannel trousers, and they might still be a gauge of battle. If so the next move was hers, thanks to old Sammy's yellow corduroys.

I'm keeping my fingers crossed, said Gawain.

So they came to the South Gate, and stopped. Gawain looked up at the curve of blunt spikes that barred the way, and wondered if Mengues guessed that these spikes had been no bar that morning. Probably, for he said quietly:

"This gate is closed, Wing-Commander. You will note that this is a private road?"

Gawain had an opening there if he wanted to use it, but what would be the good? He moved his head in assent, and, after a pause, Mengues went on:

"To you and men like you I would gladly grant a privilege."

To hell with that sort of privilege! said Gawain.

Mengues pointed a hand in his foreign way. "There is a bell outside that gate. If you care to use it you will be admitted—to bathe in Cobh Echlan, or to fish loch and river, as you please." Again he paused as if waiting, and then finished firmly yet courteously, "Anyone coming otherwise comes as a trespasser—and I can deal with trespassers."

Gawain could have told him that the law of trespass was a chancy thing in Scotland, but he had already decided that it was no use arguing a case with this man. Yet he must make one thing clear. He said:

"If I want to see you, Mr Mengues, I will use that bell. Otherwise!" His broad hand moved in a flat negative. "But having eaten your bread, you must know where I stand. You need not open that gate for me. I am Luke Carnoch's friend, and I go the way I came."

Again he flexed and taughtened his knees, and went over the top, lithe as a cat, powerful as a hound. He took the shock, facing the gate, in what looked like a formal bow.

"Good morning, sir!" he saluted, swung away, and went striding up the slope.

Sanin Mengues stood still and watched him go. A cool, adequate, likeable young man, using words sparingly but unmistakably. A grave smile came about his mouth. A young man home from war with a remarkable record of daring! He had been coming to Luke Carnoch's for twenty years—he had said—from boyhood—and, no doubt, had moved freely everywhere. Yet he had made no claim and had said no plain word of protest. But he was Luke Carnoch's friend, and there was no need to say more. He would not conform to convention, that young man. He had trespassed that morning, and, probably, would go on trespassing, and if he did, that challenge must be accepted—and dealt with.

There Mengues tapped the ground firmly. This place was his and he would hold it. Some day, indeed, he would hand it over to Iosabel—and the man of her choice. She was, somehow, sib to this glen, and it would be hers—and time might resolve all troubles.

Sanin Mengues frowned. The man of her choice! One man he did not want, but he would not influence his daughter in any way. Therein danger lay. And he would give the man a fair field—and trust Iosabel.

He turned round then, and there was the daughter of his thoughts, not twenty yards away, standing in the middle of the drive waiting for him. He walked straight up to her, and she said with suspicious humility:

"An erring daughter, sir!"

He took her arm firmly, swung her round, and the two went pacing slowly up the drive, her shoulder pressing against him.

"You saw that remarkable feat of agility, young woman?" he enquired.

"The braggart—daring you!" She kept her voice steady. "You know I met him this morning, Father."

"So I gathered, my dear. And he is no braggart. He was but showing me where he stood. You met him for the first time—?"

"Yes, Father." This was going to be pretty bad.

He shook his head. "Modern young women I do not comprehend at all."

"And I am one?" There was a note of rebellion in her voice. "Oh! why am I not a boy at your side?"

He said half-playfully: "I am glad you are not, my little imp."

She looked up at him quickly, and said a little breathlessly: "Oh, Father! You can't mean that?"

He pressed her arm. "My dear, I would not change you for any son I once hoped for."

"You darling!" Her voice deepened. "Oh dear! I do want to see you happy."

"We cannot command happiness—"

"But we can command content in effort," she said impulsively.

"That is a wise saying," he said with a little wonder. "Content in effort!"

"Why not? If things go wrong it is worth while trying to right them—I would if I saw a chance," she cried eagerly.

"So would I, my dear," he said, and left it at that.

"Now, this morning—" she began determinedly.

"No! don't tell me."

"But, Father—it was only a silly game—"

"I don't want to hear, not now. Some day, *gracias a Dios!* you will tell me, and we will laugh together. You must work out your own problems, always—every problem, my daughter. You see, I am aware of the imp that is in us. Indeed, I am acquaint of it for fifty years."

"My darling!"

"Your imp was active this morning, and I think it left you with an obligation—"

"An obligation?"

"I think so. And, if I may, I would make a suggestion—only a suggestion, Iosabel!"

"Yes, Father."

"I would suggest that we restore a certain garment to an officer and a gentleman."

Blast his eyes! said Iosabel. "Yes, Father," said Iosabel mildly.

Chapter V
THE MAID WHO FIGHTS AND RUNS AWAY

I

ANTHONY VILLIERS—or Sammy Veller—sat forward in the big car, and looked sideways at the girl's calm profile.

"You got a hell of a nose, Bell," he said, "but your mouth ain't bad from this elevation."

"Want kisses four, do you?" Iosabel said carelessly.

"No dam' fearo! I got no nose to spare." He looked through the wind-screen. "Don't friend Mick hang out here somewhere?"

"Mick who?" she said indifferently.

"Come off it! The late pantless one."

"You mean Wing-Commander Sir Gawain Micklethwaite, Baronet, D.S.O.?"

"And he can play the Mick when he wants to."

"He made a name out East?" She sounded faintly interested.

"A bloomin' legend! He was up in Kelantan with a few planes to save Singapore and bust the whole Japanesy Air Force. He didn't. He got himself shot down and taken prisoner—"

"Then he *had* a bad time."

"Someone had. The Little Brown Brother could not hold him. He got away into the Jungle, and turned up months later, and a thousand miles away—in Burma. He was wearin' a loin-cloth—I saw him—and what he came through—"

"Leave it!" She moved expressive shoulders. "I want to forget atrocities."

"So do we all."

"He stays further down this slope. Want to see him?"

"And a pair of yellow corduroys."

It was a sunny afternoon, and Iosabel had hauled Sammy off for a drive—just a jaunt she had said. They had gone down the shore road as far as the old jetty, made an inland detour by the borders of the deer forest, and curved homewards on the main road over the ridge of Ardaneigh, making for the South Gate below Blinkbonny.

Above the township, where the common grazings fringed the moorland, they passed a tinkers' camp on the left of the road, in a big narrow-mouthed bay that had once been a sand-pit. A brown-faced woman, black-haired and straight, stood at the roadside and watched them coming. A brindled dog, half greyhound, broke away from her side, and came barking, a jump ahead of the bumpers. It was a young dog and untrained. A tinker's trained lurcher knows about cars, is as silent as a shadow, and less noticeable.

Iosabel might easily have killed that dog—many motorists would kill a dog as readily as they kill bipeds—but she braked smartly, swerved, and straightened again. She cast an angry glance at the tinker woman, and had mouth open for a warm reprimand, but the woman, high-headed and black-browed, stared at her with such supreme insolence that no words came. The tinker did more. She turned her head aside and spat on the ground. The insolence of that stare, the contempt of that spit, brought the blood to Iosabel's face. She took her foot off the brake, and the car went sliding down the slope on an idling engine.

"A dollar to a ducat! that's her—the very one," cried Sammy.

"What one?"

"The one that lifted Mick's bags, and begad! she'll be awearin' of them too."

Iosabel moved her head, and there was a self-accusing note in her voice. "That woman—no! She would not descend to that. She is Malcolm MacFie's wife. I know Malcolm—and old Parlan."

They were now passing parallel to the township: that long scattered row of squat houses with the remnant of peat stacks at the gable-ends. Away down the slope, over the bright and dark-green boskage of the demesne, they could see the steep stepped-roofs of the Tigh Mhor, and, beyond, the narrow waters of Loch Easan, and, beyond that, the whin-yellow ridge of Stob Glas lifting to the grey crags, and, beyond the shoulders of the Stob, all the welter of the northern hills, brown and grey and purple, fading to smoke-blue at the limit of distance.

There were very few people moving about the township. Most of the children would be in the slated school further down the road. A shepherd dog barked at them uninterestedly; a woman turned her back and disappeared through an open black doorway; two men sowing turnips below the road gave one glance and went on with their work; a man turned shoulder and stalked round a peat stack. There was no display of hostility, but no one gave them the lifted, benignant hand that is so natural with the Gael.

"A surly place this?" remarked Sammy.

"I don't know—it usen't to be." There was a forlorn note in her voice. "It is no worse than the Tigh Mhor. I suppose you know there is some trouble between Ardaneigh and my father?"

"So I heard. Your father can ignore that push, can't he?"

"No, he cannot," she came back at once. "And I do not think that he wants to either." And she went on as if to herself. "They are an intelligent and sensitive people—not yet blunted—primitive but aware of an old culture—friendly, with a real humility, yet proud too, and I think I could understand them—if they would understand me. When I came home after the war, and up to the time of the trouble, I found I could work with and for them—and there was so much to do in this devastated land. We sort of spoke the same language, and laughed at the same things." She moved her head irritably. "Oh dear! We all live in the same glen, and why cannot we all be friendly? Blast them—and us—and all big black—! This is Blinkbonny, Luke Carnoch's place. And there's your friend in his shirt-sleeves! Go and talk if you want to—men always talk, don't they?"

The car slowed and stopped before the red gate.

"The hound!" said Sammy. "He's still sporting me fine corduroys."

II

On an open green patch at the house-end, and just below the wheel-less bus-body, a white-covered small table was set up, and a tall red-haired woman in slacks was busy over tea-cups. Luke Carnoch was coming from the house with a tray; a blond man was at ease on a long chair, a stiff leg extended; and Gawain Micklethwaite was leaning on a dutch hoe, his bare brown arms folded, and his head turned gatewards. Except Gawain, the others ignored the car at the gate.

Sammy put a hand on the door handle. "You're coming up! You gave him breakfast, didn't you?"

"No, Sammy! This is one thing I can't do—not yet." There was a touch of regret there. "You go on—please! I'm in no hurry, and I'll smoke a cigarette—after that you can walk."

He looked at her shrewdly. "All set! I'll do what I can for you."

As she lit a cigarette she looked under her brows at Sammy walking up the path, and was interested in the pantomime that followed: Gawain's gesture towards the red-haired woman, Sammy's formal bow, the sitting man kicking a leg and extending a long arm, Luke Carnoch pulling round a garden chair; and then her eyes were drawn to a movement behind and above them. The curtains of the bus had been pulled aside, and the windows lowered. Something in pink and cream was moving within. Yes, it was an arm waving to her—the quick and nervous arm of a child throwing her a friendly greeting.

Iosabel's heart lifted. That was Major Keegan's disabled child, and the little one was not of the churlish tribe that turned back on a lonely girl. This was that rare one who would wave a greeting to a stranger—to an outlaw—to a lonely devil, daughter of pride.

She threw up head and hand, and returned the greeting with interest; and her smile made her face lovely.

Gawain was the only one of the grown-ups who saw that friendly gesture, and it resolved his indecision. That lady in the car might not accept an invitation to afternoon tea, but after that salute to his little queen, she could not be left to sit alone outside the gate.

He dodged under an apple tree, hopped the tulip bed to the path, and put his dutch hoe at the slope; he was like a marching pikeman. He came through the open gate to the side of the car, brought his hoe gravely to the salute, and thudded the heel of it smartly on the ground. He was thinking: *Damn Sammy Veller! I hope he keeps his mouth shut about his blasted yellow bags!*

Iosabel was as serious as he was, and her mouth had again its sullen line; and she was thinking: *He is more foreign-looking than I am, with his black casque and his Cervantes jaw!*

He brought his hand up. "Will the dark lady—more beautiful even than she of the sonnets—alight from her coach-and-eight-pistons and partake of Chinese brew?"

He is starting to make fun of me again! Very well!

Half-turned to him, she leant back in the seat corner, and

drew in and exhaled smoke. She moved a red gauntlet in her foreign way, and her voice was cool and remote.

"Did the lady send you? No! Woman is more stiff-necked in quarrel than man." She was using his own medium.

"Thou hast said it," said Gawain weightily.

"Then I will not partake of Chinese brew, but I have some discourse to make."

"To take my hide off?"

"I hope so." She looked at him through half-hooded eyes, and, if she only knew, her insolence was more devastating than the tinker woman's. Her voice remained remote.

"Preening himself for a gallant and chivalrous gentleman! Forgetting how ridiculous he looked—!"

"In my skewbald shanks! Wait! oh wait!" He threw his hoe backwards over his shoulder, and it rattled on the concrete path inside the gate. "Out of temptation, my trusty halberd!"

She looked him up and down, and pointed a scathing scarlet finger.

"You are still wearing your underling's nether garment! Where is your own?"

"Where, indeed? A nest for a wandering hedgehog, or—"

She stopped him briskly, holding on to the initiative.

"Ha! You knew where to look then? But you were too barbarously angry to look in even one bush!" Her finger stabbed. "Ah! perhaps you did look, but vindictively decided on vengeance."

Gawain looked over his shoulder. "Stay put, O halberd!" he said sternly. He hadn't another come-back in his mind, nor time for one. The remote, taunting voice had the spell of the siren.

"This noble soldier carrying a king's commission, entitled to wear little silly rows of coloured ribbons on his left breast like all the childish war-lords who love to bedizen themselves like children—"

"Bedam, but they do!" said Gawain heartily.

"This famous soldier would not be demeaned. He would come raging coldly to the Tigh—"

"Jesu Maria!" exclaimed Gawain fervently.

"Yes, you were raging. I saw it under the whole wood of your face. You would make a spectacle of yourself, but you would put the temerarious one to shame. And then, inside the door on your ridiculous—yes, skewbald legs—you perversely changed your mind, and decided that a noble chivalry was the better part to play."

Gawain actually yelped wordlessly. And she went on:

"You would be noble, you would be chivalrous, you would be a pourer of coals on the head. You would accuse no one of stealing your ten-and-sixpenny pants—except a poor tinker woman who might get into the trouble that she is used to—"

"Termagant!" He almost bawled. "There are no tinkers—"

"Bah!" Voice and flung hand contemned him. "They are not at Corran Hook, but they are camped half-a-mile up the road at the Sand Pits—the whole MacFie clan. But, noble baronet, you cannot saddle the blame on a MacFie." Again she pointed a scarlet finger. "Do you take my father for a fool, Sir Baronet?"

"By my halidom! but I do," he cried hardily.

"But not that sort of fool. Chivalry my eye! Look! You crawled over a gate, you persisted in trespass to rough handling, you went bathing shamelessly in Cobh Echlan. Your cottons were shoved in a bush, you saw—or guessed—who did it, and you followed raging to burst into the sun-porch like a scarecrow. Wait, sir! What would my father gather? No officer-and-gentleman would trust himself so disgracefully amongst house guests unless hot on the trail. My father must know that the player of what he called a scandalous trick had come into the house—was in that room—a woman! And there was only one woman out and about that morning. Chivalry, sir?"

"I bet your father gave you hell, young woman!" said Gawain coming up for air.

"And so you lick your chops. Let be! I do not want to be too severe on you." Gawain strangled, and she pointed an imperious finger down the road. "Go and recover your property—it is still under its bush!"

Gawain put a hand on the door and the muscles of his forearm ridged. "Do I go now—with you? I know a deep place."

"No! At night—slinking under the trees—so that you be not seen and shamed again."

"And you will meet me at the Cove—in the witching hour—under the full moon?"

"No, sir! But have no fear. Go tonight, and no one will hinder you. Tonight I will be angling—for big ones—in Loch Ros Caller—under the full moon—and the man who would throw you into the loch will be with me."

A finger moved to the self-starter, and the engine purred. She leant a little towards him. "Tell Sammy to stretch his useless but clothed legs, and good afternoon to you, my poor tongueless one!"

The car moved off with one small spurt to show that she was in some hurry—the spurt of victory, or a dexterous retreat with the enemy confounded. And as she went she waved a hand towards the wheel-less bus, and a white arm answered. But above the sound of the engine, Gawain thought he caught another sound. It might be a self-satisfied chuckle.

He stood looking after her, his hands grasping his ears; and he was slowly and astoundedly realising that the playful but barbed badinage that he had blithely intended to use had been grasped out of his hands and turned into a rapier, a sabre, a bludgeon, a brick-and-a-half-and-half-a-brick.

Oh Gord! Oh Lor'! Oh, hell and damnation! Oh, you bloody little termagant! Oh, you graceless hoyden! You, the scandalous purloiner! You, the origin of all sin from all time! Turning every table in sight—and getting away with it! No! by the powers! I'll get even with you if it takes me all summer—ten days anyway.

He took a fresh thought, scratched the back of his head, and grinned.

By gum! She was good. Came out with the bell both hands swinging, and never let up till she had me down in a neutral corner. And left her hat in the ring plain for me to see!

His face stilled, and his trap of a mouth opened and shut. *Yes, sir! Angling for four-ounce trout in Loch Ros Caller—under the full moon—with our Mr Dukes! No business of mine, is it? Damn the bit, brother! You stay home, and pour scalding tea down Sammy Veller's neck.*

Chapter VI
WILL LIVE TO FIGHT ANOTHER DAY

I

LOCH ROS CALLER is two miles up from the head of Loch Easan, and then a further mile to the right up the course of the Caller Burn coming down steeply over the shelving brow of the glen; too steeply for salmon or sea-trout to spawn in, though sometimes an angler caught a silvery fish of a few ounces that looked very like a smolt.

The lochan covers an oval area of not more than a hundred acres, and is set high, a thousand feet up, among wastes of old heather scattered with low-growing, sage-green juniper and yellow whin. It is shallow—a fathom or so—except where the Ros ridge makes a promontory and lifts out of dark and deep water. It is held that monster cannibal trout haunt the under-water shelves and hollows on the deeper side of the Ros; but no angler—or poacher—had yet caught one; no fish larger than a pound had ever been landed; but a man here and there, otherwise trustworthy, averred to seeing a massive black fin cleave the surface in the gloaming; and David Keegan used to insist that he had once hooked a big one that had broken him before he could surface it. All the useful places could be cast over from the shore or by wading, so no boat was kept on the loch.

An hour before sunset, Gawain Micklethwaite walked out on the ridge of the Ros, fifty yards out, and fifty feet above the water. Twice he turned round full circle, and made sure that no one moved in all that waste. The heather ridges, one behind the other, sloped and flowed down to the loch like the waves of the sea, and the far-flung panorama of mountains was hidden behind the blunt summits. Then he turned his back on the loch, and looked into the fold in the hills where the Caller Burn had cut its way to the main river. He could follow the course of the stream for some distance to where it dipped out of sight over a steep drop, and in the still evening air he could hear the sound of falling water. That was the way he had come, that was the way anyone from the Tigh Mhor had to come, for the heather of the slopes was trackless and hid leg-breaking boulders.

The evening was sunny and still, and not a wimple or a fin broke the tenuous, silken skin of the loch. With the lowering of the sun, a flow of air might sigh down from the heather, and minute white flies come drifting with it. Then the quarter-pounders—or occasional pounders—would begin to feed, and a long line, deftly placed, might rise and hook a potable fish—but not a cannibal. Casting flies before cannibals would be a waste of foot-poundage.

Gawain hooked off his canvas fishing bag and laid it behind a shelf of rock, placed his landing net and cased nine-footer on top, lit a cigarette, and eased himself down on his back. The rock was warm after a long day of sun, and the pleasantness of it came through to his shoulder-blades. By lifting and turning head he could see down the Caller Burn, and his ears would apprise him before his eyes if anyone moved on the track by the stream.

He really had nothing much in his mind or on it. A certain young termagant-virago had said that she was coming up with Oliver Dukes to try for big ones in the full of the moon; and, indeed, a big one might take a tinselled fly or a small minnow in moonlight, if the night remained clear. Gawain had just come along well ahead, and, if given time, would catch some breakfast trout before the Tigh party turned up—or after they had gone. The night would not be too long, and fish rose in the dawn, and the heather would make a softer bed than many he had slept in over years.

If and when the Tigh party turned up he would have to keep out of sight, but there was enough heather and juniper to hide an army. And he might play a prank on the spur of the moment or the spur of chance; but unless he could do something adequate he would do nothing at all, for a certain one deserved something worthy of her style. And he told himself, as an angler, that he must do nothing to spoil another angler's sport.

His hands under his black poll, he crinkled his eyes and focussed into the cloudless blue abyss of the sky. Up there somewhere a hill lark was singing its evening song before spiralling down to hover over its mate on her nest in a tongue of grass, but his eyes could not find the black speck against the blue. As a boy, he remembered, he had never failed to follow the highest soaring of the skylark, and he recalled how once, lying under a bush, he had followed the spiral down from the zenith to the final hover and drop, and then had searched for and found the nest amongst the young spears of rye-grass. Five eggs there were, a delicate, brown-spotted grey, and he was about to take one for his collection when his father erupted and chased him across two fields, not for nest-robbing but for trampling first-crop rye-grass. Those were the great days—even if they came between two inevitable and unnecessary wars. . . . And a third war looming. . . . And all men fools and unfit to persist in a bounteous world. . . .

He was almost asleep, the whisper of running water lulling him from afar, when another whisper came far away from the heather, and came closer, and was about him; and something that was like a ghostly finger moved in his hair. It was the first breath of evening, and Gawain sat up. A faint crinkle ran slowly and evenly across the surface of the loch, and died away, and was followed by another, and yet another. The trout would be moving any time now, and, with luck, he might have an hour to fill a bag. The fisherman always fills a bag—before he starts to fish.

He took a precautionary look down the outrun of the Caller, picked up his tackle, and slipped off the ridge. Before he had his rod up the white flies were on the water, and the trout were on the move. And the drift of air still held, and the water was nicely crinkled. Small black fins tipped the surface; splashes sounded; ring joined to ring, made little sibilant whispers among the reeds, and lapped on the brown gravel along the shore. But no big fish showed itself.

Gawain had his hour, and fair sport with it. He had no waders, and kept near the ridge where there was a fair depth of water inshore. And in hopes of rising a big fellow he used a seven Palmer, with a white-splashed Heckham for a long dropper, He hooked many small ones that he put back, but had half-a-dozen or so quarter-pounders in his bag before deciding that it was time to make himself scarce.

The sun was now below the hills, the toneless light of the gloaming over the desolation of the moors, and the water smoothing itself out to a floor of wan-shining silver. Away south-and-east a daffodil glow grew above the curve of the hills, and the crest of the moon would show at any moment. Gawain would try three more casts before reeling in, the three casts that usually finish the session. It was the second cast that gave him the first thrill of the night.

A trout came hurriedly out of deep water and flung itself

a foot into the air: a nice fish, not a monster, but as big as anything Gawain had seen or caught in Ros Caller—and just about within reach. He drew two more yards of line off the reel, and lifted his tip. It was then he got his thrill. A fin, like a triangular black sail with a notch in it, came sheering through the water, and a porpoise-like shoulder showed for an instant.

Gawain steadied and made his cast, and there was the Palmer exactly where he wanted it, two feet in front of the boil. Gosh! if he hooked that tiger, he would take twenty minutes to subdue it on a number seven, and he would be caught red-handed—and probably drowned by Oliver Dukes. Dam' the care he cared.

Glory hallelujah! The big fellow would play. Indubitably that was a rise! There was the curve of the back and the flip of the broad fluke as the fish drowned the fly. And Gawain struck, and cursed himself on the instant. In loch fishing the very least twitch, a late strike, or no strike at all is the surest rule. For a split second Gawain was certain that he had pulled the fly from the very jaws of the trout. And then, with an electric thrill down to his hands, the rod-tip curved, and the line checked solidly for an instant. And next instant the reel screeched, and the hooked fish went away from there. That was not so promising, for a big fish, well hooked, plays sluggishly for a start.

For two minutes Gawain was certain that he had hooked the monster. It took plenty of line, and he was wary in using the butt. Finally, when it paused, and Gawain started to recover some line, it kept sagging from side to side, and that is contrary to the tactics of any big one. And then it came out of the water, and Gawain yelped in surprise. It was a nice fish, but it was not the monster. A pound trout and not an ounce more, and Gawain wondered if he could believe his eyes.

He guessed at once what had happened, for he had heard of it happening before. He had been premature in striking the big fellow, and had foul-hooked the little fellow that the big fellow had been pursuing. The doomed youngling had been hooked by the dropper in the back fin, and a pound trout so hooked, lively as a kitten, takes a lot of killing.

Gawain gave it all the time he could. He let it rest, and he let it sink, and tried to play it as a minnow, hoping that the cannibal would come back for its supper, swallow the bait holus-bolus, and get drawn out by the pit of the stomach. But the cannibal had taken alarm, and was sulking in the deeps somewhere below the ridge. And, at last, Gawain had to bring his fish to the landing net. He cursed it as he broke its neck—which was ungenerous, for it was the best fish, chubby and nicely marked, that he or anyone else had brought out of Ros Caller on rod and line.

Gawain did not hesitate now, and, at that, he was barely in time. He took down his rod, stored away his tackle, and turned towards the Ros above him. The outlet of the burn was out of sight, and he was about to climb up for a look down the track when a sound of voices drifted over from the other side. The gloaming was deepening now, and though the moon, round and red, was over the crown of the moors, its light was not yet strong, and he would have time to retreat out of sight along the shore if he had wanted to. He did not want to, for he had already decided that here or hereabouts was the choice observation point.

Softly treading, moving unhastily, he went up into the heather, disposed of his tackle carefully under a juniper bush—and disappeared. He was wearing a blue Harris-tweed jacket, a black pullover up to his ears, and an old brown tweed hat of Davy Keegan's. One could not say that he dropped out of sight, or crouched between the bushes, or faded into the distance. He disappeared as a ghost might disappear. He might be anywhere. Actually he was merged in a loose clump of juniper not twenty yards up. That merging immobility was the hardest part of the game he had to learn in the Jungle. All animals, except man, acquire it naturally, and many men had died in learning it in a bloody school.

II

Four people—yes, four—came out on the crown of the Ros, and halted. Gawain had expected only two, but he was none displeased to see four. From their vantage point he was in plain view in the juniper patch, but not even a trained eye could make out his outline unless he moved. And one pair of eyes was surely on the watch.

He looked up at them from between the crotches of a bush, and they bulked black against the northern glow that flowered up into a nameless litten green. There were two girls, Iosabel Mengues and another; the two men were

Oliver Dukes and Sammy Veller. Iosabel and the men were in waders, the other girl in slacks, and Iosabel, talking, was making those foreign hand-gestures of hers.

"Isn't it one perfect night for a real whopper?"

Dukes was lighting a cigarette, and Gawain saw his long nose and longer chin. He laughed unbelievingly.

"A whopper! I don't know this pond—too many sprats—"

"Pounders have been caught, and bigger ones seen," Iosabel said with some heat.

"Of course they have," he said derisively. "Bigger fish in the sea—you know. Still! Pounders are good enough if you rise 'em."

"Lead me to 'em!" Sammy Veller said.

Evidently Dukes was a fisherman. He said:

"No hurry! They're off the move now. In an hour if the moon keeps ashining you might—just might—land a pounder. But where? Down there?" His cigarette-tip glowed as he pointed with it down towards the spot where Gawain had been fishing. And Iosabel promptly said:

"But no! There are only two places on a night like this." Her cigarette-tip made a wide curve. "The lower end, down there—a curve of sand shelving out, and the fish like it at night, not big ones, but plenty of them. That's where you get your ear hooked, Dandy, you're going with Sammy. Use that big cast I tied for you, Sam, and yell for me every time you lose a fly."

"When the chump hooks my ear, you mean," said the other girl.

"Nolly, you'll take the other place," went on Iosabel, "from here to the outflow, deep and shallow water, and if you don't rise a good fish don't blame me."

"I will if you rise one—"

"I don't expect to." There was resignation in her voice. "I'll try a few casts along here under the Ros, but the water deepens too quickly. Let's get going."

Up in the junipers, Gawain's breath fluttered amusedly. This Iosabel girl had the roots of angling in her. She, self-sacrificingly, gave the two good places to her friends, and merely kept for herself the one choice place.

The anglers moved off the ridge, and Gawain eased his muscles. Few men can lie moveless for ten minutes, and it's the man who can that gets the man who can't, as Gawain knew. Then he flattened himself out comfortably, and carefully made a fresh peep-hole to look down on the pool below.

Iosabel was down there on the gravel, and she was setting up her rod; Dukes had disappeared on the other side of the ridge; and Sammy's wading boots crunched along the shore where he went with his Dandy. *Dandy Dinmont! What a hell of a name! Worse than Gawain Micklethwaite!*

Thunder! what sort of a contraption of a rod was she using? Not an eight-footer to catch a big 'un? It was. But it was a spinner strong enough to hold a porpoise. And she was for trying a minnow too. As far as Gawain could judge by the light of the slowly-towering moon the minnow was a three-inch, two-tail phantom, brown and gold: a good size and good colour for a loch in moonlight. Where had she learned this game?

As soon as she started fishing he knew where and from whom she had acquired her technique; in this glen and from Lukey Carnoch. She had his way of turning from the water as she smoothly brought her point round, and the same easy way of pivoting as she made the throw, so that she was set and ready as the minnow plopped softly five-ten-fifteen yards out. She must have made good use of her time in the glen, considering that for a year or so she had been away on some war job or other. *That's where you learned some of your language, ma'am,* said Gawain.

She certainly could fish, and she was patient. Up and down she went, twenty yards this way, and thirty yards that, and as far in as her waders would permit, covering all the places over deep water time after time. Twice she changed her lure, first for a smaller and then a bigger minnow. Twenty minutes, half-an-hour, an hour, she swung and cast and drew and reeled, and in all that time she raised nothing, big or little.

You may be a fly-off-the-handle, said Gawain, *but not at this game! I nearly pulled off a miracle, but you deserve to. Gosh! I got a crick in my neck.*

The moon was higher now, and he could distinctly see her red kerchief against the polished steel of the water. And he could see that at last she was slowing down. Dukes, at the other side of the Ros, made no sign, but the two at the far end were having a right good time. Talk and laughter and yelps came up, and the splash of a small trout splattering on the surface, and more laughter and more splattering.

Iosabel Mengues deserved her miracle, and got it. That

big cannibal had risen once that night, and, now, it rose again in the same place. One moment, Iosabel, ready to give up, was reeling in slowly, her minnow deep; the next, her stiff spinning rod bent as if she had struck a log, and the ratchet of the reel scurried. Gawain came to his knees behind the juniper.

There followed fifteen exciting minutes for Iosabel Mengues—and for Gawain too, indeed. The girl was into the biggest fish ever hooked in Loch Ros Caller, and she wanted to land it by her own sole efforts. Her eagerness to score off the scoffing Dukes impelled her to yank that six-pounder—it was at least that—right out of the water, but she restrained herself finely; in fact she restrained herself more than was needed, considering the strength of her tackle. She let the fish run too freely, and when it sulked was over-tentative in giving it the butt, and she reeled in with a touch as sensitive as a nerve. And as the fight progressed her excitement and anxiety grew. When the fish went deep close to the rocks, and sawed sullenly, she groaned aloud; when it lashed a savage fluke on the surface her agonised moan accompanied every lash, and during one fierce, storming run she prayed aloud:

"Oh, dear Lord! Oh, Mareea mother! don't let me lose him."

That prayer was answered. She did not lose her fish. And Gawain, let it be said for him, was inclined to pray with her. He was as glad and tense as she was when, after a last weakening run, the quarry showed a gleam of yellow as it came to the reel on its side.

She unhooked the landing net from her belt, and went thigh-deep into the water for the last tricky operation that is so often a failure. Gawain half-rose to his feet. If he were a man, a sportsman—half a man—he would go down and net that grand trout for her. But no! If she wanted help she had only to shout to her friends. She wanted to complete the job all by her lonesome. Gawain sank back under his bush.

She did the job steadily and neatly, holding the butt of the rod high, a little finger checking the line, sinking the net deeply, and scooping firmly. Gawain saw the broad flukes lashing in the mesh, and the whole curve of the body safely confined; and he shut his teeth on a cheer.

She backed out of the water slowly, minding her feet, and her arm astrain; and she kept backing up the gravel till she nearly tripped on the edging of rough grass. And there she dropped rod and net, and pounced. She was taking no chances and despatched her prize emphatically. Gawain saw and heard the solid clump of the stone on the trout's poll.

She took a little time to release the firmly set minnow, and then sat on her heels to admire her prize, touching the long killer's head, fingering the back fin that had a deep, healed notch in it, spanning a hand across the fat navel. But not for long. Suddenly she reared upright, and her voice pealed out, first in a wordless, mellow bellow of triumph, ringing off the ridge and rolling far across the water and up into the heather; and, then, words came.

"Nolly—Sammy! Come—come—come! I got him. Oo-ee! Come and see! Hip, hip, hurrah! Come and se-e-e!" There was rhythm in it.

An answering shout came from Sammy, and a yodel from Dandy. There was no sign from Nolly. Her voice pealed again.

"Nolly—Nolly Do-o-ks! Where are you, Nolly? Oliver—come—here is Roland for you."

Perhaps her voice did not carry over the ridge. Oliver was the man she wanted. The scoffer! The mocker! The know-all! She must have Nolly. She gave a look down at her fish as if to make sure of it, turned, and scrambled up over the neck of the Ros.

III

A shadow materialised from the base of a juniper, and Gawain Micklethwaite slipped down to the gravel; and he was cursing under his breath. He was almost hating himself at that moment. Well! She had had her thrill, her twenty minutes of emotion, her supreme moment of exultation. That was fair enough, and all right by him! But now she wanted to gloat. In gloating no virtue lay. It was unmoral. It was contrary to the nonchalance that the successful angler assumes as a thin veneer over hell's pride. It should be punished, and he was the hound called upon for the job.

But what really moved him was something that he would deny indignantly if it was put under his nose. It was not requital or retaliation or revenge. It was merely a hankering desire to keep the game going.

He hadn't much time, but he had enough: half-a-minute perhaps; and he was back in the heather and immobile in the junipers when Iosabel and Dukes appeared over the Ros.

She was still excited, and gabbling, positively gabbling all the way down to the gravel, where, under the full moon, lay her rod and her landing net—and a trout gleaming on the meshes of the net.

"A whale, Nolly? No, sir! A veritable loch trout all of seven-eight pounds! And out of this loch—your Ros Caller of the sprats! And I hooked him, and I played him—thirty glorious minutes—and landed him, poor weak vessel that I am. The true cannibal, Noliver! with half a back fin where another cannibal—or an otter—nipped him! but healed nicely. Come on, you doubting Thomas! Put your finger in the notch, see where the minnow grappled. Look! There he is! . . . Jesu!"

The last sacred word was exploded out of her, Oliver Dukes bent over, and spoke gravely.

"Quite a nice trout, Iosa! and nicely nourished. Did you say seven pounds—or eight?"

"Have you caught a better?" she managed to come back, but her voice was strangely small and breathless.

"No. A half-pounder amongst small ones." He straightened up and laughed. "You damn'd imp! You had me going for a minute."

Sammy Veller's big boots crunched on the gravel behind them.

"What's all the pother about?" he wanted to know. "Anyone bust a limb?"

"Our she-Izaak has caught the biggest fish ever," Dukes told him. "There it is!"

Sammy pushed between, and bent to look. "A nice trout!" he said commendingly. "But look here, dammit—!"

"What a plump little chap!" cried the girl Dandy over his shoulder.

"That's a seven-pounder, you juggins!" said Dukes.

"What's it made of—lead?" Sammy was inclined to anger. "Brast it, Bell! I wish you'd stop your joshing. There was me fillin' the bag—"

"Filling my shoes with water, you slug," Dandy put in.

"Shut up, baggage! And you yell your head off for us to come and admire your sprat! Is it a pound, Nolly?"

"A pound, just about," Nolly agreed.

Iosabel was not heeding them. Her back was turned and

she was eye-searching the heather. She had turned too late. A little while before she might have seen a shadowy movement in the junipers, and something or someone drifting away parallel to the shore. Now there was nothing but the wastes of heather, and the pale gleam of whin blossoms, and juniper bushes casting darker shadows than themselves, and the high serene moon above the black silhouette of the summits.

"One sometimes goes gaga with the full of the moon," said Dukes solemnly. "Poor old Iosa! She had a hallucination. Let's take her home out of the baleful influence—or she might land a crocodile on us next time."

Iosabel turned round, "Want some more fishing, Sammy?" she asked quietly.

"While the goin' is good I would," said Sammy with the enthusiasm of the beginner who has caught small ones in plenty.

"Go to it! You'll have another half-hour, with luck," Iosabel told him.

"And don't you yell your head off next time," Sammy said, and clumped off up the shore. Dandy trailed after, her shoes squelching water.

At the foot of the loch they found Gawain Micklethwaite sitting on the sand waiting for them. Sammy had always been wax in his friend's hands, and he was now. Presently Dandy was chuckling uncontrollably.

IV

Oliver Dukes was no fool. He was puzzled. Iosabel had taken this too quietly. She had brought him on the jump, and then behaved as if her silly ploy had been pricked like a toy balloon. There was something queer in her manner—and it was not due to the moon.

"What came unstuck, old girl?" he asked. "You were joshing, weren't you?"

"Someone was," she said, and he caught something in her tone.

"A ghost?" He looked towards the heather, and looked back. "Is that your fish?"

"You are not blind, are you?"

"Nor goggle-eyed either. Oh, all right!" He moved across and picked up her minnow. "A three-and-a-half-inch phantom! You never caught a pounder on that?"

"I caught it on that."

"Maybe—maybe! What's biting you, young woman?"

"You are," said Iosabel, turned her back on him, and stalked off up the shore.

Dukes hesitated, made as if to follow, paused, and shook his head. He was an angler, and he had left his rod at the other side of the Ros, where he had risen one or two reasonable fish. He would try them again for that half-hour, and by that time Iosabel's disgruntlement would be gone. She was never the one to nurse a grouch. But it was dam' queer all the same! From the top of the ridge he looked down and over the near heather carefully, foot by foot. There was nothing to see now, and even if there was he would not see it. *A ghost!* he muttered, *but I thought it might be a solid one.*

Iosabel went slowly up the shore, her boots crunching, her thumbs in her belt, and one eye lifting towards the heather. Had she been wool-gathering—or moon-gathering? Had she—? Yes, she had hooked a monster trout. Blast! her arms still ached. She had played, and netted and clumped that seven-pounder—or eight. She could see the nick in its fin in her mind's eye. And she had not turned her back for more than half-a-minute. And in that half-minute her grand fish had been metamorphosed into a one-pound sprat. It couldn't—yes, it could! It had happened almost under her eyes. She stopped and pounded fist into palm.

You blasted tomboy! Why did you open your mouth so big this afternoon? Why scarify and put a dare up to that black devil? And my hat! hasn't he taken it!

She did not understand how the catastrophe could have happened, but it will be noted that not for a moment did she doubt the identity of the culprit. She just knew. She faced round and addressed the heather.

You're no gentleman! You're a tinker! You're no sportsman! Anyone who would play such a dastardly trick would rob a church. No gentleman, I said!—and by glory! give me a chance, and I'll be no lady.

The heather gave no reply, and she turned away in disgust. *What could she do, anyway? Keep her mouth shut—even if Nolly Dukes had his suspicions. Thank heavens! Sammy—*

She lifted six inches off the gravel, and loosed a small skirl. The cause was a truly terrific bellow from Sammy

Veller at the end of the loch, and in the volume of sound that filled that hollow in the hills was a note of desperate appeal.

"Help! To me, Bella! He-e-lp! Hurry—hurry! I got him, and I don't know what to d-o-o."

Got him—got who? Punch him in the nose, and hold on for me!

Iosabel lifted up her feet and ran, and she ran well though cumbered with waders. The moonlight was so bright now, that she soon saw that Sammy's captive was not a biped, but she kept on running, for it was plain that Sammy was either into a big fish or into all Scotland. Dandy Dinmont came shouting to meet her.

"Sammy—a fish—the father of all the fishes!"

"An old boot!" Iosabel derided.

"A fish," Dandy insisted. "A troutosauras, Sammy says."

"We'll soon see!"

Sammy stood up to his knees in the loch, and his rod made a perfect parabolic curve, the tip not a yard above the water. A fish! No fish would sulk like that in shallow water, Iosabel knew.

"Can't move the brute!" Sammy gasped.

"You can't move all Scotland, you chump!" Iosabel said.

"Scotland? What the—! It's a fish—I saw him—ten foot long."

"All right! Take it easy! Take your finger off that line—leave the reel alone!"

Fish had vagaries of their own, and Sammy might be into an utter sulker. Iosabel picked Sammy's landing net off the gravel with her right hand, and for her left found a nicely-rounded stone. Then she slipped through the water right up to Sammy's shoulder. She had the impulse of the expert to take the rod from the tyro, but suppressed it—as an occasional expert will. Sammy must kill or lose his own fish—if he had one on—but a few instructions would help.

"Let out some more line, and lift your tip. More—more—another foot! Hold it! Don't touch the line—don't or I'll brain you! Let the reel run loose! Are you ready?"

"God'llmighty! what are you doing?"

"Let your fish run—if it can. Here we go!"

She could see where the line went straight and still into the water, and she neatly lobbed the stone a foot behind it. The water splashed, Sammy yelled, so did Dandy; nothing else happened.

"You felt a stir, didn't you?" Iosabel said.

"Dam' the stir!—only me heart somewhere in the roof o' my skull. What'll we do now?"

"That's easy. You're hooked solidly to the bottom." She had yet no inkling of the truth.

"Bottom your granny! It's a fish—I saw it," Sammy shouted.

"Did you rise and hook it?" she asked curiously.

"Well, no! It hooked itself sort of."

"Silly fool! Hooked itself?"

"It did." Sammy had no objection to inventing a lie, for a bit of fun in a good cause—or a bad one. "That time you started the hullabaloo I dropped everything and left my line trailing in here—"

"A fool trick—to torture wee trout!"

"Wee trout! Hup! did he stir?" Sammy was inventing some more. "Gosh! when I took up the rod again, I had something on, and tried to chuck it over my head. That's how I been doin': hookin' 'em and chuckin' 'em over into Dandy's lap. Never missed once. I did that time. Golly! I sprained a wrist, and heard the rod crack. But something did come up and I saw it, and it was the biggest thing in fish I ever saw. A fish! And down it went again, and dam' the stir has it stirred since then. Blow! I thought you could handle—"

"Wait!" A bleak daylight was breaking in Iosabel's mind. "You saw it?"

"He only says he did, the ass!" said Dandy.

"Go to hell, you!" Sammy said.

"Did you notice its back fin?" Iosabel asked.

"Has it a back fin? I saw its head and the yellow of its underside."

He told her more there than he knew. "Oh! you saw the yellow?" The bleak dawn was clearer, and the man up in the heather knew she was seeing things at last.

"Thunderin' blazes!" roared Sammy. "Am I to stand here all night and be called a sanguinary liar? Here! take the blame thing and yank him out yourself."

That is what he had been leading up to, but he did not get there, for he had won Iosabel's sympathy.

"Wait, Sammy!" Her hand touched his arm. "Hang on! It is your fish and I'll net it for you. Back up, and lower your tip. Lower—lower!" She drew him back till the line ran straight from the tip of the rod. "Hold it! Now you have some purchase. Try the reel. Go on! You've tackle to hold it. Steady—steady! He's coming."

Sammy shouted. "There he is. Do you see that yellow?"

She saw it, and she knew what it meant. Poor old Samivel! Someone had played a trick on him too. That unspeakable thug! to play a trick like that on a beginner! This was her fish beyond a doubt, but she would never let old Sammy down. She had had her thrill, and Sammy would have his too.

"Jove, Sammy! it's a fish," she cried, "and he played himself out while you were admiring my seven-pounder."

"Mine is a ton," said Sammy. "Can you reach him with the net?"

"I'll reach him. He hasn't a kick left. Hold him so, and give me more line when I ask for it. Steady now!"

She slipped by him and went out by the right of the rod. She pulled up her left sleeve, her left hand felt for the line, and followed it down to the water, and under it elbow deep till she found the gut. She put on a steady strain, scooped deeply with the net, splattered with her feet, and cried exultingly, bitterness in her soul:

"Got him! More line, Sammy!"

Sammy peeled yards off his reel. It was then that a high, interrogative voice hailed them from down the shore. That was Oliver Dukes, and he was striding along quickly.

Iosabel Mengues was quicker. She came ashore in a curve away from Sammy, the bottom of the net trailing in the water to give the trout some semblance of life, and, a yard out on the gravel, dropped on her knees and felt for a stone. She clouted heartily, hit or miss, and it was not that poor fish that she was clouting. She was clouting Sammy and Dandy and Nolly and herself—and an unspeakable pirate. Yet she got to her feet and spoke cheerfully.

"There's your fish, Mr Veller! and the best ever."

Sammy was strangely dumb, but Iosabel could understand that too. Emotion was choking him. After all, the beginner who lands a record fish will never see a finer day, and she would not spoil it for him. Actually Sammy believed that she believed that this was his fish, and he did not know what to do next. Before he could do anything Oliver Dukes shouldered him aside.

"What's going on this time?" he wanted to know.

"Can you believe your eyes this time?" said Iosabel, and stepped aside.

Dukes reared back, and expressed the view that his eternal soul would suffer a final fatality. His voice went high. "Who caught that beauty? Not Veller!"

Sammy did not care for Dukes, and would not have his bluff called by the hound.

"Before two witnesses—and to hell with you, Nolly! Take a look at him, you scoffer. See them there shoulders! Look at that waistline! Begod! I'll get him stuffed—and my picture in the papers: 'Mr Anthony Villiers and his two-ton trout'! That's us! Hurroo!"

He pirouetted, caught an armful of Dandy, and pranced down the sandy beach. It was a good idea to get out from under. Dukes sat on his heels over the twice-killed trout.

Again he insisted on his final fate. Iosabel stood over and behind him, and considered using that rounded stone once more.

"Sambo Veller! Never—never—never!" he said intolerantly.

"You saw me net it for him?" said Iosabel.

"After a fashion—I did." He shook his long head. "This is beyond me, but I'll find out. One thing I do know: Sammy—did not—catch—this fish." He spaced his words.

"That's Sammy's fish, and he's having a good time about it," said Iosabel reasonably, but she was not feeling that way.

"For about one minute he is having a good time," Dukes said. "A dam' beginner getting away with this! Never. I don't know how it happened—yet—but that is the fish you did catch back there. Look!" His finger went exploring. "Hooked in the angle of the jaw on a nine teal and silver! It could happen; but why twice loop itself under the gills? To oblige a duffer? And will you take a look at that deformed fin!" He looked up at her over his shoulder, and his light voice scoffed. "Hielan'woman! You got the second sight. How did you know?"

"Know what?" said Iosabel under pressure.

"A seven-eight pound trout, you said, and so it is, near enough. And nicked in the back fin, and nicked it is. That's second sight, ain't it? Like hell it is! I'm not going to see you cheated out of your fish, and I'll take Mr Anthony Villiers down a peg. And that's flat."

Oliver Dukes was pleased with himself. There was some mystery to be probed later, but now he would insist that this fish was Iosabel's, and so he would stand well with her. That was ever his object.

A little distance into the heather, behind a whin bush, Gawain Micklethwaite stirred and was about to rise to his feet. Already he was feeling repentant. That girl down there was assaying sterling metal, and it was due to her to come out into the open—and—get himself thrown in the loch. But before he could act things came to a climax down below.

Iosabel Mengues spoke quietly—so quietly that Dukes did not get the danger in her tone.

"Oliver Dukes, if you spoil this for Sammy I'll—I'll—"

"Nonsense! You can do nothing about it, my dear," he said, and opened his mouth to shout for Sammy.

"Can't I?" said Iosabel, and did it.

The temptation was as obvious and big as a mountain. She could not resist it. A bishop couldn't. Dukes was crouching over her fish—yes, her fish—and she stood directly behind him. He was wearing arm-pit waders and was well padded; and she was wearing stout fishing boots. She went back half a pace for distance, swung a vigorous leg, and half-punted, half-heaved with whole-hearted abandon. Dukes' torso lifted abruptly, and he went forward and down, head, arms and shoulders, into a foot of water. And that was that.

And Iosabel went striding along the shore, and though her ankle ached she was too mad to notice it. She was a first-class beater of strategic retreats. And she kept this one up, for, barely taking time to recover her tackle, she clambered over the ridge and went off down the track by the Caller Burn.

Oliver Dukes had scrambled out of the water, strangling, for he had gulped some of it. And up in the heather someone was strangling too. Sammy and Dandy were unrestrainedly laughing.

"Right between the goal posts!" cried Dandy.

"She took it out on Nolly—thank the Lord!" said Sammy.

Dukes coughed water, shook his head, and made a blind and angry movement along the shore.

"Wo there! put a hitch on it!" cried Sammy, and spread his arms.

Dukes grappled him, and tried to thrust him aside; and Dandy, after the manner of the cave-woman, cried out:

"Swat him one, Sammy! Swat the hound!"

Dukes threw him off, stepped back, and pulled himself together. No! he must not further antagonise Iosabel Mengues. Not now! There was something going on about this loch to-night, and he would keep his mouth shut until he got to the bottom of it. He wiped his face downward, and swallowed his choler.

"Forget it! You can have your dam' fish," he said.

"Sure! and I'll present it to Bell as first prize," Sammy said. "I can always catch myself another."

"A damn bungler would," said Dukes, and stalked off on the other curve of the shore.

After a while Sammy and Dandy faced the heather, and Sammy whistled softly. There was no reply.

"Come out of it, Beelzebub!" invited Sammy. He walked a few feet into the heather, right up to a whin bush, and whistled again. But there was nothing to see or hear.

"He's gone, the devil!" said Sammy, "and I'm left holding the baby."

"Good old Iosabel!" said Dandy. "I'll tell her first thing in the morning."

"That she-devil will cut my throat and I'll scrag you," said Sammy. "Let's get going."

When they were gone a figure materialised out of that whin bush, and the figure was Gawain Micklethwaite.

Chapter VII
IOSABEL WINS A GUERDON

I

THE FOUR from the Tigh Mhor had left Ros Caller, Iosabel first, Dukes some distance behind, and Sammy and Dandy trailing after. Gawain was left in possession of the stricken field, but he did not feel the glow of the victor. A cloud island had drifted up from behind the summits and swallowed the moon, the surface of the loch was grey-steel, and all the moors were withdrawn and sombre. There might be no more fishing till the dawn.

He moved round the shore to where the Caller Burn debouched from the loch, sat down on one of the many boulders bedded in the gravel, lit his last cigarette, and listened to the water chuckling remotely to itself as it shouldered amongst the stones. He was in no hurry. It was a balmy night of late Spring, and it was good to be here in his own land, under the half-dark, and with peace all about him.

Things had not been so peaceable a while ago. He had fallen to temptation, and played rather a mean trick on a fellow angler—and a woman at that. And he did not want to have anything to do with woman. Dalliance—or marriage—was not for the man who had suffered from a sick mind. He knew what he wanted to do. He had been in the hills of Burma and the foothills of the Himalayas, had flown a plane into Kashmir, and seen the Karakorams and the colossal dome of K 2. And he had read a book by the great climber, Eric Shipton. The mountains for him and the fellowship of the great boys—the never-old who made the mountains and the wilderness their own. That would be enough out of life, and let woman choose others for her bowers.

Then, let him be fair. This dark, foreign-highland, señorita-lass was a good sport, and to-night had shown a sterling core of character. She had taken the loss of her fabulous prize with fine forbearance, and she would not let old Sammy down. By glory! she wouldn't! and had so apprised that big fellow unmistakably, Gawain chuckled, recalling the satisfactory thoroughness of that propulsion into the loch. It was he himself should have suffered it, and he would have if she had had a chance. Well, she hadn't, and she wouldn't. He was finished with her now. He would wash his hands of the whole business, and, after a few more days with his friends, betake himself to the high places.

But what of little Alsuin? She had put one of her Tasks on him, and he had made a mess of it. He had acerbated the situation. He had proclaimed his allegiance to Luke Carnoch; he had made the laird's daughter in the laird's eyes lose caste by provoking her to lift a cheap pair of pants; he had shown skewbald nakedness amongst the laird's guests under the laird's roof; he had gloried in trespassing; and, finally, he had spoiled for the laird's daughter a worth-while angling triumph. Surely, he had better clear out before worse befell.

As for Alsuin, she was getting beyond the fairy-story stage. The make-believe was wearing thin, and soon she would no longer expect of him the doughty deeds of Finn or Lancelot, or even that Gawain who became a rogue. He would just play along with her for a few more days and then slip away—and he might never see her again under glimpses of the moon.

That was Gawain, master of his fate, making final decisions in the quiet of the night, the moors hushed all round him, the loch a wan sheet before him, the burn talking aloofly to itself. But no final decision was his to command, as he should have known; and there and then he was made aware of the fact with a startle. It was as the cloud cleared off the face of the moon, and a path of radiance was laid down across the water.

II

There was a resounding splash three yards out in the loch, and Gawain lifted to his feet as if plucked.

"A big one right under my nose!" he cried.

A cold voice spoke behind him. "Another where that came from! Where do you want it?"

He put his hands over his ears and crouched his head between his shoulders.

"*Geal is dearg a suas!* Up the white and red!" He gave her the slogan of the Menzies. "Between the shoulder-blades for choice." He did not expect her to hesitate for a moment, and he would cough a piece of lung into the water.

He heard her boots among the stones as she came up on his right side within two paces of him. He looked cautiously round the side of his hand, but she was not facing his way. She was looking out over the loch, and swinging her left arm; and with one final swing she sent a solid chunk of rock curving high and far into the water. It was a remarkable throw for a girl, and done with the elbow action of a boy. And she was left-handed.

"You learned that throwing the bola—no, the bolas!" said Gawain, dropped his hands, and faced round to her.

She faced round too, and her voice was desperately calm, "Wing-Commander Sir Gawain Micklethwaite, I am going to have things out with you if it takes all night."

"I had just decided to call it a day—"

"After licking your chops—as usual?"

"Glory! Had I any chops to lick last time we met?" he asked indignantly.

She gestured that left hand impatiently, moved half-a-pace, and sat down on a conveniently placed shelf of rock. He sat down too, and if he made a long arm he could touch her. Neither of them said anything for quite a while, but their thoughts were busy.

He knew that she knew from early on that he was the man in the heather; and now she had come back, alone and fearlessly, to find him and have things out with him, fair and square, man to man, cool and calm, time no object, and no holds barred. They seemed fated to tangle every time they met. Fair enough! Let this be the final tangle, then.

A few minutes ago his thoughts had been the cold thoughts of a man going into exile; now there was a warmth in his mind. He did not realise it, but if he did he might put it down to the mood before battle, not to a hidden contentment at being here in the lap of the hills, a live young woman at his side, their minds on each other and grappling for hold. And the mind is part of the body—or is it only a function—or the Master?

He waited for her to begin, but she was slow about it. She pushed her red kerchief back from her hair, and lifted her head as if feeling for a draw of air. But no breath of air moved, and the loch was a smooth shield with one bar of radiance laid across it. She was wearing a brown golf-jacket, and she moved a hand up to the breast-pocket, snatched it away again, and said "damn" under her breath.

"Sorry! I have no cigarettes either," said Gawain.

"I have some." This time her hand went definitely to her breast-pocket, and brought out a flatly-curved cigarette case. She did not open it, but reached it across, and he took it and looked at it shining in the moon—and it was warm with the warmth of her breast.

It had been freshly polished, but there was a dent or two in it that he knew. It was Chinese silver, with the Chinese dragon engraved intricately on the convex, and he had picked it up in Hong Kong for a few dollars. And it had been in the hip-pocket of a vanished pair of pants.

"I forgot to return it this afternoon," she said coolly.

"You did not forget much this afternoon," said Gawain with conviction. He flicked the case open. It was nearly full of her expensive cigarettes, and he reached it across. "Without prejudice!" he said.

Her fingers fumbled and touched his. He scraped a match and leant aside. In the pulsing flame he saw the strong bosses of her cheeks, and her strange, live eyes glinting below black lashes, and the full curve of her mouth—made for kissing.

"Thanks!" she said, and inhaled smoke. "And thank you also for that nice pound trout."

A neat opening begod! "Your fish," he said. "Some poaching fellow—"

"Leave poaching out of it," she stopped him smartly. "I have enough to resent—"

"You have, indeed, yes—yes!" he said ruminatively. "And it is a great pity someone is not more repentant."

"You never are."

"I mean—Och! I don't know what I mean, but I liked your style to-night. Does your ankle hurt?"

She sat up quickly. "Stop that!" she cried. "That is a red herring. What brought you up here?"

"You did."

She accepted that readily. "Yes—I did open my mouth! But why were you so—so obnoxious?"

"Nice word—cuts both ways!"

She leant forward, rested her forearms across her canvassed knees, and smoked for a while. "All right! I was obnoxious—at the beginning." Her arm swept an arc. "But still, you have no rights in this place?"

The gloves were off at last.

"I have," said Gawain. "I belong. Do you?"

"You mean?"

"Do you belong—does your father belong?"

"Micklethwaite—Gawain! Does that belong?" she challenged.

"Right here. Anywhere fifty miles up the coast and fifty miles down, these nine hundred years, since Margaret, queen and saint, brought a Yorkshire robber in her tail—to civilise Scotland—and got himself lost in quarterings and sixteenths and thirty-seconds of MacDonalds and MacLeans and Camerons, with Campbell for a by-blow. I belong. Do you? Does Sanin Cejador y Mengues?"

That was blunt enough, but she would not show that she was hurt.

"You, too, are a bit of a sentimentalist about your Highlands," she said.

"So was your father."

"What do you know—?"

"But I do know. He would restore at least one place in the Glens, but all he has done is to set up a small squiredom of his own, and the Squirearchy was the greatest tyranny that this island ever suffered from. Don't speak to me—"

"I don't get a chance—"

"Don't speak to me of English Freedom and Love of Liberty—capital letters—since the signing of Magna Charta! Liberty and Licence for the squire, who made the peasant his serf, and legalised abominable punishments for the least infringement of the squire's privileges. That's the liberty the Union brought to the Highlands."

"You accepted it."

He threw his cigarette away, rose to his feet, and came round in front of her. He put his hands behind his back, his fingertips holding the cigarette case, and stared down at her sombrely. And she sat up, threw back her head, and stared boldly back.

"You are having things out with me," he said, "but, this time, I am getting my piece in first. You would never guess why?"

"You tell me?"

"I will—dammit, I will!" His gaze never changed. "It is because I like you, somehow. You've got sand, and a streak of toughness, and considerateness as well, and your sense of the proper is about the fragilest thing I have ever seen broken. Honest to God! you are a bit of a tinker, and I like you." His voice was full of gloom.

She might accuse him of condescension or plain unvarnished impertinence, but she simply said:

"All right! Go on telling me."

"I will." In front of where she sat was a clear patch of gravel that allowed him three paces one way and three paces back, and as he talked he paced back and forth, and the cigarette case flashed in the moonlight as he emphasised his points. And she sat very still, hands folded, and watched the slow roll and check of his feet.

"Whatever your father had in mind, he only set up a squiredom in Glen Easan. He certainly did not re-create the clan system in a Highland glen—a return to what we used to call the Golden Age. Fellowship there was none. Chief and clansman had no meaning. The demárcation line between laird and tenant was as impassable as between hidalgo and peon. Your father was no more than a landlord in the manner of a Sussex squire after the pattern of one Rudyard Kipling, a Hindoo writer on the caste system at home and among the lesser breeds."

"There was a Hindoo man of caste in this too," she could

not help saying.

"But not to blame. The trouble was always there and only dormant. As long as the villeins kept their side of the line amenities were poured on them. When one of them offended he was treated like an offending eunuch. When the others sided with him the punishment became absolute. There was no longer the power of pit and gallows, but all amenities were taken away—and some amenities were almost necessities. The squire closed a useful road, locked his gates, put himself behind barbed wire, and turned his back on the glen—turned his back on the people of the glen that make any glen worth while. And there he is, and there you are, a captive in the house of a lonely tyrant."

He had not spared her. He had put all the blame on one pair of shoulders, and had ignored the executive servant. She took it passively and did not lift her eyes. It was almost as if she wanted all this said once and for all. Her voice remained low and quiet.

"You are exaggerating in places—and all the time you are taking sides."

He faced her again, and looked down at her black hair sheening under the shining of the moon.

"I am not taking sides any more," he said. "I decided on that a minute before you came back. In a week or so I set sail for a land where the miles stand up on end, five at a time."

"Forsaking this Scotland of yours?" she said quickly.

"Forsaking many things."

"Scotland is always forsaken by her children—but she will not die," she said, her tone deep.

"You have the roots in you," he said, and felt a stir.

III

Gawain went back to his boulder and sat down. He tendered her his case, and she took a cigarette without hesitation; and for a while they smoked in silence, and looked along the path of the moon across the water.

He thought, rather smugly, that he understood her silence. He had given her something to think about, and she was mulling it over in her own mind, and regathering her resources to come back at him. What he did not know was that the things he had said were already old and heavy in her mind.

"You were to have things out with me if it took all night—and the night is young," he suggested.

She released her breath in what sounded like a sigh, and moved a hand deprecatingly.

"Only little things after what you have said. I suppose it is natural that you should side with Luke Carnoch against us—and show your contempt in the things you do—"

"Hold it!" he cried. "One thing at a time. Luke Carnoch is not taking sides—"

"Against my father, he is?"

"He is not. He rather likes your father, and is the one restraining influence in Ardaneigh—"

"Restraining influence?" She was inclined to bridle at that.

"Exactly! Do you not know? There are some young soldiers home from war after crashing Hitlerism in blood and ruins, and they do not gladly suffer totalitarianism in their home town."

She did not know that, and it disturbed her more than he thought it would. She got to her feet and sat down again, and there was a hurt note in her voice.

"Oh dear—oh dear! Is it as bad as that?"

"No—don't worry!" he said quickly. "Lukey has Ardaneigh under his thumb—and can hang on for his miracle." He leant towards her, a finger lifted, and his voice very serious. "But wait! There is another force that Lukey cannot restrain at all, a really vindictive force."

"Another force?" she said a little helplessly.

"The MacFies."

"The tinkers—that poor wastrel crew!" Her shoulders jerked in contempt, but into her mind came the vision of that young tinker woman with her insolent eyes and contemptuous spit. Gawain went on:

"Wastrel and depraved! Maybe they are. But the MacFies have their code. They'll poach and steal and cheat and lie, and, caught out, take their jail sentence with stoicism. That's the luck of the game. But touch them where they live and 'ware trouble—to the burning of roofs, the shedding of blood, stark murder itself. Your father, or his agent, threw them out of one of their traditional camps at Corran Hook—"

"But they are allowed to camp at the Sand Pits."

"For how long? Throw them out of there and don't

blame Luke Carnoch if trouble comes."

"Trouble! A tinker against my father? Bah!"

"All right, prood Maisie! The tinker will get the worst of it. The underdog always does, but it sometimes gets its bite in first. That's all."

They sat silent for a while, and Gawain turned the cigarette case over and over to let the moonshine play on it. He had a little more to say, and he would say it carefully. She spoke first.

"You said something about a miracle?" she put in curiously.

"Leave it! A miracle strikes out of the blue, and we can do nothing about it." He turned towards her. "What I want to say is that I did not intend contempt in the silly things I did. I climbed over a gate to walk in an old path I helped to make—"

"If you told me!"

"I was playing a fairy story, and the dolour that befell me I deserved. This afternoon you told me off—"

"Some of the things—"

"Sounded like a dare."

"They were."

"So I came along to-night, and I am not too happy about it. But you may well be, for you behaved like a good 'un all the time. I am glad of that, and let that be my apology. Now we make a finish. I will not again trespass within your gates; I will not poach your waters; and in ten days I will be gone. That is all now."

He got to his feet, and so did she. They faced each other, and a sudden thought made him smile.

"You had things out with me?" he said.

"And there is no more to say," she said, and smiled too.

"But—I think—we should finish our fairy story worthily."

"Is it not—?"

"I trow not. Three times we met, and three times jousted with might and main. Victory remains with you, and I concede it. But there should be something else." He looked down at the cigarette case that turned over and over in his fingers, and his voice was strangely diffident. "There should be something to show for it, an honourable award, a guerdon is it not? Something to recall what might in retrospect be a gay ploy—" He stopped and did not know how to go on, and the cigarette case winked in his fingers. But she understood, and her face lit and smiled, and was lovely. His head was down, and he did not see how desirable she looked.

"Knight, yclept Gawain, though I deserve it not, I accept your honourable guerdon."

She picked the battered silver case softly from his fingers, smoothed a finger over it, and slipped it back into her breast-pocket. Then she reached him her hand, and hands and eyes locked for a moment.

"Good night—and goodbye!" she said, her deep voice steady, and she turned from him and went. And he let her go.

He faced round to the loch, and heard her feet, amongst the stones, fading down the track. It was better so, to make a quick finish between them—for all time. But life was a lonely thing for a man, and now he knew it. Life without love! and he must not fall in love. That old sickness of mind—that might return—forbade love—forbade marriage.

Chapter VIII

IN THE CAMP OF THE BROKEN CLAN

I

GAWAIN MICKLETHWAITE and Sammy Veller met, not quite by accident, on the road to the township of Ardaneigh, and a smart shower drove them into the local inn, or, rather, the local public house. It showed no sign, carried no coat of arms, and was known to all as Dinny Sullavan's; for, strangely enough, the landlord was a stray Irishman, who farmed a croft and grazed sheep, and let his wife, Peigi, run the pub as a side-line. Her father had owned the premises, and she had met and married Dinny in Glasgow.

Dinny Sullavan's was one of the thatched houses of the township, for the new laird of Glen Easan did not approve of public houses, and had done nothing to modernise the amenities for fairly temperate drinking. Dinny did not mind, nor did his customers, for it was an intimate, old-fashioned place in the tradition of the glen. The bar, the bar-parlour, the snug, the lounge, the saloon-bar were all comprised in one big room that was also the kitchen and living-room: a wide, long room filling half the cavity of the house from flagged floor to rye-thatch. The black rafters glistened in peat crust, and from the collar-braces hung flitches of bacon and bunches of salt ling tough enough to sole boots. At one end was the huge, open fireplace under a mantel-bar six feet up, so that in cold spells the customers could get inside the cavern of the chimney corner. At the other end was the low zinc-covered counter outside the scantily-stocked shelves—scantily stocked in these hard times when the whisky that Scotland has made world-famous is not only rationed but duty-penalised beyond the means of the plain Scotsman.

Gawain was an old friend of the Sullavans, and Peigi, a sonsy Highlandwoman, greeted him with both hands, dusted a couple of straw-bottomed chairs, and pulled a small deal table between them in front of the strongly-scented peat fire. On this table she placed two glasses, a jug of water and a soda siphon, and looked interrogatively at Gawain, her eyes crinkling.

"Whatever you say, ma'am!" said he. "I'm leavin' it to yerself."

"You schemer! Wait now!"

She went through a doorway at one side of the ingle, and came back bearing a black quart bottle without a label.

"Dinny heard from the Major and Lukey how you were on the road, Bart.," she explained, "and he went a piece of a journey to see a friend who obliged him. Don't be afeared of this, sir," she said to Sammy. "It is a distillery whisky out of Islay. Help yourself, and welcome!"

She placed the bottle on the table, and went behind her counter to work at a stock book. The two men had the whole place to themselves in the quiet of the afternoon. Dinny, his two sons—one home from war—and daughter, with most of the township, were away back in the high moors cutting and footing peats; and until the end of the working day the bar would be deserted.

Sammy sampled unblended malt whisky and cleared his throat appreciatively. Gawain lit a cigarette, and listened to the rain on the four panes of the small window.

"You spoil good whisky with soda-water, Samuel," he said. "Is it true that you been catchin' big fishes?"

"One." Sammy lifted a blasé finger. "Just one—but a

nice fish—six pounds eleven ounce—on a small fly! Took me fifty-two minutes by the clock, and Bell Mengues netted it for me. I got two witnesses."

"A sound liar like you should make an angler," Gawain said. "Did you give it back to the lady who caught it?"

"Blast your daylights, Mick!" exploded Sammy warmly. "You got me into trouble." He brought a palm down on the table. "I'll never trust a woman again."

"Which one?"

"That viper, Dandy Dinmont."

"Is that really her name?"

"Is it? No. Danice Din-dun. Danice Dinwoody—that's it! Dandy for short."

"A hell of a name too. What did she put across?"

"She blew the gaff."

"One of you had to?"

"But not premature. That night—two nights ago wasn't it?—we pulled the quick one—and damme! I should ha' known you better than go in a game with you. I didn't see Bell that night again—gone to bed in a huff or something, and wasn't I glad! Next morning I thought better of it. Dandy and I made up a plan to save our skins. 'Mum's the word,' sez I, 'cut your throat!' And she did, the rip! We sent the trout off packed in ice to be mounted. You know?—stuffed out large as life, and put in a glass box with a silver plate—'Record Native Lake Trout, 6 lbs. 11 oz., caught in Loch Ros Caller by Miss Iosabel Mengues, Tigh Mhor, Glen Easan'— something like that—"

"That was a real nice idea, Sammy," said Gawain commendingly.

"Wasn't it? I thought so myself, and threw my weight about, for I owed old Bell a coupla jabs in the midriff. She thought I thought I caught that whopper, and I kept rubbin' it in like salt in a wound. And do you know what that cussed Dinmont called me?"

"An ungrateful hound."

"Frog-spawn, she made it, and if I did not draw it mild she'd blow the gaff. So I scragged her—"

"Choked her, you caitiff?"

"A bit of manhandling—she's used to it. And she kicked me in the shin and went straight off and told Bell."

"Any decent girl would."

"Damn your eyes! I left. That was an hour ago. The two of them were makin' an encircling movement with a baffy and a number three iron."

"They'll get you—"

"They will, brast you! That's why I'm imbibing Dutch courage." He reached for the bottle. "Say, Mick, did she really know that was her fish?"

"Of course. She knew it by the nick in its back fin."

"She's a good sport, begod!"

"Dukes knew it too—"

"That for a yarn! He'd call me down pronto—"

"The lady wouldn't let him. I was listening. That's why she kicked him into the loch."

"Ho-ho-ho! Did you see it? Twenty-five foot from the take off—I measured it. An' that's why he's goin' round with his mouth shut, and a face like the wrath o' God."

"Why?"

"'Cause the sly dog don't want to counter her. All the same he's goin' the wrong way to work—all the time. I know."

"Like hell you know!" said Gawain offensively.

Sammy poured another drink carefully, for Gawain had taught him that malt whisky should be treated with respect before nightfall. He seemed to change the subject.

"You know the old hidalgo has a tribal war on with the aborigines round here—includin' your man, Carnoch—and some tinkers."

"A bloodless war, Sammy!"

"Maybe. But the sly Mr Nolly Dukes thinks he'll stand well with the daughter by siding the father against the *canaille*. He's talkin' now of a double watch on the fishin' reaches, an' throwin' the tinkers out of their camp up the road."

Gawain sat up. "Throwing the MacFies out?"

"That's right! But his high-handedness won't help him with the girl. No suh!"

"Why not?" Gawain hid his interest.

"Because she is on the other side—not openly—but she is. She told me so herself."

"When did she tell you—today, yesterday?" Gawain asked quickly.

"Le' me see! That afternoon I called on you—why, that was the evening we went to Ros Caller! That very afternoon. Gosh, Mick! she nearly cried on my shoulder."

"Something hurt her?"

"I saw it. We'd been a motor run, and a black tinker woman came out of that sand-pit up the road, and spat at her. You wouldn't mind a tinker, but this township lot were worse: slinkin' indoors, slippin' round corners turning backs on her. She might ha' leprosy the way they acted. She wasn't a scrap mad, and that wasn't like her. These were her sort of people, she said, and a fine crowd they were. She said herself and this here crowd spoke the same language, and pulled the same fast ones to laugh at. She said she could work for and with them—and something about repairing the devastation. Damn the devastation I see! She was nearly in tears, and I'm tellin' you."

Nearly in tears, and ten minutes later she took the hide off me! thought Gawain. *I came in the way of the discharge, and that was all.*

He poured whisky slowly, but his thoughts were so busy that he kept on pouring till Sammy said, "Hoy!" For a moment he had thought that his lecture at Ros Caller had borne fruit, but he had been preaching to the converted all the time—and indeed, it was the only sort of preaching that was ever listened to. He might have known! The sound metal in her would ring to the sound metal in the glen. Pity someone couldn't help her. He couldn't—not in a week, and another week was all he had. . . . But there was a thing he could do, and he thought of it only at that moment. He could look over the danger point—just a look and no more. He got to his feet, and tossed off his whisky in one clean gulp.

"Lawr! how do you Hielan' men do it?" cried Sammy.

"The shower is over," Gawain said, "and I am going up to see my old friend, Parlan MacFie. You go and take your medicine!"

"I might lure Dandy up the river and drown her," Sammy said hopefully.

Gawain threw a pound note on the table. "You're paying for the drinks, Sam."

Sammy pointed at the note. "What's that for—a tip?"

"No—that pays. I found it in the back pocket of these yaller pants." And he moved for the door.

"Scotland for ever!" cried Sammy.

II

At about that time two young people, a mile apart, each took out a dog for training and exercise.

One was Donal MacFie, age fifteen, and he went slinking

covertly amongst the coverts, for he was on preserved ground. His dog was a brindled lurcher bitch, aged nine months and full of noisy enthusiasm for the game. When trained its enthusiasm would not be abated, but in silence it would pursue and kill and bring its quarry to the feet of the god that had trained it.

The other young dog trainer was Iosabel Mengues, and the dog was a black-and-white springer spaniel, some six months old. She went boldly in the open, for every place within sight was hers. That springer, when trained, would never be silent, but it would be a good dog amongst partridge, springing like a springbok over turnip tops, and occasionally tailing a-yelp after a coney.

Iosabel had another dog along too. That was big Oliver Dukes, who was willing to pretend to come to heel. They went round by Cobh Echlan and up the glen by the river, where there was cover of blackthorn and whin, with plenty of rabbits and an occasional water hen. Now and then she brought the pup to heel for discipline, giving it the end of the leash in a safe place or threatening it with the long hazel crook she carried.

So they came over the rise on the right, outside the barbed wire of the demesne; and here, in dampish ground, there was a scattered cover of sallaghs and brambles. After a while Iosabel said:

"We'd better leash Rory. He's getting near the heather, and we can't have him amongst the nesting grouse. Head him off, Nolly! That bark is getting excited."

She was breathing freely after the rise from the glen, fine colour in her cheeks, but she was not winded, and she went off nimbly amongst the sallaghs, avoiding the brambles. Nolly went to the right, long-striding. The pup did not respond to Iosabel's clear call or Dukes' whistle. It was discovering a new interest in life, and its bark receded, lifted interrogatively, and stopped.

"Dash! he's found a burrow," Iosabel called. "We must find him now, or he might smother."

In half-a-minute Dukes' voice lifted warningly.

"'Ware poacher! Your left front." He slanted towards her. "Fellow in a red kilt! a grey dog with him. I didn't see Rory but his last bark was that way—towards the common."

"Damn! that is the way he would go," Iosabel said disgustedly, striking at a bush with her crook.

"We'd better hurry," Dukes called. "The tinkers are camped up there, and that pup is a valuable one. I'll try and head it off." He curved off at a gallop.

Young Donal MacFie was not trying to steal Rory. Donal, who had seen Dukes long before Dukes saw him, was manoeuvring himself and his lurcher off preserved ground as fast as he knew how. It was not his fault if a spaniel dog and a lurcher bitch had met in a covert, and taken a fancy to each other; and it was not his fault if the spaniel kept lolloping lop-eared after the lurcher. He was in too much of a hurry to shoo the dog off—and anyway, it was a nice wee pup. He chose his line of retreat as the son of generations of poachers would, keeping well out of sight and dodging from cover to cover; but, in crossing the road below the camp, he had to come into the open for a moment. And Dukes' voice lifted:

"There he goes! and Rory too begad! No confounded tinker can get off with that!" And he ran as directly as the ground permitted for the fold in the hills where the sandpit was; and, as he ran, he said: *This is the chance I wanted*

Iosabel slowed down. She knew Oliver Dukes up to a certain point, and was prepared to make use of him; and she was quite cold-blooded about it, as women are when making use of a man. She might now see how the MacFies reacted to the high-handedness of the laird's agent, and that might give her a line on any danger threatening her beloved father. If Nolly got a bloody nose in the issue, that was his business; he was ready enough to blood a nose himself, and if he couldn't, that was just too bad for him.

III

Gawain sat on the tail-steps of Old Parlan MacFie's caravan, nibbled a buttered farl of oatcake, and drank boiled tea. Boiled tea did not sit well on malt whisky, but the ritual of friendliness had to be carried out in this camp that Gawain knew of old. He had a standing amongst the MacFies. They accepted him for the easy-going tolerance that made no demands and gave what it could in a natural way of fellowship not touched with condescension. He was as nearly a friend as any out-lander is ever likely to be with the real clan-tinker.

That small tribe of MacFies was the last remnant of one of the great broken clans. Old Parlan, the chief, could trace his blood back three hundred years to Murroch who was chief of Colonsay, and to that Malcolm betrayed to the Campbells by Coll Kitto, father of Montrose's famous Major-General. That betrayal had sent the clan to the road, and here it was, now, not far from the end of it.

Parlan sat on a straw creeple facing Gawain, and made courteous talk. His native tongue was Gaelic, but he used Beurla-English to Gawain, who also knew Gaelic, but not fluently. He was a lean angular old man, and lean-faced, and, though beardless, he had never needed to shave. Neither had he any hair under his black glengarry bonnet with its badge of oak. He was wearing patched home-spuns, not the kilt of red and green.

His granddaughter-in-law, Sileas, presided at the black tin teapot, and buttered oatcakes on the tail-piece of the van. She was a flaming, black woman, still lovely, and her face was so richly brown that minute freckles barely showed. She it was who had spat her contempt for the people of the Tigh Mhor some days before.

Her husband, Malcolm, leant a shoulder against a corner of the van, and drank tea out of a tin panny. He was a veritable throw-back to some Pictish forbear, the formidable Pict who had held Rome behind the Wall for three centuries. He was under middle height, but had the shoulders, chest and arms of a gorilla; the frustum of his neck started under his ears and sloped far out on his shoulders; he was black and crisp in the hair, sallow of skin, and his deep-set smoke-grey eyes were slightly aslant. Those slanted eyes, flat cheekbones, and open nostrils gave his face an almost-Mongolian cast. He was wearing an old battle-dress, for he was not long back from Germany. His father had died at Cambrai in 1917. Malcolm was an outcast and a landless man in the land that he and his father had fought for; and that thought was beginning to trouble Malcolm's mind. He and Gawain had known each other from boyhood, and had done a few lawless things together in this glen.

Gawain looked round the scattered untidy camp, ragged with nettles and briar, and noted that the three or four vans needed paint, and that the half-dozen wedge-shaped tents had been patched and patched again with old sacking. The other members of the little clan—twenty or so—were having tea round small fires of whin roots and peat, and the smoke drifted and curled up the scaling, sandy walls of the pit. High up, at a place where the strata was firm, the bluff was pitted with the nest-holes of sand-martin, and the little birds darted in and out, careless of the tinker crew.

On the far side, an old road came through from the main road and went on through a gap at the back. That was one of the old droving roads, and it went straight as a rush some fifteen miles to an old camp at Cloun Aiternach, and another five miles, again to join the main road. It was still a right of way, used by the MacFies to get to Cloun Aiternach, and by the township to get to the peat banks.

Gawain reached his cigarette packet to Sileas, who shook her head, and smiled to show her white teeth. White though they were, she smoked a pipe in her own van. Malcolm took a cigarette, but Parlan shrugged his bony shoulders and brought out a black pipe of Irish clay. Gawain, making talk, said carelessly:

"This is not your camp the season that's in it, Parlan?"

And Parlan replied smoothly, translating from the Gaelic:

"It does be one of our camps, and a change-round is good for the health, *mo buachail*." *Mo buachail*—my boy—and said in joking friendliness.

Gawain used the old rogue's idiom. "Delicate you are getting in your old age, and you needing a grouse's egg for your breakfast."

These people appreciated the sly hit, and Sileas and Malcolm laughed at their grandad. But, serious as a judge, he came back:

"It could be, indeed! But the garcoch (the embryo) does be in the egg the season that's in it, and that is bad eating."

"And good eating below at Corran," Gawain said, "the salmon running free, Saturday to Monday, round the hook point—four miles from here."

"And what is four miles to young fellows like us, and we wanting to bathe our feet in the salt water?"

The other two laughed at Gawain that time. But Gawain had found out a little. The MacFies had been ejected from Corran camp, and Parlan would not be drawn about it. That was not so good. In any everyday resentment Parlan would curse the new laird in seed, breed and generation, and leave it at that. This went deeper, and Parlan would not say anything—even to a friend—that might be used later against the MacFies. A bit more probing was called for, and he might win confidence if he hunted his own bout with authority. He said:

"Speaking of bathing your old feet in salt water, I came on a locked gate the other morning, but I bathed in Cobh Echlan all the same."

"Do you know," said Parlan, "it is a great puzzle to us

still, the tartan of the short kilt you were wearing for a while that morning."

"You ould divil!" said Gawain, startled, and chuckled with the others. But he would try a little more. "That shameless story did not finish that morning, Parlan, but you would know nothing about the rest of it."

"Not a word, indeed," said Parlan agreeably, "and how could I? You are a good man in the heather, my friend, but you was not born in it."

And that was so. Gawain was a good man in cover, and his life had depended on that more than once, but he could not hope to match a tinker, born and reared in the heather and winning sustenance from its harsh penuriousness. He turned to Malcolm.

"You couldn't call your soul your own with your oul' fellow, Malcolm," he said.

"He has the loose tongue in him." Malcolm had the rumbling, throaty voice of one sparing of speech. And he was, maybe, reprimanding the old fellow for telling too much. Evidently the adventure of the purloined pants was known to the tribe, and, almost certainly, there had been another man in the heather that night at Ros Caller. But Gawain had been told more than that. He had been told that the MacFies were keeping a close watch, day and night, on everything that took place within and without the policies of the Tigh Mhor. But why? A mere poaching precaution, or the hatching of a plot against the tyrant? Parlan would never say openly.

Parlan sucked at his old pipe; Malcolm blew a thin stream of smoke; Sileas went round to the other end of the van with the tea-things; no one spoke for a while. The old primitive was watching Gawain slyly. Gawain had come looking for information, and he had been given it in the indirect way in which he had asked for it. What did the tall man want? In the days not so long ago he was a friend to the MacFies. What was he going to do now to befriend the MacFies, hunted from pillar to post?

"Damn the thing," said Gawain, and jerked his half-smoked cigarette away. It was an apt answer to a silent question, and no one noticed the strangeness of it, for their minds had been in touch all the time. "There are a fine lot of fools in this place," said Gawain, "and to the devil with them!"

"That's the airt they're going," said Malcolm's rumble.

Gawain turned and thrust his head at Malcolm. He had a

 strange affection for this gorilla of a man.

"Don't you be one of the dam' fools, Malcolm! Haven't you been in hell long enough?"

"Show me a road out, brother," Malcolm said. "I'm lookin' for it."

"Ay—ay, indeed!" said old Parlan remotely. "A time there was that three men I know had great power over every road in this place."

Gawain knew the three men: Luke Carnoch, David Keegan and himself. And it was true—but no longer.

"You schemin' old Turk!" said Gawain, and rose to stride out of camp. But he checked himself, and sat down again. A high imperative shouting came through the opening from the main road, and it was coming nearer.

Gawain turned that way, and looked over the ridge of a squat tent; Parlan pivoted slowly round on his creepie; and Malcolm said dispassionately: "That foolish wee loon! I'll take the skin off him." But that shouting was the shouting of a grown man.

IV

A young fellow in a ragged kilt came sneaking in at the road-opening, sort of pretending that he was on his own business, in no great hurry, and not to be noticed by anyone. But he never paused, as he sidled along the left margin of the camp, and dodged into an opening in the sandy bluff. Gawain knew there was a steep track in there, leading up to the heather; the tinker's "briar-patch."

Two dogs were on the young fellow's heels: a lurcher and a spaniel. A spaniel? The men of the road would never use a spaniel. It was too slow and too noisy. But they might lift one in the by-going, and barter it fifty miles along the road. That young fellow had trouble on his heels, too, and here came the trouble now.

A taller and a bigger fellow came in a hurry through the road-entrance, and Gawain sat up. He knew this man: Dukes—Oliver—Nolly Dukes, who had a habit of thrusting himself in where angels feared to tread; and here he was, now, barging into a hornet's nest.

This is no place for me, thought Gawain, *but I'm lyin' low and saying nuffin!* He lit a cigarette, leant back on the steps, and crossed his knees.

Oliver Dukes, who had been in a hurry, slowed down, stopped, and looked coolly and searchingly all round him. There was no sign of the young tinker or the spaniel, but he had expected that, and, indeed, was rather pleased about it, for he was glad of the opportunity to prove his authority, and deal drastically with the tinker's sly deceit—and he might have some fun too!

Gawain watched him stride forward to where a small man had risen by a cooking fire. The red toorie on the tinker's blue bonnet wagged to a headshake, and an arm pointed in the general direction of Parlan's van. Everyone in camp had seen the fool Donal come in and disappear with a strange pup, but this was business for their Old Man, the fount of great wisdom and noble lying.

Parlan's van, as had been the custom in more dangerous days, was strategically placed at the back of the camp, so that intruders, to get at it, had to twist and turn amongst the tents and other vans. Dukes, with assured leisureliness, moved this way and that, and brought up four paces short of Parlan. That was near enough for the reek of peat and bog-myrtle. Behind him the women and weans disappeared into vans and tents, and the men drifted forward here and there, so that a line of retreat was no longer open.

Dukes did not order Parlan to his feet. The old death's-head was in his dotage, a black pipe sucking in his teeth, and his eyes set vacantly somewhere in the distance. A chimpanzee-thug was leaning against a corner of the van, his hairy ape's forearms folded below a breast that showed a mat of fur in the opening of the shirt. That fellow would have only a rudimentary brain behind that craggy brow! A brown gypsy woman, with looks, was peeping over the ape's shoulder.

The third man sitting at ease on the bottom step? Dukes knew that man. That flying officer, Micklethwaite, who had burst in so outrageously at the Tigh Mhor. An officer and a gentleman? A friend of Sammy Veller's—but Veller was an oaf! Dukes had his suspicions of this fellow. There was something between him and Iosabel! And he did not know what it was, yet—or how far it had gone! But he would ignore him now, consorting here with the scum of the Gael, of no use to King or country. Dukes had had a particularly safe job at home, while Malcolm and Gawain were facing terrible foes and breaking them. But he was no coward.

Gawain, for the first time, had a good look at Oliver

 Dukes: the high, square shoulders, the narrow face, the long straight jaw—or was it inclined to recede a bare degree—the red-brown eyes, lustrous enough, but, simian-like, without expression or liveliness, and that dark-red hair with a dry matt surface. Gawain might be wrong, but that fellow had a queer streak in him somewhere—something not to be trusted.

Dukes took his time; he had been running, and waited until he could give orders without panting. And Parlan, the talk-master, could wait a year until he got the slant he wanted. In the pause, Gawain reached his cigarette packet to Malcolm, but Malcolm, without looking, moved the packet quietly aside. That was not so promising. Malcolm had been away too long, and the subdued rebellion of the out-cast no longer suited his forthrightness. He had been a soldier and a sergeant in a famous regiment, and had taken and given orders, and he would allow no man to contemn him in his own camp. Well! that was Malcolm's own business. Gawain would just look on and smoke.

Dukes addressed no one in particular, and spoke with a chosen restraint.

"I am looking for a dog—and a dog-stealer. They came in here."

Parlan brought his old eyes down for a moment, and looked into remoteness again.

"Could it be that you lost a dog, sir?" he asked mildly, and with no particular interest.

"I did not lose a dog, gran'fer," Dukes said.

"Oh-h-h! Your pardon, sir! 'Tis how you want to buy a dog?" Parlan's interest brightened.

"Not a tinker's dog," said Dukes, and laughed. His laugh was high like his voice, and had a metallic quality. He shook his finger at the dour old dodderer. "This particular dog is a springer spaniel—black-and-white—and it belongs to Miss Mengues of the Tigh Mhor. It was lifted by a young tinker in a red kilt, and seduced in here." He crooked a forefinger. "I am having it, old boy—and the young tinker too."

Parlan was taking time by no forelock. He, too, had seen young Donal, and was giving him time to lose himself and the dog. He said:

"The young lady would be sending you to look for her dog, sir? A springer, black-and-white—a grown dog he'd be? No then?"

Gawain looked towards the entrance. No, she would not

trust or thrust herself in here, but she might send in her Mr Dukes. He was interested in her—and she might be interested in him, but the imp in her could not be much interested in the safety of his skin.

Dukes thought it was time to show the teeth of his authority. His voice went a tone up.

"No one sent me, you old fool!" he said. "You should know who I am, I am Mr Dukes, the Factor of this Estate, and I am here to give orders." He glanced round, and swung a long arm. "I do not see red-kilt, but he'll be hiding in a van with the dog, and I am having the two."

He was so sure of his power that he did not particularly notice that the tinker men had closed in in a wide curve.

Damn that young Donal! thought Gawain. *Why did he not hide in a van? I'd ha' hauled out that spaniel myself and told Dukes to take him to hell. This is a dangerous fool!*

Parlan wasn't finished yet. "It might be a young dog, sir?"

"You want to play some more, do you?" Dukes said. "Yes, it was six months old."

"And it would be a dog or a bitch?"

"I'm hanged if—! No, wait! it was a dog."

"A young dog-pup like that," said Parlan consideringly, "would be finding his nose at this time, and if he would be meeting up with a young bitch he would be apt to be seduced along, till she bit his ear—and the humour on her."

"Very nice work, old boy!" conceded Dukes. "I'll play along with you. There was another dog—a lurcher—and the spaniel might have followed along. Very good! Produce the spaniel, and I'll keep the poaching for another day."

"And a very fair offer, sir," said Parlan. "I promise you that every search, far-and-wide, will be made for the pup-dog as described, and when it is found—as it will be—it will be taken back to the young lady—and a fine young lady she is as we all know."

Parlan could not offer more than that, nor could he offer less. The dog had to be returned, because it had been seen into camp. But young Donal had to be found first—and have his jacket dusted.

But Dukes wasn't to be put off. His voice sneered. "Want to save your face, do you? Not this time! That dog is here, and if you don't find it, I will, and that's final."

This was bad. This meant trouble, and if anyone could stop it he should try. Gawain rose to his feet, and lifted a hand.

"Excuse me, Mr Dukes!" he said quietly. "Take the old gentleman's word. The spaniel will be returned—I vouch for that."

"Mind your own dam' business, sir!" said Dukes, his metallic voice brittle, but his red-brown eyes still expressionless. He took a short step nearer Parlan. "Stop this nonsense! Do you want one of your young toughs in jail for stealing and hiding a valuable dog—and for poaching? Get me that dog—or I shall!"

Parlan's wide-armed gesture presented Dukes with the whole camp.

"There it is for you, sir! And you can search it up-high and down-low." His voice rose and rasped. "And no *man* will dare put a finger on you—as I will call this gentleman to witness."

Oh, you old devil! said Gawain. *Oh! you plotting old scoundrel! This was in your mind all the time: keeping the men out of it, and getting your enemy to throw himself to the she-wolves. You'll learn something now, Mr Dukes! But my lord! you might kill a woman.*

V

But Parlan and Gawain had reckoned without Malcolm, Malcolm who would no longer conform to the tinker's wily policy, Sergeant Malcolm MacFie who could no longer stomach the slow degradation that was aye the fate of the broken clans.

His eyes had never left Dukes, and now he straightened from the van. His massive shoulders tremored queerly and his strong-moulded face went rigid. His voice rumbled from his throat, and he spoke as if he had difficulty in finding words.

"That man will not search the camp. He will go away now."

"You would make me, you big ape?" said Dukes contemptuously.

"It is what I will do," rumbled the deep voice.

Plain bloody slaughter! said Gawain. This was much worse than anything he had expected; this had to be stopped now, this instant, or it could not be stopped at all. He took one long stride to face Malcolm, and he knew that he was taking his life in his hands, for he knew of old that, in a matter of seconds, Malcolm would be beyond all control: berserk.

The woman, Sileas, was looking at Gawain over her husband's shoulder; there was sheer terror in her eyes, and all the blood had drained from her face so that the minute freckles stood out on the tan.

It was that face of fear that moved Gawain to action. He didn't think he could do it, but he did. He put his big hands down on Malcolm's shoulders, exploded all the power and drive that was in him, and walked Malcolm backwards and round to the other end of the van, where the cooking fire was dead in ashes.

Malcolm had not struggled, had not exerted the least force, and did not exert any now. But Gawain's arms were tingling to the elbow as from a galvanic shock. Some terrific force was heaving inside that squat torso, and in a moment it might break loose. Then Gawain would be flung aside like a rag, and Oliver Dukes broken to pieces. Gawain had to get hold of this man's mind before the berserk madness possessed it.

"Man, let me go!" the deep voice rumbled remotely. "I will break him in my two hands."

Gawain put all his will into his own two hands, fighting down the turbulence coming through. He kept his voice steady and insistent.

"You can break that man in two—and you can break me in two—and me first! And what then? You lose everything—your woman, your son—everything—and freedom—freedom—freedom! You have suffered enough, my brother."

Malcolm was listening as from afar, and Gawain knew that he had got a toe-hold. He had to get complete control now at all costs. Suddenly and forcefully he pulled the great barrel of chest close to his, and bent so that their heads touched. His steady whisper was in Malcolm's ear.

"Take it easy, brother! You are not a broken man any more. There is a place for you. Give me time—only a little time—and I, and you too, will make this a place to live in without fear or favour. Listen! Let me deal with that man. He is my enemy. I want him, and you know why—you know why! He will not search this camp. I will take him today—or some day. Give him to me?"

The big oak-brown paws came up over his. "He is yours. Leave me alone now. I will be all right."

Gawain loosed his grip, and stepped back. Malcolm swayed on wide-planted, bowed legs, turned away, and sank down in a crouching posture, his hands up to his sunken head; and his whole body shivered as the electric force drained away. Sileas brushed by Gawain's shoulder, put a firming knee against her man, and a steadying hand in his black hair. She turned head to Gawain and nodded. Her mouth was still trembling, and she could not speak, but the fear had gone out of her eyes.

Gawain went striding rapidly round the van. Inside him he was no longer the cool Gawain. He was experiencing a feeling that he had never felt before, even in the savagest fighting. A disturbing feeling and, yet, pleasant, and behind it a flaming urge to let it rip. He had, indeed, subdued Malcolm, but Malcolm had, in turn, smitten him; had actually transferred some of the qualities of the berserker, the exaltation, the exultation, the desire to smite and rend, to hurt and be hurt. But the old Gawain, Jungle-fighter, had practised control in many a difficult place and time, and would not now loose a bigger charge of explosive than was necessary.

He came round the side of the van, and the first person he saw was Iosabel Mengues. She was coming between the tents behind the curve of men, a long hazel crook in her hand. So here she was at last—the cause of it all—to recover her messenger and her dog. Fine! She was just in time to get her messenger delivered into her hands—all in one piece if possible. *Where are you, Mr Dukes?*

He was there, and Gawain was barely in time. Dukes had paused for a minute while Gawain was rushing Malcolm round the van, but he was determined to search the camp, and now he was beginning. A van was set at right angles to Parlan's, and Dukes was on the steps, his hand reaching for the closed half-door. Earlier on Gawain had watched four or five active women disappear into that van.

Gawain hesitated for a moment, and the thought in his mind was: *All right! Let them take him apart.* But next moment came another thought: *Mygod! he'll kill one of them.*

No one could tell how Gawain moved—in strides, or bounds, or a hop-step-and-jump. But he was on the steps, had Dukes by the back of the neck, and both of them were in the air coming down. They were two active men and they did not tumble and roll. Gawain swung Dukes with all his might and let him go, and Dukes spun five yards, touched the ground with his fingers, and came round raging, crouching, and ready. He saw who was his attacker then.

"By God! I'll deal with you, too."

"You'll deal with me," said Iosabel Mengues, and was between them. She was as prompt as that.

Her back was to Gawain, and she was facing Dukes, her long crook held like a quarter-staff.

"Stop this nonsense!" she ordered imperiously.

Oliver Dukes pulled himself upright. He was, indeed, lacking in ruth, but he was not berserk. He would break Gawain gladly, but he would not do it over the body of Iosabel Mengues, or even after brushing her aside.

"Your dog is here, Iosa," he said. "Look! Let me—"

"No—my dog is not here," she told him, "I know where my dog is—and you are coming away from this place now. Come on!"

He found his arm grasped firmly, and he was facing the other way, and he was going; and he made no attempt to break away and demolish that cursed hobnobber with tinkers. Moreover, no blow had been struck—and a more suitable occasion might arise.

Parlan, on his feet, made a wide gesture with both hands, and his tail of men scattered apart, and came together again behind Iosabel and Dukes, who went their way, and out through the entrance to the road.

It had all finished as innocuously as that.

VI

Gawain relaxed, and the tingle went out of his arms. That swing and throw had helped to discharge the spleen in him, and then the girl had stepped in and averted an unnecessary show-down. That was all right. Things had finished not so badly, and he had stopped the MacFies getting deeper into trouble. He would be feeling smug in a minute.

But the tinkers were not at all satisfied with the tame ending. They glowered and grumbled at this interfering man—and a friend too—who had stopped the women from dealing with their enemy. One of them, a lathy lad with a dead-white, wicked face, took two steps forward, and dashed his heavy-peaked cap on the ground at Gawain's feet. He spoke through his teeth.

"Would you be turnin' against us, too, at the end o' the day?"

Gawain looked him over. This was Murrich, another grandson to Parlan. Contrary to tinker fashion, his black hair was so closely cropped that the white of the scalp showed through. *You are the lad that had a month in jail!* thought Gawain, and put a flat palm forward hip-high.

"Murrich," he said pleasantly, "many the time, when you were that high, I belted your backside. Do you want another belting now?"

"Give the jail-bird a good one while you're at it, my gallant man," Parlan encouraged from behind.

Gawain kicked the cap ten feet, ignored young Murrich, and faced round to Parlan.

"A great pity you are too brittle to be belted, you old devil!" he said, not so pleasantly.

He came forward, sat, again, on the tail-steps of the van, and lit a cigarette. He would give the girl and her man time to get well ahead. Parlan sat down on his creepie, scraped out his black pipe, and spoke wisely.

"The thing that does be in my mind is that a woman, young or old, is the start of all trouble, and then, as often as not, she will not be letting the men finish things as they was meant to be finished be God and the divil. All the same, it could be, that young woman of yours did a good day's work—"

"It was a good day's work, but she is not my young woman," said Gawain with commendable patience.

"And how would I know what two young people would be talking about an hour at a time?" Parlan said.

"Listen, Parlan! For this day's work you may get thrown out of this camp."

"That man—he never would?" Parlan sat up. "Not the second camp, and the grouse only nesting?"

"It is in his mind already, Parlan, I am sorry to tell you," said Gawain quietly.

"My father's bones!" said Parlan in distress, "and me an old done man not able to hold the young fellows, and they wild."

Yes, if trouble were brewing, Parlan, even if he had a mind, could not deal with it. Parlan had another wily thought.

"Look you, sir! That young lady—I have good reports of her—she might have power over that big man—"

"She might have."

"And you have power over her—?"

"Oh hell!"

"She has a liking for you, and didn't she save you from the father of a leathering a minute ago?"

Gawain thought he would take the war to Parlan.

"The sort of leathering you are going to give young Donal?" he suggested.

"The skin off him!" boasted Parlan.

"Yes, indeed! I have heard of the terrible, savage beatings you used give the young ones."

That was a calculated insult. Parlan, like most primitives, was extraordinarily considerate of children, and it was on record that he had once outlawed one of his tail for thorough-beating a son who needed it. Parlan reared up, and voice and hands appealed to heaven.

"Many hard words have come my way, but this from a friend—" He pointed an accusing finger. "Was I hearing you right?"

"You was." Gawain moved a careless thumb. "It was Murro MacDuffie told me. He said, when Malcolm was young you used to beat him with a piece of string a foot long—you old tyrant!"

Parlan sat down, and rubbed his bald skull under his bonnet. "You was always for your bit of fun, my friend," he said softly, "but will you tell me this now: are you wanting that young woman, and she as bonny as a tinker in her youth?"

Gawain got to his feet and spoke soberly. "No, Parlan! I don't want that young woman—or any other young woman. And don't look to me for anything! In a week I'll be on a road longer than yours—and more lonely."

"Very well so," said Parlan. "A week is a long time, and you could settle your affairs easy."

"What are my affairs to you?"

"What indeed!" said Parlan agreeably, "but it is a thing we often noticed: your affairs are the affairs of most of us, here or hereabouts."

What was the use of talking? These people had been watching him as well as the Tigh Mhor, and they had some extraordinary notions. And so had others: little Alsuin, Luke Carnoch—and how many more? But they could not change his resolve. There was a risk for him in this place that he would not contemplate, and in a week he would be gone. He ground his cigarette under his heel, and, looking at no one, walked out of camp.

VII

He walked slowly down the road, hands deep in pockets, and head down. That was another incident finished—or was it a ring in the linked rings of the past few days?—and the makings of a fairy story for Alsuin, who was beginning to see through make-believe? The last ring, then! In a week there had been some excitement on occasion, and a spice of fun thrown in, and a display of good metal here and there. That was fine. And now for a few quiet days with his friends and then—Heigho! and away we go. And thank the Lord! he had avoided another encounter with that disturber of the peace, Iosabel Mengues. . . .

A dog barked at the other side of the road. Gawain started, turned, and stopped in his tracks.

"Glory be!" he said aloud. "A black-and-white springer pup! The poor lonely little first cause!"

Clicking fingers and tongue, he moved slowly forward, and the dog twisted its hindquarters, cringing a little, and not yet sure of this biped. It was tied by the leash to a coping stone on the low dry-wall.

Gawain had the explanation in his mind already. Cute fellow, young Donal! Not to incriminate himself too much, he had tied the dog here after its mistress had passed, and was now trusting Gawain to take it along.

The pup sniffed at the quietly-tendered hand, and was satisfied. Gawain smoothed a curve of brow, and pulled at a long ear; and the pup contorted itself, and strained at its leash.

"A bonnie wee pup! A bonnie wee dog!" he addressed it. "Myself, I wouldn't mind stealing you."

"Not while I have my eye on you!" said a quiet, deep voice from the other side of the road.

"From the rear—always from the rear!" said Gawain, and turned slowly.

Iosabel Mengues was sitting on the stone wall over there, and she was alone. And Gawain had a thick sort of feeling somewhere at the back of his throat.

He walked, slow-footed, across the road, the spaniel whimpering behind him; and his lean face had a saturninely-resigned look. The evening sun, shining aslant between clouds, made her green-black eyes alive, and her generous mouth was not sullen, but grave almost to sadness. She was wearing white doe-skin jodhpurs, a loose black suede jacket with a white soft collar turned down over it, and her black hair was held loosely by a white ribbon. That combination of black-and-white made her extraordinarily vivid.

"I do want to talk to you," she said. "Will you please sit down?" That was a request, not an order.

"I will, ma'am, but I like where I am fine. Could I ask you one question first—may I?"

"You will."

"This is it. Did anyone ever tell that you are lovely as well as beautiful?"

She took that coolly. "You did first time. Please sit here?"

He sat on the wall within a yard of her, and pointed at her long crook across her thighs.

"I threw away my halberd, remember?"

She leant the crook on the wall between them.

"At your service, ma'am!" said Gawain. *Darn! that's what I say to the queen.*

She was slow to begin. Her hand, of its own volition, moved up to her breast-pocket and brought out the dented dragon cigarette case, fingered it idly, flicked it open, and reached it across. He took a cigarette, and lit hers, and looked at her mouth below the down-tip of her nose.

The showers had sheered off, and the sky was clearing. If it did not cloud up again in the night, there would be a ground frost, and Lukey would root him out at four o'clock to spray the potato shaws. But, probably, there would be more rain, for "the distant hills were looking nigh." The ridges and chorries of Stob Glas stood out boldly, and looked near enough to put a hand on. It was only by looking down the long slope and over the woods and across the water that one could put the mountain back in its place. That double-perspective made a fool of space, and gave a strange sense of imminence.

Still she was slow to begin, and Gawain would help her. He pointed across at the spaniel, sitting up and watching them eagerly, yet forlornly.

"Did you find your dog tied in that place?"

"I tied him there myself."

"Oh!" said Gawain.

"Oh-and-bah-and-stuff-and-nonsense—!"

"I made a bad beginning," said Gawain.

"While foolish men were playing at heroics, someone had to do the obvious: slip round on the flank and collar Rory. I nearly collared a young tinker too. He'll be over a couple of horizons now."

"Up in the heather looking down on us. Hush! we are being watched."

"Nonsense! Look here! Did Nolly—Oliver Dukes—?"

"And where is our Mr Dukes?"

"I sent him on."

"As an old friend of mine would say, we do be noticing that someone does be ordering that young man about, eye or hand or—" he looked down—"that's a neat boot you're wearing!"

"Oh, shut up, for heaven's sake!" She pointed her cigarette at him. "Will you please tell me did Oliver rub these people the wrong way?"

"He didn't think so. He took the direct method, and that is not the way to take a MacFie of the devious mind—if you know what I mean?"

"I don't—I never do."

"You will—words of two syllables. Your dog went into the camp and out again. All of us saw it come and go. Your Mr Dukes arrives, and there is no dog. But the dog is there, right there in camp, says Mr Dukes, and the dog has to be produced at once, pronto, imm—no, that's three or more syllables—and if not a search will be made. That's the direct method. And you know the dog could not be produced." He chuckled. "Silly fools, sure enough! and you doing the obvious, slipping along to the bolt-hole, nobbling your pup, tying him over there, and strolling in to see how your champion was faring in a frontal attack—"

"And finding him being assaulted by the tinkers' champion. The way you flung yourself up those steps and threw Nolly into the air was the savagest thing I ever saw—and the most unnecessary."

"Wow!" exclaimed Gawain. "Leave it at that! You got your dog." Let her have the wrong impression, and she would go off in a dander—and never trouble him again.

But she would not leave it at that. She said reasonably, "Why not let him search, and make himself out a fool? The tinkers were not interfering. Why be brutal about it? I saw you stop Malcolm MacFie in time, but in another second you and Nolly would have been tearing at each other like dogs. Why—?"

"You're talking turkey, ma'am," said Gawain.

"But why?" She reached a hand out, and placed it on his sleeve, and sent a new tingle up his arm. "Please tell me why?"

And Gawain thought it would be no harm to tell her indirectly. "Listen then! A thing like that happened once before in Parlan's camp. Luke Carnoch told me; he was there and saw it. A certain man down at Corran lost a bit net—forty yards of it, all leaded and corked and ready for a draw on Sunday morning, for he was that sort of man—and he accused Parlan, in Parlan's own camp, of stealing it, and, as they say, if he wasn't right he wasn't far wrong. And that big husky man threatened to search the camp. And Parlan says: 'If I took the net it is here, and you can search if you have to search, and no *man* will put a finger on you—and I have Lukey Carnoch to witness.' And the man searched, and in time went into one van that had five women in it—and the door shut behind him. Lukey says the van went up and down like a coracle in a steep sea; and the roof lifted a foot. And in time the man was pitched out, and—let a veil be drawn—but the women chased the bare legs of him—and bare legs you have seen—half-a-mile up the road—with nettles. But he got his net back Monday morning, and it was wet."

He put his hands on his knees and started a preliminary chuckle. But she looked at him with wide serious eyes, far from smiling.

"You boys do love brutal horseplay," she said reprimandingly.

"It was the ladies that time, God bless 'em!" said Gawain and started to laugh.

She would not laugh, she would not even chuckle, but she had to clear her throat with a sort of syncopated whinny, that she controlled abruptly.

"Stop it! Would that have happened today?"

"I counted the five she-wolves—"

"Then you did save Nolly from a disgraceful mauling?"

"Ma'am," said Gawain, "I couldn't care less if they took Nolly's hide off."

Iosabel had her own ideas. Her eyes crinkled thoughtfully and her voice was thoughtful too. "Yes, Nolly would take some persuasion, and yes, you were not interested in saving his hide. I know what you were interested in: the tinkers. You wanted to stop them getting into trouble."

"They are in trouble," he said seriously. "Sons of men with nowhere to lay their heads, don't blame them if their minds turn towards a tooth-for-a-tooth."

"What can the poor wastrels do?"

"You'd be surprised." He seemed to go off at a tangent. "I told Parlan—their Old Man—that I was trespassing at Cobh Echlan, and he was wondering what tartan I was wearing for a short while after—"

"A check, not a tartan," she told him, her mouth twitching.

"So. I told him there was a bit of a sequel to that disgraceful story, and he said I was a good man in the heather but that I wasn't born in it. Anything to put your finger on?"

"Yes. You are being watched. But why?" Her eyes opened at him.

"You are watched, too—we are watched now—the whole place is watched. Why? And what can you do about it?"

She moved her hands impulsively. "But what can *I* do?"

"Nothing. And that goes for me too. Not in a week! And you and I may never meet again." He slipped off the wall, and simulated carefreeness. "But if we do meet again, say in twenty years, grey in our hair or no hair at all, you and I will laugh with each other. Things have a trick of happening every time we cross each other's bows. By glory! it was the pleasantest week in six barren years, and I would not miss a minute of it."

She moved quickly and lithely, taking the grass margin in her stride. "I can't pin you down," she said exasperatedly, "and I am not going to try any more."

She strode across the road, bent to her dog's leash, and the dog licked her nose. Then she marched off down the slope, and found that Gawain was marching at her shoulder.

"I am bringing along your crook, ma'am," he said.

She slowed down then, and they went on sedately side by side, and not saying a word to each other. There was little need.

Chapter IX
THE QUEEN HAS A VISITOR

I

THE BIG open car came slowly through the South Gate, and slowly accelerated up the brae. Where the banks broke down and sloped back, Iosabel looked upwards on her left, and there, on the rise, was the squat house of Blinkbonny, its windows aglisten in the sun between showers; and all the windows of the bus-summerhouse glistened too. The chintz curtains were looped apart, and something moved inside.

Iosabel knew what the movement was: a child's arm saluting her. She lifted her hand in its red gauntlet and returned the salute. Poor little mite! A sick child watching the road, and ready to salute all who passed! And for months she herself had passed and ignored that friendly greeting.

The car took the curve, and slowed and halted before the red gate; and Iosabel turned head and looked at the solid, white house through the screen of fruit trees. No one was at work in the front garden where the tulips were already blowsy; and no one sat on the patch of green in the angle between house and sunroom. She had hoped that Wing-Commander Micklethwaite would be about in the open, for, then, without getting out of the car, she could have finished her business with him—and gone her way out of his life. That is what she had set out to do, and that is what she would do.

After a while, she tugged off her red gauntlets, picked up a flat, neatly-made, brown-paper parcel from the seat at her side, and got out on the road. She paused at the red gate, her hand on it, and hoped for someone to appear, but there was no movement anywhere, not even in the sun-room, though no doubt the child was watching her.

Very well! I can leave this on the doorstep.

She walked slowly, but not hesitatingly, up the concrete path, and paused below the white door that was invitingly open. She did not like to lay her flat parcel on the scrubbed doorstep, nor would she like to knock on the open door of a man who was an unfriend—her father's unfriend. But there was Major Keegan! There was no quarrel with him—or with his sick child. That was a good idea.

She smiled at herself as she moved to the right along the front of the house to the open patch of green with its rustic table and chairs. The hour for afternoon tea was not yet come, but, of course, she would not have afternoon tea.

The bus body was without wheels, stood on piles some three feet off the ground, and was varnished over bright green. Near one end, four wooden steps led up to a white door closed on a latch. Iosabel, from ground-level, could only see the underside of the roof done in light cream. Curtains were moving lazily in a soft draw of air.

She mounted the four wooden steps, tapped a middle-finger on a white panel; and through an open window floated a soft eager little voice:

"Come! Oh please, come!"

Iosabel, taking care not to be abrupt in any movement, pressed the latch, opened the door steadily, stepped within, and, without turning her back, shoved the door shut behind her. She heard the latch click.

It was bright sunlight outside; in this pleasant sun-room the day seemed even brighter. The cream roof, the glistening glass, the bright chintz, the rose-red rugs wooed and enriched and diffused the light. And on a low couch under a silken pinkish coverlet lay the little queen of this sunny place, head turned aside, brown eyes devouring the visitor, and no smile yet on the solemn little face.

This is not a sick child! The brown hair had the lustre of life; there was colour in the delicately-moulded cheeks, and tiny freckles across the bridge of the nose; the brown eyes were shining; and the two hands, resting on the coverlet, were shapely as a resting butterfly. She lay very still, and only the shells of her nostrils were twitching rabbit-like to show her eagerness and curiosity. Iosabel's serious mouth trembled and smiled.

"Good afternoon, little lady!" she said softly. "I hope you are very well. My name is Iosabel Mengues."

Alsuin's face lit up to answer that grave smile. "Oh, this is so very nice!" she whispered, and moved one of her hands; and the vitality of the movement struck Iosabel, who did not realise that the gesture was one she frequently used herself.

Iosabel moved across between two wicker chairs, and the little one remembered good manners.

"Good afternoon, Miss Mengues! My name is Alsuin—

Alsuin Keegan—and I am very well, thank you—only my back, but I can move my toes now, and I have pins and needles."

"That is indeed splendid, *loada sea Dios*!" said Iosabel.

Alsuin reached out that impulsive hand. "You will please sit down?" It was an order as well as a request.

Iosabel had not intended to sit down. She laid her papered parcel on the coverlet, sat down in a straight-backed chair at the couch-side, and gently took the delicately-shaped hand.

"That is my knight's chair," Alsuin said, "but you are very welcome."

Iosabel did not need to ask who the knight was. She did not begin to make child's talk, for she felt that this little maid, secluded so long to only thoughts and dreams, would have her own way of approach. Alsuin, in her fashion, held on to Iosabel's hand, brought her own other hand over it, lightly fondling and massaging the fingers in that way she had. Iosabel noted the soft coolness of the hands, but in a little while she, too, got that thread of temperature coming through. The little one was not as well as she looked, but, possibly, her trouble was working itself out through that little abnormal heat; and, probably, those delicate hands had a habit of sensing the nature and worthiness of her visitors. Iosabel hoped so, for the little one whispered to herself: "This is very nice—I like this."

Alsuin turned her head, and looked through an open window down the slope. There below was the curve of road, and, beyond it, the trees in new green, and the dappled purple and green of the firth, and the strong front of Stob Glas towering into the blue. That is what she saw all day long, under the sun or under the clouds, and in it there was beauty, and loneliness too.

"I saw you coming there, dear lady, and you waved back to me. That is three times now, but—" a finger pressed—"I had to wait a long, long time."

Iosabel put her other hand over the child's for a moment. "I shall not forget ever again, Alsuin dear. Do you always watch that road?"

"Ever and always! But it does be empty now—unless you come—and it used be such a lovely road for people, and I knowing everyone, and some used come up the field to talk to me—and now you come. The road going down to Camelot, Gawain calls it. I read about that lady—so sad—but I am not afraid to look."

She turned her head to Iosabel and looked at her with a possessing intentness. "You are the lady I put magic on to come. The lady that sings in the wood. Sir Gawain said that you had great beauty and great heart—it is sand he said—but I did not know how beautiful you are."

This was not precocity. This child was fey. A little woman who had read and listened, and thought about things, and had learned to express the fineness in her with naturalness. She had paid her visitor the finest compliment ever paid her, and Iosabel took it naturally as her right. She knew now that she possessed at least something of that quality called beauty, but she was not sure wherein her beauty lay, and she hoped that this young seer was referring, too, to some inner quality worth while. Inner quality, indeed! She—the imp—the tomboy—the proud-tempered—the graceless tinker! That reminded her of her errand, and she placed one hand on the flat parcel on the coverlet.

"Speaking of your knight, little lady," she said. "He is—in residence?"

Alsuin chuckled softly at the turn of phrase she knew so well. "He will be in the kitchen with Lukey and my daddy, I think. Lukey is showing them how to put the dress on a fly that he calls the *Bluidy Terror*—all silver and peacock, but not half as nice as your lovely dress of flowers. Sir Gawain was here with me, but he thinks—they all do—I must have a sleep all to myself before tea comes."

"Oh dear—oh dear! I am sorry—"

"No—no! This is nicer than ten sleeps. Whisper! I do not often sleep, but, of course, I pretend when they peep in at me." Her hand tightened. "You will not go yet—no?"

"No. This is most nice for me too." She moved the flat parcel. "This is some of your knight's—panoply—that he overlooked."

"Panoply!—that is a grand new word, but I guess its meaning—" She took the parcel into her arms possessively, and her sensitive hands felt it over. Then her nose and her mouth crinkled, and a light came into her eyes that Iosabel recognised. Her whisper was conspiratorial.

"Is it—it is—his trousers?"

Iosabel nodded solemnly, and was surprised. "You knew?"

"Only you and me! I see with my eyes. That morning he went down my road in grey, and in yellow he came back. It was not to be hidden, so he put it in a story—he tells me stories always."

"And in the story I was without manners—?"

"But no! It was not you that had no manners, he said. You had to deal justly, he said. He said, for an act of presumption you took away his—cuishes and his greaves. He looked up my big book of words—it is the big book there on the shelves—and he said that. And, of course, I looked too. And also I had to see the meaning of another word—skewbald it was."

She chuckled softly, and Iosabel chuckled too. The chuckles were irrepressible, and bubbled into laughter and more laughter. They were two tomboys enjoying a trick played on a presuming boy. Iosabel put a hand over her mirthful and lovely mouth.

"I laugh now," she said. "We laugh always looking back; but I did not laugh then, and I did not laugh later when I was most severely punished—"

Alsuin became serious at once. "But that was very, very, very bad. I scolded him—I am scolding him every day—and he is very, very, very sorry. Your im-mense trout! and you so noble and good. He tore two great handfuls out of his hair, and threw them out the window there. He wants to put his two hands under your feet to be forgiven. But, indeed, we must not forgive him for a whilie yet."

She laid her parcel at her side, repossessed herself of Iosabel's hand, and resumed her soft kneading. Her eyes were wholly serious.

"I am wicked too," she said, and patted Iosabel's hand in gentle reproof. "Yes! you were a little teeny-weeny wicked, and I am too. I am deceiving him, and I do not want him to find out—not for a long time. He thinks I still believe in fairy stories."

"I believe in fairy stories," said Iosabel firmly.

"Oh yes! This is one, I believe in this one too." She was doing her best to explain, and her eyes were shining with thought. "But I am old now—I am eleven years two months and four days old—a lot and a lot of days—and it could be that there are no fairies, or knights, or ogres, or princesses. Sir Gawain always—always made me fairy stories. You know the rhyme of Gawain, darling Iosabel?"

"I know of Gawain of the Round Table."

"But there was another Gawain too. You will know:

"'Thanks to Saint Bothan, son of mine,
Save Gawain, could ne'er pen a line.'"

"That rhyme I do not know," said the wondering Iosabel.

"Gawain, he puts it in front of all his stories to me. And he can pen a line." She gestured her rounded chin towards a shelved table. "He wrote me all those letters tied in a blue ribbon—stories of his adventures—east of Suez, he said—and some of them hurt inside me, for there was a weight on them that was in his mind. Look now! Some day I will let you read his letters."

A child to make Iosabel flush! She said quickly, "That is a great shelf of books you have, darling."

"I have more in my Winter Room within there, and I know all about them. Gawain pro-pounds the questions, and we make up lists of lovely names—he calls it a litany: Arthur, and the Queen I do not like, and Lancelot du Lac, and Galahad, and Gawain of course—but not such a fine Gawain—and Cuchulain and Fyoon MacCool, and Maeve of Connacht, and Diarmuid and Grainne, and Deirdre and Naisi, and Robin Hood and Maid Marian, and Robin and Mary, and Robert and Sarah, and Paola and Francesca, and Bran and Sgeolaing, and the Grey of Macha, and Tristan and Isolde, and Héloïse and Abélard, and Dante and Beatrice, and Petrarch and Laura, and Edward and Pamela, and Paul et Virginie, and Gerard and Margaret, and Blamaan and Mongfin Fairhead, and Rebecca and Ivanhoe, and oh! so many more." She paused to draw breath.

"Many of these I know, but not all," Iosabel said. "You are cleverer than I am, Alsuin."

"But I am not very clever—not clever really. I am only as far as long division, but I can spell good, and I know the capital of Spain-and-Portugal: Lisbon, where they are all good Catholics and had a miracle at Fatima—and Gawain says that in Spain they have too many butchers' stalls and stony temples, and he argues with my daddy."

"I know Spain, and your Gawain should be ashamed of himself. It would be just to put a Penance on him."

"A Task I call it. I have a Task on him now—the greatest Task of all—and it is very hard on him." She turned the trouble in her face towards the empty road and the forbidden land.

"A secret between you?" whispered Iosabel, who had already guessed it.

Alsuin turned her head back, and her hands gripped with surprising strength.

"A secret, but I will tell you, and you will not tell anyone. It is that he makes a peace in the glen and opens my road for me."

"And a noble Task," said Iosabel softly.

Alsuin's hands relaxed, and she moved her head sadly. "He is troubled about it. He says he can do nothing without help from one place, and in that place one who would help is bound by—a fealty. That word I had to look up too."

"Fealty opens a road—and shuts it too," Iosabel said.

Alsuin did not get that, and she was on her own road.

"There's Lukey now! He is as wise as a salmon. He does be saying (she used Lukey's very accent): help here, help there, and take it where you find it, but at the end of the day the man who closed the road must open it out of the goodness of his own heart." She paused. "It was your father, darling Iosabel."

"My father has a good heart, Alsuin," Iosabel said gravely. "But—Oh dear! Oh dear!"

II

Iosabel's exclamation was caused by the sound of voices coming through the glass-panelled door in the end-wall of the house. Her instinct was to get away at once from a situation that might be embarrassing. She stood up, and drew on her hand, but Alsuin clung to it with a sudden warm impulse, and there was appeal in her voice and eyes.

"But it is nothing, darling lady! My sleep, it is over, and they come to take tea with me. It is the thing we do. Please, oh please! Have tea with me, darling Iosabel? Just with me, Alsuin, who loved you—at the drop of a hat, as Gawain says. Please!"

Iosabel relaxed, and, having relaxed, found that she had not wanted to run away.

"I will partake of tea, little tyrant," she said smilingly. "Indeed I do want tea, having talked so much."

Alsuin chuckled. "You are making fun. Gawain says I talk too much. Ho, Madam Kate! I have a guest for tea, my very own choice."

The end-wall door had opened, and a laden dumb-waiter came trundling in. The motive power behind it was tall Kate Carnoch, her red hair shining above her white nurse-housekeeping coat. She spoke pleasantly and coolly.

"Good afternoon, Miss Mengues! It is nice of you to visit our little woman."

"A pleasure, Mrs Carnoch," murmured Iosabel, and could think of nothing else to say.

Luke Carnoch stood hesitating in the doorway, and there was an extraordinary warm shyness in his melancholic face. Suddenly his head jerked up, and he stumped forward, and got out of the way. In his place stood Gawain Micklethwaite tall and saturnine, and no one would have guessed that he had just punched Luke between the shoulder-blades. He said, his eyes gloomy on Iosabel:

"The Queen holds afternoon court!" He stepped aside and moved an introductory hand. "Have you met Major Keegan of Ours, Miss Mengues? He's Irish, poor fellow!"

Iosabel was a shade embarrassed. She did not know how an unpredictable Irishman would take her. He was of her Faith, and he was blood-kin to the Scot, she knew; but his branch of the breed had ever been at war with the landlord; and she did not know that it had mostly been the landlord's fault. She inclined her head, and her mouth was uncertain. And Keegan did the characteristic thing. He came straight across from the door, dot-and-carry-one, took her hand firmly, and bowed over it. His voice was warm.

"My dear young lady! I am very happy that you come to see my daughter."

Iosabel's heart lifted. Here was a kindly man seeking to put her at ease. Her confidence returned, and she looked at Luke Carnoch. He stood awkwardly inside the door, overwhelmed with shyness, and he would have made a run for it if he had a scrap of courage.

And Iosabel, in her turn, did a characteristic thing. She walked directly at him, and reached a warm and vigorous hand. "How are you, Luke?" she said.

He took that impulsive hand, and could hardly let it go. His mild eyes were flickering with emotion, and his mouth was ajar under his straggling moustache. He struggled for words, and they came inadequately in a fine understatement. "Gosh, Miss Iosabel! it is good to see you here."

"Thanks, Luke!" she said, and looked at Gawain.

"Let this be a peaceful occasion," he said calmly, "and let's have some biled tea."

"If Miss Iosabel will pour it," said Kate wisely, "I'll attend to this little lady."

Presiding at the tea-cups a woman controls the situation, and Iosabel was now completely at ease. She realised that these four people had known all the time that she was in the house, and they had come in to treat her nicely. That gave her a pleasant feeling. But did three of them know of her encounters with the knight-at-arms? Four times! and none of them a peaceful occasion. And Jerusalem! did they know about his trousers? She looked up from the cups, and glanced discreetly at the couch. The brown-paper parcel had disappeared.

Kate Carnoch was packing a pillow to prop Alsuin's head, and Alsuin looked at Iosabel over the woman's white shoulder. One brown eye hooded itself impishly, and a warning finger came up to softly-pouted lips.

And so the usual ritual of afternoon tea was performed. In a mixed company it is the one brief hour in which British people relax completely. Small talk flows easily, and momentous subjects are forgotten. That is only in mixed company of male and female. When the females take tea together no man is allowed to discover what they talk about, but rumour has it that a few of the subjects are: bachelors, husbands, absent wives, scandal, slander, calumny, defamation, aspersion, backbiting, detractions, obloquy, reproaches, odious truth, damnable innuendo, and children-brats.

Little Alsuin was over-excited, and her cheeks flushed. She only nibbled an arrowroot biscuit, but drank two cups of light tea. Iosabel felt repentant.

"I am sorry, Mrs Carnoch," she said. "I fear there was too much talk."

"Someone is happy," said Kate.

"Talk!" said Gawain, and thrust his chin at Alsuin. "That one would talk the leg off a pot."

Alsuin merely wrinkled a freckled nose at him. She was very quiet, but her brown eyes were watchful, and did not fail to see how her knight's eyes kept straying towards the presiding lady. He was standing at the end of the couch, a cup and saucer cradled in a broad hand, and his gloom seemed to be as black as his black hair. But his thoughts were not altogether gloomy.

Holy Powers! does she know the way she looks in that astonishing flowered dress? The way her neck rises out of it?—the ivory of her face, the strange colour of her eyes—the wide cheekbones that allure must have? Thanks be! I am leaving next week.

There came that pause at the end before men extricate themselves from the female rite, and Alsuin made use of that pause in her own way. She knew what she wanted, and she knew how to get it in the courteous but inescapable way that queens have. She began:

"Lukey darling, isn't it a grand afternoon?"

"The grandest I ever spent, ma'am," Lukey agreed.

"The weather I mean, Lukey?"

"No need to mention it, whatever," Lukey said suspiciously.

"Oh, but yes, Lukey! Yesterday, when it was raining, you said it was a great pity, for you wanted to be earthing up our early potatoes."

"Yes—yes! But the weather has a settled look at last, and to-morrow will be a fine evening as well."

"With the wind where it is, it won't," Gawain hit him.

"You for the poor mouth!" said Lukey. "Ah well! Orders is orders in this backbreakin' house."

He heaped cups on the dumb-waiter, said a shy word of thanks to Miss Iosabel, and went trundling off kitchen-wards.

"Daddy Keegan," said his daughter, "you will take your walking practice, up the brae and back—and no stick this evening."

David Keegan jerked his artificial limb, and heaved himself upright out of a wicker chair. He was smiling broadly.

"This is an unlimited monarchy, Miss Iosabel," he said. "Coming, Mick, to pick me up when I fall on my nose?"

"No, indeed!" cried his daughter. "You would be having a rest at Dinny Sullavan's—and I have business with Gawain."

Kate Carnoch straightened up from lowering and smoothing Alsuin's pillows. "Weel! if it's business, I'll go and wash a puckle dishes. Miss Iosabel, you will be visiting our little woman again?"

"If I may, Mrs Carnoch." She had not come to visit the little woman, but in future she would—but not until a week had passed.

III

Thus in the space of a minute the little autocrat had dismissed the three people that she did not want at the moment.

Gawain wanted to go too, or so he told himself. It was evident that these two females were in a conspiracy that concerned him; and he had talked too much to both of them in the past few days. Yet, he sat down aside on a corner of the couch, and gave his queen a wary eye; and he would never admit that he was obeying her because it was so hellishly easy to stay in the same room as Iosabel Mengues.

Iosabel did not want to stay either, and she was quite sincere about it. This child was too wise, too intuitive, too frank, and might say something to put a proud devil to shame.

Iosabel was on her feet, and speaking quickly. "I must be going, and you will rest, my little one. Really I must be going."

Alsuin reached her a quick hand, and Iosabel found herself sitting down again.

"There is the im-portant business of—of your visit, darling Iosabel?" Alsuin whispered. "Look, Gawain!"

She slipped a hand under the coverlet, and brought forth the brown-paper parcel. She felt it over with sensitive fingertips, and examined both sides. And Iosabel felt herself flushing.

"There is no name on it," she said. "Must we look inside to see who it is for? Must we, darling lady?"

"That is a very hard knot!" suggested Iosabel hopefully.

"And Gawain has iron fingers. Here, sir!"

Gawain, on some occasions, was as dense as a man could be. He suspected nothing, for he was sure that the parcel contained some feminine gimcrack that the lady had brought along for Alsuin—and a nice thing to do, too. He picked open the granny knot of the string, and carefully unfolded the brown paper on the coverlet. Then he lifted to his feet with a jerk.

"I'll be two times damn'd!" he said, "and I am begging no one's pardon."

Alsuin carefully spread a pair of flannel trousers on the coverlet and smoothed them affectionately. They had been washed or dry-cleaned, and stretched, and pressed, and would grace any pair of legs at a garden party.

"A changeling!" cried Gawain, and pointed a spurning finger. "Them's no' mine! Not never! Mine were circular tubes with a tumour on each knee. Them's straight off a hand-me-down shelf."

Iosabel, head downcast, looked under her brows at Alsuin, and murmured, "A hedgehog—I think it was a hedgehog found them for a new nest, and—well! I had to do some—renovating."

"Of course, dear one! Foolish old Gawain!" She drew the pants to her, and started a careful examination.

Iosabel, though on tenterhooks, was sure the little one would know nothing of needlework. But Alsuin said admiringly:

"Lovely—lovely! I can sew too. Kate makes me, three times a week—and crochet—and the heel of a sock—she says it is good for my arms and hands. Look! I have very strong hands."

"You have, indeed! What other exercises—?"

But Alsuin would not be drawn off.

"This is better sewing than I can do—or Kate even—and look, Gawain dear! this button, and this and this have been sewn on again—and here's a new one at the back."

"I couldn't find a match for that one," murmured Iosabel.

Gawain accepted the inevitable. "This is surely a coal on my head. Madam, my thanks to you—and to your laundress!"

Iosabel was inconsistent. She had hoped that her renovations would not be noticed, but if credit had to be given, it should be given where due.

"Laundress, your grandmother!" she said rudely. "Do you think I would let anyone know—" she stopped.

"Know what?"

"Know that I knew anyone who owns such a disreputable garment," said Iosabel smoothly.

"I asked for that," said Gawain. "You did all—"

"Of course she did, and bah! to you!" cried Alsuin, her hands actively refolding.

"Bah and bosh and stuff-and-nonsense!" growled Gawain. "I withdraw anything I said about a laundress. But look you, fair damosels!" He pointed a finger. "I know about amateur washing. I tried it myself in a far place, and the result was a two-foot shrinkage. Them there things won't fit even Lukey."

"Let the gentleman eat his words—after trial," said Iosabel coldly.

"Every single word!" said Alsuin. "Forgive him, dear Iosabel! Sometimes he has no manners at all, but," she sighed resignedly, "I suppose we must take him as we find him—and if we have time—"

"Viper in my bosom!" grumbled Gawain, and looked down. "Ah well! I am grateful, of course, but I was sort of getting these yaller corduroys moulded to a nice bagginess. Do they go back?"

Alsuin chuckled, and made a wide circular motion with her hands.

"The gentleman—the nice funny man who was here—Sammy—he was the owner?"

Iosabel nodded. "And he wants' em back too."

"I am so sorry! He will not wear them ever—no, never! Look, dearest! It is a secret between us—the three of us now." Her hands shaped a triangle, "I had to take an im-mense gusset out of the back, but I hadn't time to sew it up." She pointed a finger at Gawain's midriff. "It is only held by two safety-pins."

The black and brown heads were close together, and bubbling laughter filled the room. And then Gawain was laughing too.

"Fine—fine!" he said. "Someone will have to break the news to Sammy."

Iosabel rose to her feet, folded Alsuin's hands one over the other, and held her own cool cheek for a moment against the too-warm one.

"My thanks, Alsuin! You will take your sleep now?"

"I will sleep now, and you will come again like a fine dream." Her voice commanded. "Sir Gawain, you will see my lady to her car."

"Yes, ma'am!" said Gawain, and went to hold the door open for the lady, who did not look up at him as she went by.

But they walked down the garden path side by side, and Gawain felt that there was something he should say. "Yes, I am rather a brute, and I have no manners. I feel abased about that silly garment of mine, and you have put me in my place afar and low down." The antic spirit moved. "Mind you, in a week's time—only I'll not be here—I'll be upbraiding you, with reason."

"Yes?"

"There was never a woman born," said Gawain, "who could sew on a gallus button and make it stay."

"The best huss'ife thread, sir! and you'll see."

Gawain took half-a-stride ahead, and squared his shoulders. "Do you know, I think I'll withdraw all apologies. I am not one scrap sorry for anything. It has been a good week, and I am glad to have met you, Iosabel y Mengues."

She said nothing, and he admired her for that too. He opened the red gate for her. He opened the car door, and she slipped in and picked up her red gauntlets.

"This is the end of the play," she said quietly.

"Plays do come to an end, do they not?" he said tonelessly.

"They do. You are going away, you know."

"That's right! I am going away." His hands gripped the top of the door. "Look! That was a lie I told you half-a-minute ago."

She faced him, her eyes steady, and her mouth without a quiver.

"Yes?"

"I said that I was glad to have met you. That was a lie. I wish to God I had never set eyes on you."

He turned on his heel, strode through the open gate, and up the path, and across the front of the house, and up the steps into his little queen's sunroom, throne-room, fate-room, death-room. The low purr of the powerful engine went round the end of the house.

He stood at the couch-side, hands behind back, and looked down the slope through an open window; and Alsuin watched him with something sad in her brown eyes. And then the car appeared, gliding smoothly towards the gap in the slope. Alsuin turned head, and her arm moved slowly in a last salute; and the red gauntlet made a saltire in reply. Gawain kept his hands behind his back.

That is an end then—and God be thanked! But at the moment Gawain was far from sure that he had anything to thank any Deity for.

It was not quite the end. For out of the woods lifted a voice in song. It came on a drift of air, the contralto notes clear as a bell, but it had no words. A strange song, a foreign, barbarous, ancient song, with the rhythm of drums, full of desperate triumph, and exultant sadness.

It died away down the slope, and Gawain turned eyes to Alsuin. Her delicate, blue-shaded eyelids were closed over the brown eyes, the black lashes made no least quiver, and her breathing came quietly, gently, wearily. Gawain touched a broad palm on her soft hair, and tiptoed into the house.

And one brown eye opened and watched him go. She was finished for that day. She was old beyond her years, or perhaps she was living all her life in this brief period. There was a shining of moisture over that limpid eye, and when she closed it, her lashes were wet.

Chapter X
ORDERS TO QUIT
I

DINNY SULLAVAN S kitchen-cum-bar-cum-lounge was not crowded, but it was comfortably full. The flavour of peat and homespun was strong—but not noticeable to nostrils used to it. The cavern of room had been wired for electricity, but the supply had been cut off at the source, and, now, the light, murky enough, was from a brass lamp hanging from a pulley chain.

The customers were a quiet lot of people as a rule, and quiet-voiced by nature. Later in the evening voices might be raised in song and chorus, and some fun poked pawkily, but now there was only a low murmur of voices. The city lounge-bar with its chromium and shell-boarding is no more than a sounding-board for women's voices; here there was no woman other than Peigi Sullavan behind the counter; and the sod-roof under rye-thatch swallowed most sounds. A healthy peat fire burned on the open hearth.

Dinny Sullavan, a thin, flexible-mouthed man wearing dark-brown side-whiskers, never served behind his own bar; that was a job for his wife and elder son. Dinny moved about, with a word here and there, or sat straddled over a chair, listening, smoking, and spitting cleanly into the red peats; and sometimes he would richly narrate an extraordinary story to illustrate or confuse a point. And, after a good story, he would stand a drink on the house—if Peigi let him.

The drink on sale was the thin British beer of a quality to arouse no man to enthusiasm on any subject whatever.

At one side of the fire Major David Keegan sat on a straw-bottomed chair, a leg thrust forward stiffly. Luke Carnoch sat at the other side, and brushed froth off his straggling moustache with the back of his hand. Gawain Micklethwaite sat on a chair heeled back against the dresser at mid-wall, and looked disgruntledly through a thick glass half-full of muddyish-brown ale. Dinny had a small reserve of malt whisky hidden away against a special occasion, but this was not one. Gawain didn't care who heard him.

"My curse on the year of our Lord, seventeen-hundred-and-seven and all its works and pomps!"

"Seventeen-hunder'-an'-seven! What year was that?" wondered Luke Carnoch.

"You ole fox!" said Gawain. "You know all about the Act of Union. That was the sad year that looked forward to this disastrous evening for us all." Gawain was on his favourite grouse now, and everyone listened.

"The evenin' is a bit showery, that's a'," said Lukey.

"Ay! and on this showery evenin' we are compelled to swallow a muddy brew instead of warmin' the cockles of our hearts with our own clean whisky. Bloody wars—and we have fought 'em—and our good malt spirit is used to buy American dollars to nourish the poor English, God help' em! No foreign government has the right to stop us savouring our own special product on an evening like this—or any other evening."

There was a murmur of understanding, and a chuckle or two.

"Fair play is a jewel, Sir Gawain," said Dinny, straddling a chair. "Don't let us be too hard on the English, an' them in a tough spot. Sure they are a nice people, and a friendly people—if you give them their own way."

"Too dam' nice, and too dam' friendly," said Gawain, "and the poor beggars never got their own way from the few that ruled them. Too easy-going, too forbearing, too easily led, they stood—not withstood—the worst caste governments since Adam was a boy. But they did manfully stand up to two wars the seeds of which their rulers sowed—and now the bawbee has become their lord and master."

"A few bawbees in your hip-pocket is no' a bad thing!" said Lukey provocatively.

"No' a bad thing, Lukey, no' a bad thing at all—just plain Hell! The Gael don't know how to handle money—he either despises it or hoards it. The meanest miser of all is a Scot or an Irishman."

"Not forgettin' the Jewman?"

"I'm not. Moses knew his people and forbade usury. And the Gentile clapped Jewry into a Ghetto and forced it to fight the oppressor by the oppressor's own methods—that's all."

"That reminds me of my father, God rest him!" said Dinny, his elbow on the back of his chair and a hand under an ear. He had the story-teller's voice.

"Leave your poor ould father in Purgatory," advised David Keegan. "You've been resurrecting him shamelessly for ten years."

"And why not I? He p'ints a moral as good as a bishop any day. He ownded a nice bit of a pub away beyant in Kerry at a place that gave its name to an earldom. An' begob, sir! an' wonders will never cease! One of his best friends was a Jewman out of Dublin, that would be visitin' the town in the way of business once or twice a year. And he was no miser, that Jew!

"And it so happened that one day—in June it was—down comes Ephrim—that was his name—and found every shop shut, and every man wearin' his Sunday suit, and it wasn't Sunday either. 'John,' says he to me father, 'there ain't nothin' wrong wi' the place, no?' 'Wrong, nothin'!' says me father. 'Don't you know the day that's in it, you haythen?' An' the Jew considered. 'Well!' says he then, 'in Dublin it would be the twenty-ninth day of June in your callinder, but in a lost place like this whatfor do you mark a date at all?' An' says me father, 'The twenty-ninth of June is right, and is that all you know?'"

Dinny extended a reproving hand. "An' what do ye know, ye poor Ould Testament Calvinists of John Knox's breed? If ye had the makin's of a Christian in ye, ye would know without bein' told that the twenty-ninth of June is the Feast Day of SS.Peter and Paul, the founders of any faith that is left in the world. 'You'll do no business today, Eph,' says my father, 'for 'tis a holiday of obligation same as Sunday, everyone at Mass, an' I'm off meself this minute. Go 'way upstairs to Mary—she has a drop in the bottle and two chickens in the pot.' And the Jew says, the darin' divil, 'It wouldn't be any harm, ain't it, for me to go with you to your service, no?' 'No harm in the world,' says me father, 'but it will be a dull pastime for you.'

"So off they went, and right up to the front seat in the chapel, for me father was an important man. Now, begorry! that was a special day an' all, for there was a special collection for the purpose of puttin' a new roof on the school—but the Jew wasn't aware of that, poor fella! Yes, sir! we was given to edication, the same as yerselves, an' we didn't grudge money for it—much.

"Well, sir! when the collection plate started at the front seat, me father, and he was a warm man, to give it a good lead, slapped a five-pound note on it. And me bold Jew, not to be shamed be a Gentile friend, slipped another fiver on top of it—the foolish man! He did, he was a dacent spud—an' him hopin' to recoup himself at penny nap later in the day in our back parlour. And so the plate went round, an' Eph's eye after it, and at the end, when it was brought up to the altar rails, he had a good look at it. Begobs! he near lost the sight of his eyes, for, listen to me! it was heaped as high as that with bank-notes and gold sovereigns—there was gold them plentiful days—and only a small share of silver; an' dam' the copper coin to be seen.

"Look now! When Mass was over, an' the two of them on the street, me father noticed that his friend, the Jew, was in a state of perturbment, an' shakin' his head in a sorrowful sort o' way. 'There was nothin' said be the good man to trouble you, Eph?' says me father, the kindly man he was. And Eph stopped him in the street. 'Tell me, John,' says he, 'ain't it so, your Christ, the Lord you worship, he was a Jew?' 'Well, yes! in a manner o' speakin', he was a Jew on one side,' me father concedes. 'And this feast you celebrate today—the founders, Peter and Paul—they were Jews?' 'Both o' them were Jews sure enough,' agreed my father, amicable. 'Well, then!' says the Jew, spreadin' his hands disconsolate, 'how did we come to lose the business?' Ay, faith! What'll you drink, Sir Gawain?"

"What I won't get—ask me to-morrow!" said Gawain.

"That was a story," said Keegan, "but it was apropos of nothing."

"Dom' the thing I see in it," said Lukey.

The Highlandmen took five seconds to savour the story, and then rewarded it with appreciative laughter. It had a quality that appealed to them.

II

In the midst of the laughter, the latch clicked, and the door was pushed open to admit four men, the leading man forthright, and the others slidingly, suspiciously, after the habit of roadmen coming within-doors. The leader was Malcolm MacFie, broad and solid as an oaken trunk; the others were wiry young tinkers in ragged tweeds, and with the long-peaked tinkers' caps pulled down over one eye.

The laughter stopped short. Men turned to each other and talked in low voices, ignoring the tinkers. And the tinkers ignored them. It had always been so, and it had always been the tinkers' choice. There was an occasional exception: old Parlan, the chief, was one, and his grandson Malcolm was another. But, as a rule, the men of the broken clan chose to be outcasts, living on the land that had failed them, taking what they needed in hidden ways, covering their operations by a bartering that was not often important, despising the settled people, and avoiding trouble until touched in the core of their life, and then—!

The people at the bar moved to give them room, and the four MacFies set their bellies against the zinc.

"Four half-pints, ma'am!" said the deep rumble of Malcolm.

Young Batt Sullavan placed the four frothy half-pints, one after the other, on the counter, and the tinkers waited.

"Slainge!" said Malcolm. The four glasses were lifted in unison, and the beer disappeared in one smooth flow down four open gullets. Not a throat muscle twitched, and the four glasses clicked on the zinc with a single click.

"Four more, ma'am!" said Malcolm.

And four more went the same road, and, again, four more.

"Four more, ma'am!" said Malcolm.

Peigi Sullavan hesitated, and Dinny lifted to his feet. Four quick half-pints are nothing in the capacity of a tinker, who has been known to down thirty pints at an Irish fair; but even thin beer has to be rationed amongst customers these days.

"This will be the last one, Mrs Sullavan," said the quiet rumble of Malcolm.

Dinny nodded to his wife, and young Batt refilled the four glasses. These final drinks did not go the sudden road of the other three. Malcolm did not touch his drink at all. He stood bow-legged, his back to the room, his gorilla arms hanging loose, and his massive head hunched forward; there was something static and lonely about him as if he were the last of an old breed stranded amongst a weaker race.

The three lathy lads sipped their beer, lit three cigarettes with one match, inhaled deeply, trickled smoke through a nostril, and turned a shoulder to the bar. They were like marionettes on a single string. From under the peaked caps the live, wicked, tinker eye looked sardonically at the tame men of settled Ardaneigh.

Gawain saw, for the first time, that these three lads had much more deadly stuff inside them than peace-time beer. The pallor below the tan, the twitch of mouths, the surface glisten of the eyes told plainly of raw illicit spirits or, worse, wood alcohol—a wholly maddening and unpredictable drink.

These lads are ripe for mischief—and are looking for it! thought Gawain. He looked anxiously at Malcolm's broad back, and hoped that that terrible man was not under the baneful influence. But Malcolm, solid-planted as a post, seemed in some remote world of his own.

One of the three was now half-singing, half-crooning, and, though his voice was drunken, every note was true. Gawain recognised him as Murrich of the wicked, viperine face. He was singing the *Song of the Broken Clan*, in tinkers' Gaelic which is part Highland, part Irish, with a scattering of Romany words. The three voices lifted together in the chorus:

> *"'Our road it is a long, lone road*
> *That nowhere has an end.*
> *It turns away from house and fold*
> *Where no man is our friend.*
> *And all we own is that long road*
> *Where once we owned the Glen,*
> *And we'll seek it, and we'll keep it—and*
> *to hell with settled men!'"*

"Ay, indeed and indeed!" said Murrich, addressing no one. "Settled men all about us, and what good are they—even to their own selves?"

"God be with the old days!" said the second, "when it took more than a'e tyrant-laird to frighten a township."

"They would be for leaving things to the men of the long road, so they would," said the third.

"Ay! but they're sly and sleekit," said Murrich.

"Ay so!" agreed the second. "Doing a mischief on the quiet—and who would get the blame?"

"It could be a lad of the MacFies," said the third, "and he twenty miles away."

"I wouldn't put it past them," said Murrich, "especial if they had red hair."

"Them's fighting words, Murrich," said Gawain, and they surely were.

A short, firmly built, red-haired young crofter moved his shoulders against a corner of the dresser, and straightened up. Murrich caught the movement, and his viper's head went forward snake-like.

"Is it the itch troubling you, Duncan Rua?" he said softly.

"You will be minding what you say, Black Murrich!" Duncan Rua said dangerously.

"Will you mind it for me, red-head?" said Murrich wheedlingly.

"I will," said Duncan Rua, "and not the first time."

Murrich took a stride forward, and Gawain brought the front legs of his chair down on the flags. But Malcolm moved first. He took a stride back and one aside, and was facing his cousin, Murrich; and Murrich drew back against the counter in line with his two mates.

Malcolm moved a great hand towards the door, and his deep voice was casual.

"Bedtime for loons! Go to it!"

He strode to the door, pulled it wide open, and moved a definite thumb. The three cockerels hesitated. The alcohol was stirring in them, and they were on the edge of mutiny. Gawain and others recognised the barrack square in Malcolm's mastiff bark.

"'Shun! Get out!"

And they went, heads down. They weren't afraid. They just knew. Murrich was last through the door, and as he went Malcolm flicked his ear with a middle finger, slapped the door on his heels, and turned round, his massive head ashake.

"Murrich is just out o' jail—he couldn't lift a herring," he said. "You could ha' more sense, Duncan Rua!"

"Dom' but he could!" agreed Lukey. "Them two ha' been boxin' each other reg'lar once a year."

"Sorry, Malcolm!" said the red lad, who was sound metal, and grinned over his glass. "But Murrich belted me proper the last time."

Malcolm picked up his glass, that was still full, walked to the front of the fire, lifted finger to Major Keegan, and stood looking into the heart of the glowing peats. Gawain looked consideringly at that strange Mongolian profile. The bosses of the cheekbones hid the smoked eyes, and the tip of the nose barely showed. He had come down to stop trouble, and he had done so with complete mastery. But he had come for another purpose too, or he would not have stayed behind, and Gawain had a fair idea of what the purpose was.

Malcolm got at it in his own way. He swallowed a mouthful of beer, and turned slow head to look down at Luke Carnoch.

"Not so long ago, Luke," he said, "I was going to ask you for a job."

"And not so long ago, I'd ha' given you one for the asking, Malcolm," Luke told him promptly.

"If anyone offered me a job I'd take it," Malcolm said slowly. Many here in the kitchen knew of Malcolm's revolt against the wandering life. Dinny Sullavan leant over the back of his chair, and spoke:

"We are busy at the peats, Malcolm, but it would be only for a short while."

Lukey brought the front legs of his chair clump on the floor.

"Hoots! that's no' a job for Malcolm of the soft palm. There was a job goin' and it might be goin' again—but I have no' the givin' of it."

"Not yet—what sort of job would it be?" Malcolm asked.

"A job might suit you, Malcolm."

"Yes, Lukey?"

Lukey considered for a space, and Gawain knew, as of old, how his thoughts were running.

Lukey flung a hand wide. "You know the Aiternach, Malcolm?"

"I know the Aiternach, Lukey."

"Ay, do you! Sixty thousan' acres of deer forest, and you know them all, and a shame for you, you rogue. A job? Ay, a job for a poacher turned keeper!"

Lukey, you scoundrel! thought Gawain. *Enlisting a MacFie against a MacFie's mischief!*

Lukey went on. "Ay! sixty thousan' acres, hill and hollow—and the fawns droppin' next month—and only one ranger in it this minute—a tyke up from a park in the North Riding, and I'd send him back wardin' tame red deer. There's the stalkers' lodge and four bothies besides, and a man would not be tied in one place all his days. And a good man he'd need to be, used to the open, knowin' the lie of the land, the airt of the winds, the ways of the stag and hind, and acquaint of some bonny lads no' far from here to be kept their own side of the wire."

Two or three of the bonny lads stirred and laughed.

"Is that the job you would give Malcolm, if you had the giving of it?" asked David Keegan.

"The very job! It would keep a man on the loose foot, and not tie him under one roof. And the weans coming down wi' the bus for the schoolin'; and the wife wi' the pony once a week for the groceries, and to sell a few patties of butter and a puckle eggs—an' be robbed by Dinny Sullavan in the ordinar' way o' business. That's the job—and ochone the day!"

"Malcolm's mouth is watering," said Gawain. "Could I get a job like thon?"

"Find the wife—and weans first," said Lukey with some meaning.

There was some sly laughter then, and Gawain felt hot under the collar, but he made no retort. Instead he said:

"Try another beer, Malcolm?"

Malcolm faced Gawain for the first time, and nodded his massive head. "Yes, friend! I will take a drink with you. You made a bit prophecy, and it has come true."

Here at last was the business that Malcolm had come for. He took a cigarette neat-handed from Gawain's packet, bent to the lighted match, and his smoke-grey eyes were intent on Gawain's.

"You heard?" he queried.

"You are here to tell me," said Gawain.

"Just so!" He straightened up, took the full glass from Batt Sullavan, inhaled a lungful of smoke, and drowned it with a mouthful of beer. He spoke deeply but without emotion. "The MacFies got their marching orders."

"Out of the camp at the Sand Pits?"

"Out of everywhere. Three days they got, and after that out they go, never to camp again in all the lands of the Tigh Mhor. That's the order."

"That is bad news," said Gawain.

Malcolm stepped back, but the smoke-grey eyes were still set on Gawain. "And what are you going to do about it, brother?"

Blast you! what can I do about it? I am going away. But aloud he returned question for question: "And what are the MacFies going to do about it?"

"In three days they'll be twenty miles away."

"Well away from mischief!" said Gawain.

"So you say!" Malcolm finished his beer, put the glass on a corner of the dresser, inhaled deeply, and threw his cigarette in the fire. He took a stride towards the door, and glanced aside at Dinny Sullavan.

"One could be trying his hand at the peats, kind man," he said, "but I am a tinker for three days yet."

He opened the door and turned, his squat massiveness outlined against the dark. A breath of fresh hill air came into the room, making the peak reek more noticeable. The roadman's voice had the sombreness of an iron bell.

"And what is Ardaneigh going to do? Have ye not heard? The Old Road—the drover's road—the tinker's road—the road to the peats, it will be closed on us and ye to-morrow morning—closed by barbed wire for good and all. And when the tinkers are twenty miles away, ye'll be here, and let the Tigh Mhor look to itself." That was the real news that Malcolm had come to tell.

The door shut firmly, and no one spoke for a moment. Then young Duncan Rua stepped away from the dresser, and there was a savage note in his voice:

"Iosa Chreesta! No one can shut that road."

And young voices growled agreement with him.

Dinny Sullavan was smoothly ironic. "Us people that do be in Ardaneigh these times are used to the long way round. A two or three miles extra to draw in the peats by the county road won't knock a feather out of us."

The red-haired Duncan was the mouthpiece of the young men. He spoke boldly.

"That road will not be closed on us. If the tinkers don't open it we will."

"And you so ready to go to the floor with a tinker a short time ago!" Dinny said.

"Wait now!" Lukey sat up and moved his arms appealingly. "The laird would know nothin' about the closing of the Old Road. He's not at the Tigh these two days."

"He closed one road we know," said David Keegan.

"I'm not blaming him—not for a while yet," said Lukey, obstinate in moderation. "That factor, Dukes, has to do with this. Listen ye! Big Malcolm was hintin' that the MacFies would be takin' the law into their own hands—"

"They can burn the Tigh Mhor for all I care," said Duncan Rua roughly.

"An' would you have the wild MacFies interferin' in the affairs of Glen Easan?"

"Someone has to—we've been patient too long."

"Then be patient a whilie longer," Lukey's hands were eloquent. "Ay! we' been patient, and let us not spoil things now. There was stalemate day-in, day-out, but things are on the move at last, and I'm feelin' it in my bones. Give them a chance. Hold ye the glen secure till the MacFies are gone—three days—and then we'll be seein'. That's all."

Many oblique glances were cast in Gawain's direction, and Gawain noted that. But he gave no sign. He rose to his feet, put his empty glass carefully on the dresser, moved casually to the door, said *Oidche Maith* (Good night) over his shoulder, and went out into the night, closing the door softly behind him.

He would not be drawn into direct or oblique discussion of the affairs of the glen. Let the men of Ardaneigh look after their own affairs. And whatever happened in three days—or four days—or ten days—one thing would happen for certain, and he knew what it was. He would be out of Glen Easan, and on the loose foot for all his days. And that was that.

Chapter XI
ANOTHER ROAD IS CLOSED

I

IT WAS getting on for eleven o'clock in the bright forenoon, and Gawain was striding up and down the bus-sunroom by the side of Alsuin's couch, and Alsuin, head turned, was admiring his nicely-creased flannel trousers.

"Shrunk to glory!" he said.

"Not an inch. But, indeed, Mr Sammy's corduroys were just as nice."

"Do they go back?"

"But no—not as they are." Alsuin considered. "You must give him a gift in return, I think. But yes! A gift. It will be a good excuse for you."

"Excuse?"

"To go down to the Tigh, and talk to my darling Iosabel. You will tell her to come and have tea with me."

"Sammy don't get no gift," said Gawain.

"You refuse? Sir, I am the queen who cuts off heads."

There was a tap on the glass door in the end-wall, and Luke Carnoch sidled in.

"That's my head saved," said Gawain.

"'Mornin', your Majesty!" greeted Lukey. "Could I have a word or two with you?"

"A complaint, Lukey dear?"

"A word of authority from you, ma'am."

"Yes, Lukey?"

Gawain was not trusting Lukey—nor Alsuin—these days, and he made a movement towards the door. Lukey's lank figure straightened up, and he spread his arms wide.

"Hold him, ma'am!" he cried urgently. "Use your authority for a'e minute."

Alsuin pointed a quick hand. "Sir Gawain!"

Gawain obediently returned and sat on the end of the couch, lit a cigarette, and looked suspiciously at Lukey over the flame of the match. Lukey took Alsuin's delicate hand in his for a moment, and felt the thread of heat.

"It is this way, ma'am," he began. "I have it in mind to go down to the Tigh Mhor."

"The Tigh Mhor, Lukey?" She was pleasurably surprised.

"On a small bit business—of a peaceable nature."

"I understand, Lukey."

"It is that I am a shy sort of man," went on Lukey.

"Yes, dear Lukey, you are."

"Same as a brass monkey, he are," said Gawain.

"Maybe, not so shy as cowardly," amended Lukey.

"Accepted," said Gawain.

"If I had a sort of valiant knight—"

"Help!" cried Gawain.

"—to hold my hand," said Lukey.

"Gawain, darling?" said Alsuin.

Gawain saw that she was excited, and he would not excite her further by mock argument. He rose to his feet and saluted.

"It is an order, Lady?"

"An order. No, Lukey! do not tell me. When you come back, Gawain will tell me all."

And that is how Gawain, against his will, went down the road with Lukey. Alsuin watched them from her couch, their long shadows sliding in front, and was glad to see that Gawain was holding Lukey's arm affectionately. She could not know that Lukey was being cursed solidly and with imagination all the way down to the lift of the bank. There the two turned and waved back to her spirited waving.

"The pother over," said Lukey, "I would have you know that the Old Road was closed first thing this mornin'—larch posts and thorny wire."

"And the MacFies did not tear it down?"

"That's what's troublin' me. They might be lookin' to us to do it for them."

"Why not?"

"Takin' sides wi' the tinkers?"

"I would."

"Ay, would you! But look at it this way! If something ugly takes place about the Tigh—and it might—the lads that tore down the wire will have the finger pointed at them."

"So you're playing Parlan at his own game."

"If Parlan is in it."

"And you propose to interview Mr Dukes?"

"The laird came in by the mornin' boat," Lukey said.

"You'll talk to the laird?"

"If he listens."

"He will not listen, Lukey," said Gawain soberly.

"Then I have you for witness," said Lukey.

Gawain slapped a hand on Luke's shoulder. "Right, my old Greek! I'll be your witness—and keep my dam' mouth shut. Well, here we are! Do we climb over?"

"We'll try this way first."

They stood looking up at the tall, inhospitable gate. Inside, the lodge door was shut, and one chimney sent up a wisp of smoke that wavered and curled away in the soft western breeze. The drive ran straight, and dipped out of sight, and beyond, under the arch of beeches, Gawain saw the green waters of the firth. It seemed a long time since he had looked through these bars, and vaulted over, and met Iosabel Mengues. Would he meet her today? He hoped not. He was sure that he hoped not. He was going away and—well, yes! why prolong the agony?

Lukey had a flat thumb on a round brass knob in the stone gate-post, and Gawain could hear a bell tinkling somewhere inside the house. And it went on tinkling because Lukey kept his thumb on the knob.

"The bluidy thing's no' workin'!" said Lukey. "Ah! there's Mrs Thompson now. 'Mornin' to you, Mrs Thompson!"

The persistent ringing had brought Mrs Thompson bundling waddlingly from the lodge. She was a squat woman and fat, but she was not genial—not on the surface. And she had no manners. She ignored Lukey's mild salute.

"What is it?"

"I'll be goin' in, ma'am," said Lukey.

"What for?"

"A word with the laird—"

"By an appointment?"

"Not exactly that—"

"No appointment, and you stay out—Mr Dukes' orders." She turned tubbily to Gawain. "Sir Gawain Micklethwaite?"

Gawain nodded. He would be brief too.

"Mr Mengues instructs you are to be admitted on request." That was a quotation. "Do you want in?"

Gawain nodded. *And the ole fox brought me along!*

"You come in, no one else." She produced, from a fold of the many folds in her skirt, a twelve-inch key, that was attached to a leather strap round a waist notable by its absence.

She used the key firmly, and drew the gate open by a bare foot. *None of that, you old bitch*! said Gawain reprehensibly, stepped forward, unsighted her for a moment, and then slipped by.

"Stay out, Luke Carnoch!" she ordered,

"Dom', but I'm in!" said Luke in surprise.

"Out again!" she ordered.

"In a short time, ma'am."

"Now." She lifted voice for the first time. "Sam—Sam!"

"*Powder an' paint!*" said Gawain.

The Sam that appeared was Thompson the chauffeur-mechanic. He was a new hand, and Gawain had not known him in the old days. He was wiping his mouth and chewing; a big figure of a young man, his mighty legs in dark-grey breeches and black-shining leggings; and his shirt-sleeves folded to show muscular brown arms.

"Yes, Ma?" he said and swallowed, keeping eyes away from Lukey and Gawain.

His mother pointed a stubby finger at Luke Carnoch.

"Forced his way in. Put him out!"

"Yes, Ma!" said Sam agreeably, and strolled forward, his carbon-engrained thumbs in the loops of his braces.

Begod! a nice beginning! I'll have to knock his block off—and I doubt if I can. Gawain's hands slowly clenched, and he picked a spot on Sam's jowl.

But Sam Thompson had other ideas. He faced Lukey placidly. "Goin' out, Lukey?"

"Not for a while, Sam," said Lukey mildly. "I'm going down to the Tigh."

"Are you sure, now?"

"Ay! sure enough, Sam."

"Very well so!" said Sam. "If your mind is made up no man could stop you this side o' hell." And he turned on big feet and moved off to finish his forenoon tea.

"You big hulk!" said his mother.

"Have sense, Ma!" he pacified. "Do you want me busted in two halves?"

His mother surprised him, and she was fluent for once.

"You're not foolin' me, you blockhead! Think I don't know you're under Lukey Carnoch's thumb, same as the rest o' them—an' makin' rags of your breeches over the gate twice a week."

"Goad be here!" cried Sam at the door.

Her stubby fist threatened his vanishing back. "An' if anything mischancy comes o' this, Mr Dukes'll hear it—and whether or not I'll report you to Miss Iosabel."

"It is what I would do myself, ma'am," encouraged Lukey.

"'Tis what I am doin'," said Mrs Thompson, and waddled for the lodge, leaving the gate open.

Lukey and Gawain moved off down the avenue, and Gawain was chuckling.

"Nice work, Lukey! And I kept my mouth shut?"

"You did—that time. Och! Sally Thompson is all right—just savin' her face."

"And now you are using her to get someone to smooth your way?"

"No then! I was only thinkin' you would like to talk to that someone."

"Damn your eyes!" said Gawain.

II

Down at the Tigh Mhor, Iosabel was in the morning-room making out some orders, for she liked to play at housekeeping. She was not feeling too bright this morning, and it was such a fine morning too. Life, somehow, was same and zestless—and tidy, without a loose string anywhere.

She heard the 'phone ring in the hall, but was not interested, not even when their English butler tapped on the door and opened it.

"For you, Miss Iosabel—Mrs Thompson at the South Lodge."

"I'll take it, Bouse," she said listlessly, and strolled out, not speculating on what Sally Thompson might want. She yawned, and reached for the receiver.

"Speaking, Sally!" Her cool, deep voice was indifferent.

Mrs Thompson's voice was harsh in her ear. "That Lukey Carnoch, Miss Iosabel—forced his way in—a minute ago."

"Lukey Carnoch!" Iosabel's voice livened up.

"The same, Miss. That tall, dark gent is with him—"

Iosabel's heart missed a beat, and made up for it. "You mean Sir Gawain—?"

"I do, Miss. I opened the gate for him accordin' to orders, and Lukey slipped in wi' him. That fool o' mine, Sam—"

"Where are they now?"

"Up the drive, Miss. Lukey says he wants to see the laird, but he has no appointment—" She went on speaking into a dead 'phone.

Iosabel stepped back, ran her fingers through her black hair, and felt for the white ribbon that held it. Then she looked down at herself critically. She was in a white, black-flowered dress, and her ankles were as neat as ninepence; she would pass anywhere in plain company—and that blame nose of hers wasn't shiny. She did not hesitate for long, but hurried out through the hall, and down the steps by the sun-terrace; and her eyes went over the flower-beds and shrubberies towards the distant side-gate on the curve of the drive. No one was in sight yet—thank goodness!

Glory be! what a grand morning it was, with the first touch of summer adorning it! Who could be gloomy on a morning like this, when life was full of zest—and with many bright ends to be tied?

She walked across the gravel and on to the smoothly-clipped lawn. Sammy Veller and his not-so-dumb darling were playing miniature golf amongst the flower-beds, and golf-clubs were scattered about untidily. Iosabel picked up a cleek or a driving-iron or a mid-iron or a jigger or something. Why do modern golfers use numbers instead of the expressive old Scots names? Sammy had made a marvellous long putt to within a yard of a hole—even if it was not the hole he wanted. Iosabel walked up to the ball, took an open stance, and let go: a hefty smack, with the virile whip and follow-through that showed good training. The ball sailed over two clumps of rhododendron, and ran to within ten yards of the drive within the side-gate.

"Hoy!" yelled Sammy. "Blast it all! That's my best ball.

Goramighty! look at the divot!"

"Sorry, old boy!" Iosabel called cheerfully. "I'll retrieve your one-and-only for you."

She walked smartly across the grass and round the clumps, swinging her iron as she went. She was careful not to look far ahead, but kept her eyes moving as if searching for the ball which was nicely set up in plain view. She came to it, stood over it, and listened with all her ears.

Yes, there were footsteps and a murmur of voices on the drive just beyond the gate. But she did not look up. Instead she faced half round, set herself, and swung: a full swing this time and a follow-through up to the shoulder. The ball sailed in a great arc, pitched on the gravel outside the sunroom, and bounded high. Sound travels some eleven hundred feet in a second, and in about that time there came the crash of glass, and, a split-second later, an astounded bellow from Sammy Veller.

"That's your ball for you, Sammy!" said Iosabel, not lifting her voice. "Go look for it!"

The bang of the gate behind made her turn with a nicely-simulated start. Gawain and Lukey were standing inside, staring open-mouthed across the lawn. She walked across to the edge of the path.

"Well now! this is a pleasant surprise," she said barefacedly.

"A surprise, Miss Iosabel!" said Lukey, bringing his eyes back. "Gosh! what a wallop!"

"Is there a local rule," enquired Gawain, "or do you now play the ball where it lies?"

She laughed, but Gawain did not. His eyes were cool on her, but he did not feel cool. My lord! the shape and face of her struck him afresh every time, and was more vivid than his memory of her. That black-and-white dress was alive; and that rich and generous mouth, that strong-cheeked broad-oval face would turn the heart over in a man—as his had turned over. Yet his voice remained cool and remote.

"Without armour, this adventure. The lady got a peon woman's message?"

Iosabel saluted with an iron. "Damn! I thought I might pull it off." Then her voice changed and grew formal. "Queen Alsuin's forthright knight, yclept Gawain? What deed of derring-do do you do dis day? Bet you couldn't say what!"

Gawain moved a hand. "I be dragged at the chariot tail

 of the great warrior, Conal Carnoch."

"On what venture?"

"I was wantin' a word with the laird, Miss Iosabel," said Lukey in plain language.

Iosabel came forward a few centuries. "You have an appointment, Luke?"

"No, Miss—I was kind of hoping—"

"Oliver Dukes—you could see him?"

"'Tis the laird I would see," said Lukey, who could be as obstinate as a mule.

She shook her head gravely. "I am afraid he will not see you. But"—she brightened a little—"could I help you in any way?"

"I'm depending my life on you, Miss Iosabel," said Lukey.

Forthwith, she slung the golf-iron across the grass, came out on the gravel, and slipped an arm through Lukey's. Frankly she reached her other hand to Gawain, and frankly he gave her his arm; and the feel of her hand reached as far as his throat.

"You are in my hands," she said. "Let us go!" She had not asked Lukey what his business was. That she would not do.

The outraged Sammy Veller was storming across the lawn, his Dandy cackling at his shoulder. He came out in front, and solidly blocked the way, indignation struggling for expression. Then his eyes blinked, and he looked Gawain up and down, and words came to him in a roar:

"Where are my yaller corduroys, you hound?"

"You'll pay for that pane of glass you broke, you handless lout!" said Gawain coldly.

"Oh, Gord!—"

"It was your ball did it," his lady told Sammy.

"Shut up, dumbbell!"

"That's Danice Dinwoody, the brains of the team," Iosabel said. "She's my friend."

"Shut it!" shouted Sammy. "Where are my pants?"

"What did you pay for 'em—a guinea?" Gawain enquired.

"Four-and-a-half, made to measure—"

"Thirty bob cash down—second-hand to me?"

"Thirty!—say, are you offerin' thirty?"

"Twenty-five."

"Thirty! and I leave it to Mr Carnoch," said Sammy.

"Thirty-five," said Lukey, who had known about the pants all the time.

"Hand it over—I heard what happened 'em," said

Sammy.

"Get out of our road! We're going places," ordered Iosabel in some embarrassment.

Gawain shouldered Sammy out of the way, and the three forlorn-hopers went on, out into the gravel bay about the tall house, and aslant round one end of it, to where a single-storey modern Estate Office had been built on as a lean-to.

III

The Estate Office contained three rooms: a big one for the estate clerks and technicians, another big one for the laird Mengues, and, behind that, a smaller one for secretary-factor Oliver Dukes.

This forenoon, Sanin Cejador y Mengues was in his own office, and Oliver Dukes was with him, giving an account of his stewardship. The room was a commodious one, looking down on Loch Easan through wide windows; and the reflected light off the water filled it with a fine even glow. It did not look like a room in which any work was done. There were a polished parquetry floor, an outsize flat-topped desk of some foreign dark wood, several straight-backed, cowhide chairs, but no filing cabinets or other appurtenances. Covering the whole of one wall was a six-inch-scale, contour-coloured, ordnance-survey map of the whole estate.

Oliver Dukes, big tweed-clad shoulders leaning forward, sat at the flat desk, a forefinger moving over a folioed document, and his light voice a monotone. His laird stood looking over his shoulder, and smoked a long thin cheroot. Dukes was hiding indifference, for he knew that the laird was not interested, and that was all right with Mr Dukes, who was now practically in full control.

The laird, indeed, was not interested. He was merely holding on and not yielding an inch. He turned away and paced slowly back and forth behind his secretary's chair, his fawn-leather face saturnine, and his red-and-white kilt swaying to his walk. And Dukes' voice went droning on, but it had meaning no longer.

Presently Mengues moved across to one of the big windows and looked out over the loch to the breast of Stob Glas. The freshness and strength of the scene, as ever, impressed him. It had not the awful desolateness, the appalling imminence of the Cordilleras that make men little and secretive. It was strong but it was intimate, and it invited man to share its vigour. But he felt that it no longer shared anything with him.

He had turned his back on the glen, and the glen had turned its back on him. He was beleaguered in a fort-alice of his own making, but the beleaguerment was passive and invited no sally. The people of this Glen Easan were an agreeable people, but they were stubborn too; they persisted, and they drew their qualities out of the place and out of old time. They would co-operate, but they would not yield. He could work with and for them, and he wanted to, but he had failed. And all he could do now was to shelter behind his privileges, while the life of the glen went on, a little lamer because of him, and with some resentment added, and, perhaps, a little pity for the man who had failed them at the first prick of caste pride.

He knew that, basically, it was his own fault. But no man will wholly blame himself. The people were to blame, too, for their impulsive act of loyalty to their own man, an act that tied his hands and gave him no chance for reconsideration. And he blamed Oliver Dukes, who, using the laird's authority, had jumped in with both feet, and made the rift wide beyond repair. The one man he did not blame at all was Luke Carnoch.

He turned from the window, and looked with some distaste at the back of his secretary's long head. Dukes was monotoning no longer; he was turning folios, and waiting for any comments on work well done. There were seldom any these days, and that was just fine.

A movement at the door made laird and secretary lift heads. The wide door opened fully and rather quickly, and two men came in abreast. It was an oddly abrupt entrance, as if someone had pushed from behind. And that is what Iosabel had done.

Gawain Micklethwaite kept a straight face, but he was bubbling inside. Her method appealed to him. *As good a method as any! Get in the game and stay with it!*

After that abrupt entrance Lukey and Gawain were inclined to hesitate. But Iosabel was at Gawain's side, and he felt her quick nudge, transferred it to Lukey, and the three came steadily across the floor that clicked sharply under their heels. Iosabel's voice was cheerfully careless, but her words had been chosen.

"Father, I have brought these two gentlemen in to see you. You know them, of course?"

Her father's courtesy did not hesitate. "Why yes, my dear! Will the gentlemen be seated?" His hands welcomed them.

Gawain turned to Iosabel, bent head, and swung a hand to the back of a chair. It was as if he had spoken. *Stay with us, O gallant one!* And the way she at once took the chair said, *You could not put me out—not with a battle-axe!*

Gawain and Lukey sat down facing the desk; Gawain relaxing his shoulders against the back of the chair, Lukey upright, but not on the edge of the seat. Sanin Mengues half-sat, half-leant on the high window-sill, his attitude wholly detached. His cheroot had gone out, and he laid it on the sill beside him. Dukes sat forward very definitely, his forearms on the desk, his mouth tight above his long jaw, and his eyes expressionless. He knew that this was no casual visit; these fellows were here for some purpose. Well! he could deal with Carnoch adequately, and he would like to deal with Micklethwaite—if he got a chance.

There was a pause then. The laird's bearded face was composed, but something was moving inside him. His daughter had brought these two men to see him. Was that remarkable daughter of his already at work? Luke Carnoch, he knew, represented Ardaneigh; and this Wing-Commander stood for something wider, stood, indeed, for something in all the glens. Here was where one moved carefully.

Dukes had a trick of letting the other man begin; but his laird spoke quietly.

"Is this a business visit, gentlemen?"

"Business, Mr Mengues," said Lukey in his mildest voice.

Dukes lifted a forefinger off the desk. "I attend to business, Carnoch."

Lukey was looking over Dukes' head. The laird was the man he wanted to talk to, but he could not insist on it. Nor would he try. If he could talk to him through Dukes his purpose might be served, for the laird was the man in control at the end of all.

Mengues noticed Lukey's hesitation, and said courteously:

"Mr Dukes will listen to anything you have to say, Mr Carnoch."

And you'd better listen too, Mr Laird! thought Gawain.

But Lukey put it more diplomatically. "And I would like you to listen too, laird."

This was playing the game right into the laird's hands. He bowed his head stiffly in assent.

Luke Carnoch could beat about the bush as well as any Highlandman, and better than most. But now he was simply direct, his voice mild as ever, and only a friend would recognise the steely glint in the pale eyes. He said:

"It is the Old Road—the clan road—what is now called the Tinker's Road. You closed it this morning with thorny wire, Mr Dukes, and it should not be closed at all."

This was news to Sanin Mengues. His own private road had been closed, but he would not readily close an old traditional road—the road the clans had taken to war, the road of the black and dun cattle for the Border, and now the road of the wandering men. But his agent had closed it, and his agent would have a reason. Dukes was talking with easy confidence.

"Yes, I closed that road this morning. What of it?"

"No man has the right to close that road," Lukey said slowly.

Dukes spoke for his laird's ear. "But it is no longer a public road under the County Council or Road Board. It is under no authority, whatever, other than that of the Proprietor, Mr Mengues. I exercised that authority for a definite purpose."

"It is not possible, sir," insisted Lukey. "It is a Right of Way time out o' mind. It is, as well, the shortest road to the township peat moss. It canna' be closed."

"And what do you propose?" Dukes queried.

"I am askin' that the road be opened again."

"When?"

"This very day that's in it," said Lukey firmly.

"And if we refuse?"

But he could not get Lukey to show his hand that easily. "I didna' come to any gentleman's house to say what we would do, or wouldna do. I am only askin' that the wire be cleared this very day."

"And I am witness to that," said Gawain quietly.

"No witness is necessary, sir," rapped Dukes coldly.

"Depends," said Gawain.

Dukes leant back in his chair and tapped a forefinger with a pencil. "I don't mind telling you, Carnoch, that the Old Road is not closed permanently."

"It should not be closed at all," persisted Lukey.

"It will be reopened within—yes—three days," Dukes conceded.

"I am askin' that it be opened today—and left open for good."

"Witness here," said Gawain. "Old Road open today and left open!" *Put in the form of a request mild as buttermilk and tough as steel.*

"I see that I must explain," said Dukes. Ordinarily he would not explain anything to this fellow Carnoch, but he felt that it was necessary here and now to justify his actions to his laird.

He got to his feet, and walked across to the big wall-map. He put his pencil point on the spot that marked the Tigh Mhor, traced a line down the shore and tapped the map.

"That is Corran Hook."

Tautology! said Gawain. *Corran means hook—a reaping-hook.*

"The tinker MacFies camped there," said Dukes.

"For three hundred years they have," said Gawain.

"Three days!" snapped Dukes. "In three days I threw them out." The pencil tapped the map. "The salmon on the run come round that point close in, in deep water, before coming along here to the estate stake nets. Fishing or netting is forbidden at the Point—it is too deadly. Salmon can be taken there in an ordinary bag net, pulled out with a stroke-all, thrown out with a long-handled gaff—"

"Witness here! I've done it myself," said the cool lazy voice of Iosabel. She was leaning back in her chair, knees crossed, and her long leg drew the eye.

"Iosabel, please!" said her father coldly.

"Contempt of court!" said Iosabel.

Iosabel was right, Gawain noted. The atmosphere in the room from the very beginning was that of a courthouse. A case was being presented to Laird Mengues, who listened like an aloof judge. Dukes went on making his case.

"The tinkers camped there at the Hook during the height of the run, and did uncountable damage. I ordered them off. Why not?"

He paused challengingly. Gawain glanced at Lukey, and met an appealing eye. Lukey had said all he had come to say, and now it was Gawain's turn. *And dammit! if this is a case, someone should give a proper perspective to his honour, the Justice? Fair enough!*

"The fish run that Point literally in thousands, Mr Dukes?" queried Gawain.

"This is no concern of yours, sir," he said.

"Nonsense, Nolly!" cried Iosabel. "The fish run the Point

 in thousands? They do. I saw them—millions of them. Go on, Gawain?"

"The point I would make," said Gawain with quiet reasonableness, "is that the water-bailiffs keep a particularly close watch on the Corran, and that a very expert tinker-poacher might snig one fish—or two—or three, but not more." Malcolm MacFie had once snigged three, with Gawain as a look-out.

"A tinker has no right to snig any," said Dukes firmly.

"A fish out of the untracked sea for a poor wandering man! Wo-wo-wo!" There was such a depth of feeling in Gawain's voice that Iosabel could not help herself.

"Good man yourself, Gawain!" she said impulsively.

Mengues flicked an eye at his daughter. This flying man should be a mere stranger to her, but she had called him by his Christian name—twice—Gawain? A little quiet enquiry was called for! Mengues' interest was really alive now.

Dukes hesitated. This soldier-fellow had cramped his style—and damn Iosa! But, still, the laird objected to wastrels, and could not object to their being ejected from the estate. And now was the time to enlighten him. He traced his pencil back at a slant, and again tapped the map.

"These are the Sand Pits, at the mouth of the Old Road, and the tinkers are camped there now. I did not interfere with them until two days ago when they tried to steal a valuable young dog—"

"Hosses—hold 'em!" cried Iosabel scathingly. "The dog was mine and was not begun to be stolen. Young Rory went off with a lurcher—"

"And the lurcher, with a young tinker, was poaching at the time," Dukes came back, and went on quickly before that devil, Iosa, could come in again. "I had to take action, Mr Mengues, because my authority—delegated from you—was flouted. And, moreover, the Sand Pits is not the tinkers' camping place until August—"

"Who threw them out of Corran?" queried the irrepressible Iosabel. Dukes ignored that.

"Until August!" he said, "when the grouse are on the wing, and we know only too well what happens then."

"Counsel for the defence intervening!" said Gawain. "Poaching grouse on the wing is not so profitable for poor devils who are not allowed to own shotguns. The time for poaching grouse is October-November, when the grouse are packing the stubbles, and, whoever poaches your grouse then, the MacFies do not. They are not here."

“And see where they are!” said Dukes triumphantly. He swept his pencil across the map where the Old Road, scorning all gradients, made a chord to the great arc of the main highway. Two-thirds of the way along the chord he made a firm point. “They are there at Cloun Aiternach, in winter camp, right on the flank of the deer forest.” He sneered. “Venison on a tinker’s table!”

“And nothing to kill it with,” put in Gawain, “but I’ll be fair—a weighted hind in November or a stag getting over the wire in a blizzard.”

Dukes ignored that. He turned round full, and his voice rose. “I have given the tinkers three days’ notice to quit. They are going for good and all, and they are going by the main road. I have closed the Old Road so that they cannot get to Cloun Aiternach. Three days—that’s all.”

He came back to the desk, sat down firmly, and began to arrange his papers. The interview was over, and there was no more to be said. And Gawain wondered cynically if anything had been gained by what had been said.

He rose to his feet, so did Lukey, so did Iosabel. And Sanin Mengues, straightening up from the window-sill, spoke quickly.

“Have you anything to add, gentlemen?”

Lukey showed what a tough old fighter he was. He was boiling inside, but his face was as gently melancholic as ever, and his voice never changed.

“I am only asking that the Old Road be opened today,” he said. It was as if Dukes had never explained.

“Three days,” snapped Dukes.

“And you, Wing-Commander?” queried Mengues.

Very well! Things had been put before this laird. Why not complete the picture? Then the laird could do his damndest in full knowledge—and the Lord have mercy on his soul! Gawain took one stride forward, and kept his voice in control.

“I will state the obvious, Mr Mengues: the MacFies must camp somewhere—”

Dukes interrupted him, his voice showing his temper.

“They are a wastrel crew, serving no purpose, entitled to no consideration. In these days when there is work needed from everyone, they should not be tolerated; drones and rogues living by poaching and petty pilfering—parasites on the public body—and the sooner they disappear the better.”

Gawain ignored the special pleading, and went on

 steadily.

"The MacFies come of an old race—the old race, Mr Mengues. They trace back into the darkness. They were broken, as a clan, three hundred years ago. Some of them joined the clan that broke them, some joined other clans; a few would not conform at all, or shake the hand of the betrayer—and can you blame them? That few took to the road—it was all that was left to them. They have a song, Mr Mengues, the Song of the Broken Clan, for they had singers and pipers amongst them always, and one singer made this:

"'Our road it is a long, lone road
That nowhere has an end.
It turns away from house and fold
Where no man is our friend.
And all we own is that long road
Where once we owned the Glen,
And we'll seek it, and we'll keep it—and
to hell with settled men!'

"They serve no purpose, says Mr Dukes! But they served. They fought in all the wars. They marched with Montrose, they charged home at Killiecrankie, died at Culloden, stood staunch at Waterloo; they were volunteers in 1914; and some of them up there in the Sand Pits are back from this last war—and some will not come back at all. And so, the last remnant, under old Parlan MacFie, wanders the Highlands, taking a little toll here and there; underdogs getting the worst of every quarrel, biting if they must, and getting the worse for that. And now have they come to the last degradation where you forbid them a place to lay their heads? Why persecute them, Sanin Cejador y Mengues? The responsibility is wholly yours."

He pulled himself up, turned on his heel and stalked out of the room. Iosabel's breath was quivering in her nostrils.

Gawain walked across the gravel stiff-legged, and he was not too pleased with himself. He, that would be a silent witness, had talked too much, and had displayed some emotion—uselessly; and he was afraid of emotion. Well! there would be no need to say anything more after this. Dukes was inviting trouble, his laird had been warned, and things would have to take their own course now.

A petulant voice was lifted behind him. "Hoy there—hoy! Goshikins, man! are we no' wi' ye?"

Gawain swung round. Lukey was coming in his long,

loose-kneed strides, and Iosabel Mengues was failing to keep in step with him. Gawain's mood snapped over as if switched by a lever. There was one spunky kid! In her stern father's face she had taken their side, and had kept the issue open in spite of Dukes. She would do to take along—but where? He had chosen a lonely road, perforce, but already the thought of a companion was intruding itself in his mind.

He took three long strides, and had Lukey by the lapels of his old tweed jacket.

"You ruthless old Highland weasel! You wily old dog fox! You schemin' auld hoodie craw! I was your witness of the shut mouth, and you got me to whistle a jig through a milestone. Bah!"

"He'll have my head off in a minute," Lukey cried protestingly. "Look, Miss Iosabel! Did I ask him to open his mouth once?"

"I did, Lukey," said Iosabel. "And glory! didn't he open it? We played a pretty sound game, I think."

Gawain noticed the "we," and liked it.

"The game was yours, damosel, from the moment you heaved us through that open door."

"Thank you!" She met his eyes boldly. "The game is not mine, but I am in it—till the cows come home."

IV

Sanin Mengues came down the steps from the Estate Office, slanted across the gravel, and drifted out on the lawn, his hands, as usual, behind his back. But the weight of depression was no longer heavy on him, and his attitude was meditative rather than indifferent. He went out the side-gate, across the drive, and down the track to Cobh Echlan. He stood on the platform fronting the bathing house, and gazed across the land-locked little bay to the stark ridges of Stob Glas above the orange-gold band of furze. This secluded yet wide prospect had always appealed to him, but now he scarcely took it in, for something else occupied his mind.

Things were beginning to move out of the old obstinate impasse, and that incalculable daughter of his was playing a part—for him, against him, or trying to break the deadlock that he himself had brought on Glen Easan? He had delegated authority to Oliver Dukes, and Dukes had implied today that his authority must be supported. But had Dukes gone too far in this matter of the Old Road? That had to be decided this very day, and the responsibility was his, as that flying officer had said. But first he would talk to his daughter. . . .

He moved back to the main drive, and faced towards the Tigh. A clear halloo from behind made him turn. Iosabel, swinging a hand at him, was coming up from the South Gate.

She moved well, that girl of his, full of young life—and she had a live and lively mind that sometimes moved her to madcap activity—and her brand of language was not always ladylike, but always apt. There was a boylike quality about her, but she was all woman too, and desirable. Presently she would find herself a mate. Once he had thought she had found Oliver Dukes, but after today he doubted that. Gawain Micklethwaite was again in his mind.

He waited for her, and she came to him, one arm swinging, her head up, and her eyes clear.

"Am I in trouble again, O my Father?" she came to the point. But he ignored that point.

"You have been seeing your friends off, I see!" He emphasised *friends*, and she took him up promptly.

"They are my friends—yes!"

"And so I want to talk to you, my dear."

"I know, Father." But did she know? Would this father of hers probe into a place she was keeping secret?

He took her arm in his usual way, and the two of them walked on the lawn, moving leisurely, skirting round the shrubberies, and circling back again. And she found that he was leaning a little on her, borrowing, somehow, from her youthful vigour, and she gave him the prop of her shoulder, affection glowing in her.

He came directly to his subject, as she knew he would.

"You seem to know Sir Gawain Micklethwaite—fairly well, Iosabel?" He spoke almost casually.

"Fairly well, Father," she agreed. *Fairly well* was about right, though once or twice, for a minute or two, she had thought she knew him very well—and then he had withdrawn into himself abruptly—almost as if afraid.

"You have met him more than once?"

"Our paths have crossed a few times," she said, and knew it was only half the truth.

There was a pause then. Iosabel plucked a bay leaf from a bush as they passed by, bruised it in her fingers, and smelt the dryish-sweet scent of it. Her father was waiting, and she found it hard to tell him of her five (she knew the number) encounters with Gawain Micklethwaite. But she must tell him something. She spoke brightly, sticking to the half-truth of a woman.

"You are to blame, old-Father, for my meeting him again."

"Oh, indeed?"

"Oh yes! You put an obligation on me over a nameless garment, and I had to call at Blinkbonny—I had to—and oh, Dad! I met the most wonderful child."

"Major Keegan's sick child?"

"Yes. I had afternoon tea with her. Eleven she is—two months—and four days. No, she is not a child. She is fey. A little witch—a little imperious queen, who wants to rule with a peace abounding! Sir Gawain Micklethwaite is her knight-at-arms."

"He has that quality."

"And Alsuin—that is her lovely name—puts what she calls Tasks on him. He is on a Task now—the very hardest. She is not sick—I mean ailing—it is her spine in plaster. You can feel the thread of febrile heat—and Gawain fears she may not get well—and that is terrible."

"Very terrible indeed."

Iosabel was on a good line now. "She lies there in her little sunroom, a brown mite, looking down through her windows, and watching her road. This road, beyond the South Gate, is her very own road. She is the Lady of Shalott, without the mirror. And her road used to be a most entertaining one, busy all day long, and everyone knowing her and waving to her, and some going up the slope to talk to her through the open window. I did not wave for a long time, but I wave every time now; and she has invited me to tea this afternoon." Iosabel paused for breath.

"This little one blames me for closing her road?" he asked quietly.

"No! She blames no one. She would love you, her serious, serene hidalgo. She wants her road open of course, but she wants peace in the glen first."

"Peace!" said her father deeply. "Peace is hard to win. Pride is its enemy." And abruptly he brought her back to the point. "I think, my daughter, that you like Sir Gawain

 Micklethwaite?"

That was nicely put, and she would answer now. He felt her arm stir; and she looked straight ahead.

"Yes, Father, I like Sir Gawain Micklethwaite—and he likes me." She had to be clearer. "But look, he is not—" she changed that—"we are not paying each other court—not even in the mildest flirtation. He is not that sort."

Flirtation, she knew, was a horrid word. There should be another word to express another shade of meaning; for it was certain that, in some subtle way, Gawain was paying her court—going so far and, then, stopping abruptly.

Iosabel would be still more definite. She spoke evenly: "He is going East next week—going away for good."

Mengues was surprised. "Has he not a home in Scotland?"

"Sammy Veller says he has not." In her own way she had screened some information out of Sammy—with Dandy to help, and now she retailed some of it to her father. "He is a poor man really. The title comes from one James the Sixth, and means nothing, for the family place on Loch Linnhe was lost—oh, generations ago. He is an engineer by profession."

"And going East—I see!" and he added a question. "And what about this Task?" He had not forgotten, and he knew the Task.

And she answered promptly. "He leaves that to you and Luke Carnoch."

"Luke Carnoch! You like Luke too?"

"Everyone likes Lukey." And then she flared, shaking his arm. "Blast Nolly Dukes! and blast the township of Ardaneigh!"

He checked, and his voice sterned. "Has anyone insulted you, girl?"

"No—no! They treat me as they treat you—as you treat them—turning their backs—oh! very politely, but unmistakably. They are the stiff-necked ones."

"There is resentment—"

"Only amongst the young men home from war, and Lukey can hold them."

"He bears no resentment?"

"Not he. But he is afraid."

"Afraid?"

"Afraid of the MacFies."

"That poor remnant?"

"The underdog that bites!"

"And gets the worst of it—as your friend said—the poor devils! What can they do?"

"I don't know, but Lukey—and Gawain—are afraid."

"For me?"

"For the whole glen, which is one,'' she said firmly.

They were on the edge of the gravel in front of the house. He loosed her arm and patted her shoulder.

"Thank you, my dear, for all the information. The responsibility is mine."

He left her, and moved aslant across the gravel towards the Estate Office.

Chapter XII
GAWAIN DECIDES TO PLAY

I

IOSABEL had been invited to take tea with Alsuin, and she came up on foot that afternoon. She came in such a hurry that she had passed Alsuin's approved saluting point before she remembered. Then she went back ten paces soberly, gave the proper salute, and saw Alsuin's answering arm.

Alsuin chuckled softly. "Darling Iosabel! She nearly did not remember. It would be something on her mind—and see the lovely flowers she is bringing for me."

Gawain, standing at the couch end, was looking down the slope too. "The foot of Diana—no, Artemis—the foot of Roman Diana was not light enough—"

"Quit your haverin'!" said David Keegan, kicking a left foot. "She's only a tea addict, and in a hurry to it."

"She has news, the dear one!" said Alsuin confidently. Gawain quoted an old saw: "'Bad news comes on the swift foot'—I hope not."

He had the door open for her, and she smiled to make him blink, and handed him her flowers.

"For the queen. Queens always arrange their own flowers."

"And you to help, dear one," Alsuin piped. "Gawain pops them in as they come."

Iosabel greeted the little one, cheek to cheek, shook hands with Dave, sat in the knight's chair, and surrendered her hand to Alsuin. She was wearing an afternoon frock of delicate silver-grey, that showed only one ornament: a big jet and silver plaque, with a spray of larch in emeralds, on her left breast. In that demure, silver sheath she was the complete Patrician lady, without any evidence of the antic streak.

"Where is Lukey?—I want Lukey," she said, and, indeed, Lukey was the man she wanted. Already she felt at home with this household.

"He is not where he should be—at his taties," Gawain told her, "but he'll be here with the tea-cups."

"He's trying a Castle Connell splice on a rod broken at the stud-lock," Dave said, "but he'll never get the balance."

Alsuin patted her hand. "He was looking out the window for you all this afternoon," she whispered.

But when Lukey came in behind his wife and the tea-trolley, Iosabel did not say what she wanted Lukey for. It was not until tea was over, and she was arranging flowers with Alsuin in Alsuin's vases, that she remarked over artful hands:

"You were looking for news, Luke?"

"Me, Miss Iosabel!" He simulated surprise. "I could see you in a hurry—but how would I know—?"

"There was that request—or was it an ultimatum?"

"Not the Old Road!—Gosh—?"

"Yes, Luke! My father has given orders to open the Old Road—unconditionally. It will be open today—this evening—before nightfall." That was her news.

Lukey smacked his knee resoundingly. "The laird is a just man, and didn't I always say it?"

"Justice stared him in the face through your eyes, Lukey," the laird's daughter said.

"The Old Road—not my road?" Alsuin was plaintively eager.

Iosabel patted her hand. "Not your road yet, darling—but we move." She turned to Gawain and said sadly, "Your plea—I am sorry, Gawain—! The MacFies may go by their old road, but they go."

Gawain said musingly: "And they will camp one night at

Cloun Aiternach—it is as far as they can get."

"Mr Mengues' hands were tied," said Keegan reasonably. "He was just. He opens the Old Road because his agent had no authority in law to close it. But his agent had authority to order the tinkers out of their camps, and he cannot go behind his agent, unless—" He paused and frowned.

"Unless what, Major?" Iosabel was eager.

"That's the devil of it, young lady!—I don't know."

She turned hopefully to Lukey, and Lukey was cheerful.

"Och! The MacFies will clear out—Scotland is wide—and there'll be nothing more about it."

Lukey knew he was wrong; but he was not going to disturb Alsuin, this fine day, by discussing the danger from the tinkers. The tinkers had a grievance that went right to the roots of their lives, and they could be implacable in hitting back. And in hitting back they might try and involve Ardaneigh? He saw no way out either.

Gawain Micklethwaite was taking no notice of anyone now. He was in one of his brown studies, and his eyes were uncannily vacant, though they seemed to be directed at Iosabel. He was so deep under, that he forgot his manners. He took out a cigarette packet, did not offer it to her, put a cigarette in his lips, and forgot to light it; but in his own mind he was inhaling and exhaling smoke. Iosabel's eyes crinkled amusedly, and Alsuin, drawing on her hand, pulled her down close.

"Hush, dear one!" she whispered. "He is on the Task. He is that way always—and then it is done! You will see!"

Iosabel had a queer feeling that was almost eerie. This man had gone right away from them into a world of his own, so far that he might never come back. Some day he would go like that, and not be able to come back. She had a strange intuition that that is what he was afraid of. And she would not be there to draw him back. . . . She would not try to draw him back now. She got to her feet, put the last vase on a side-table, and came to bend to Alsuin's ear.

"I will go now, darling, and leave him where he is."

Alsuin squeezed her hand, and nodded. "You will see what he will do—for you are there too."

And Iosabel saw in half-a-minute.

When she got round to the concrete path, she heard a step behind her, and Gawain was at her shoulder; but he did not seem to know that he was there. They walked down the path side by side, and through the gate that Iosabel opened, and down the road that curved round the house. His hands were hanging limp, and his gait was slow and short and stiff-kneed; his head was back, his eyes vacant, and he was still blowing imaginary smoke. Iosabel felt inclined to take his arm to guide his automaton feet.

A more frightening and deeper abstraction she had never seen. So deep was it, that he would have passed Alsuin's saluting point without noticing. But Iosabel would not permit that, lest it hurt the little one.

She put a quiet, holding hand on his arm, and he started as if out of sleep. He looked round him perplexedly.

"Blazes alive! how did I get here?"

"On two stilted legs," Iosabel said with relief. She was waving up the slope, and he, too, made his saltire. He had come back—all of him.

He threw away his damp cigarette, lit one for her, and for himself, and gave his head a final clearing shake.

"Sorry! I was wool-gathering," he said, and heel-tapped the road under his feet. "Don't some of you want this road open?"

"We all do."

"This road may never be open if someone don't kill two birds with one stone," he said cryptically.

"Why not—you and me?" she said hardily, a little excitement moving in her.

"Let's walk and talk, then!" he said.

He took her arm frankly, as her father would, but more impersonally, and they went on slowly walking: down the slope, through the South Gate, and up the drive as far as the side-gate to the Tigh. And Gawain did most of the talking, once Iosabel had started him.

"Did you gather any wool in your ultimate dim Thule?" she began.

"A bit here and a bit there, like rags on a bush. Do you know what I was trying to do?"

"Resolving a Task, Alsuin said."

"Maybe! I was trying to get inside the skin of a tinker."

"Did you find it difficult?" she said slyly.

"You should know, damsel!" He chuckled, shook her arm and went off on a side-road. "I suppose I could call myself an old campaigner?"

"In war or peace?"

"War! A particular kind of war: war-under-cover and no quarter. One learned quickly in the Jungle, or went out—sometimes not so quickly. We were up against a brave, wily, intelligent and ruthless foe—but not quite as ruthless as we bloody Occidentals, once we learned the game—and you can take it from me. We Europeans of the West have such a savage streak in us that two thousand years of our Lord haven't rooted it out."

"The females too?"

"Worse if anything—the inciters. In the Jungle the man who stayed put longest lived longest. Get inside the other fellow's skin, force his hand, get him to make his move at a place appointed, and his day's work is done. A rotten game! and I hoped never to play it again!" His voice was gloomy.

"Inside the other fellow's skin—a tinker's skin—poor devil?"

"Ruthless streak at work, lady!" He waved a hand, and appeared to go off on another aside. "I know this 'ere glen pretty well, and it knows me. It is not my native glen, but I have been here often as not since boyhood. The old laird's wife was a cousin of mine. And when the old laird died, and the place was being rented to sporting tenants, I still kept coming—to Lukey's with Dave Keegan, whose wife was Highland and died in this glen. I taught Alsuin to walk—and she may walk no more."

"Oh dear!"

"Such is life! In them days I lived with and on the glen. I grew up with the lads, and I introduced a thing or two. We play shinty where I come from, but it had died out here. Shinty—the old game—hockey is an emasculated form of it. I helped to restore it here, and we had a darn good junior team before the war. Some of that team will never come back. To adapt Dave's song:

"'In far foreign fields from Dunkirk to Belgrade
Lie the soldiers and chiefs of the Highland Brigade.'

"You know that side-road down to Cobh Echlan? That was my first feat of engineering—and a nice bit of grading, though I say it myself. To trade, I am a sort of engineer, civil and mechanic. From the beginning, with Lukey pulling a quiet string, Blinkbonny was the focal point of the glen. The Tigh Mhor was in the hands of a done old man, or empty, or occupied by sporting tenants, and someone had to lead—"

"And I suppose the transfer of leadership was never really made to my father?"

"It was being made. Lukey saw to that. And then came that wholly ridiculous incident—"

"I know! My father was forced into his citadel—but was he to blame?"

"As much as Luke, that blasted old Pale Face! It was Ardaneigh that took the bit in its teeth. And there you are!"

"And here *you* are!" said Iosabel meaningly.

"You are like the rest of them. Very well! There are two good things: there has been no regrettable incident so far, and peace appeals to everyone. But no one has made the first move towards peace. Your father will not, Lukey cannot, and Ardaneigh just hangs on. There are left Dave and myself—and we used be the live wires. Dave is helpless with his gammy leg, and, besides, he's Irish."

"So you are elected?"

"From the beginning, darn it! and it has been put up to me constantly, if not in plain words. I am of the glen, and yet not of the glen. Of-the-glen I cannot ask the glen to eat humble pie; not-of-the-glen I am a free agent, and I can play any dam' ruthless game I like."

"You will play one?" She was really excited now.

"And two-three days to play it in. I haven't worked it out yet, but look, Iosabel! I would be taking a hellish chance—"

"Would it bring peace?" she asked quickly.

"If I pull it off—"

"Then, my dear Gawain, you simply must pull it off," she said firmly, and added quietly, "and I am in it with you."

He touched his breast with dignity.

"Knight-at-arms—and you a lady?"

"You big, selfish bully! and to blazes with your chivalry!" she cried indignantly. "You couldn't keep me out of it."

He laughed and shook her arm. "In this hellish game you take help where you get it—even if it hurts. You are part of the game and, as I see it just now, at one point everything will depend on you."

"Thank you, partner! When do we begin?"

"Now," said Gawain promptly. "Will you take orders?"

They had walked up to the side-gate, and walked back to

the lodge, and, now, they were again at the side-gate. Gawain loosed her arm, and she stepped back and saluted.

"At your service, sir!"

Gawain returned the salute gravely, and considered. "Three nights!" he said then, "and to-night is one of them. To-night we take precautions. Your part is to watch the Tigh Mhor."

"But it is impregnable!"

"Not against a tin of petrol and a lighted match through a window."

Her eyes opened. "As bad as that?"

"Hope not! But we are taking care. You'll watch till dawn inside and close round the house. Get Sammy to spell you—no one else—and tell no one but Sammy, and don't tell him much. Other watchers will not be far away. That is all."

"And to-morrow?"

"To-morrow you will get further orders—"

"Is that all you are telling me, you—?" And then she remembered discipline.

"I have to do two things before giving any orders," he told her gently. "To-morrow night—" he stopped. "This is an order: meet me at Cobh Echlan to-morrow afternoon at four o'clock. Dismiss!"

She saluted smartly, turned on her heel, and took four paces.

"Just a moment, Iosabel!" he stopped her.

She did the about-turn neatly and waited. He was looking at her steady-eyed and very seriously.

"There is something I would like you to know before we begin."

"Yes, Gawain?" she said evenly, but her heart turned over.

"You know who I am doing this for?"

"Alsuin—her Task."

"I am doing it for you."

"For me?" Her heart turned over again.

"For you. Playing out the game together, and not at cross purposes, so that we'll have a friendly thought for each other five thousand miles apart."

"A friendly thought—a gay thought—a gallant thought! You said that—something like that before. Thank you, Gawain."

She turned about again, took a short stride, hesitated, and swung back decisively.

"Wait, Gawain!" Her hands went up to her left breast. She kept her voice pleasant, almost jocular. "You presented me with a guerdon at Ros Caller. Does not a knight on a Task for a lady wear her token—her glove in his casque, or something—?"

He walked close up to her. "I will wear your badge, Iosabel."

Her jet and emerald plaque was in her hands. She turned up the lapel of his old Harris jacket, pinned the plaque on, and patted the lapel down.

"A secret between us," she whispered.

She was very close to him, and he caught the faint perfume that she used. He could put his arms round her. If he twitched a finger he could not hold himself. So he kept his arms stiffly at his side, and, when she was done, turned on his heel, and marched down the drive.

And Iosabel walked across the lawn, head down at last, and she was saying to herself:

Five thousand miles apart! Why—why—why? Why did he not take me into his arms and crush me? Five thousand miles! and I would go with him to the world's end!

These two foolish young people were so concentrated on each other that they had not seen or heard Oliver Dukes come up the rise from the harbour. He had got within twenty yards of them, and stopped to watch, his eyes expressionless, but his mouth malevolent. He had seen Iosabel pin on her badge. He knew that plaque well—jet and silver, and a spray of emeralds—and he was to remember it later on.

Chapter XIII
GAWAIN CHOOSES A SIDE

I

GAWAIN, coming in from the fresh evening air, was hit in the back of the nose by the reek of peat, homespun, and pipe-tobacco. He noticed, at once, that there were more customers than usual in the smoke-drifting room. The older generation, unable to get the national spirit, would not stomach thin beer, and were not often in Dinny Sullavan's. Many of them were here to-night.

The interest alive in the room was obvious. A silence had fallen with the entrance of the three from Blinkbonny, and, now, many side glances were cast in their direction as they sampled their mugs of Alloa ale. News in a Highland glen spreads quickly. Everyone already knew of the visit to the Tigh Mhor that morning, and of the reopening of the Old Road that evening; and the two events made one whole in everyone's mind. Something was happening at last, and other things might happen too—and would happen if a certain friend of theirs took hold. Here he was now, heeled back in his old place against the dresser, and they were his men for the asking. But he was taking his time.

It was the old schoolmaster, one Colin Cameron, that started the ball rolling with a sly remark.

"Is it true that Sam Thompson of the South Lodge got himself into trouble this morning?"

"Ay so, begod!" said Dinny Sullavan, his thigh over the back of a chair. "Sam's ma went as near as dammit to gettin' him a bloody nose."

"And me sheddin' my ain blood this evenin'!" said Sam himself at the corner of the bar. He was in his overalls, and the hand round his beer-pot showed a long scratch on the back of it.

"Do you know," said Dinny of the illustrative anecdote, "'tis often enough a man's ma or wife runs him into a drop of his own blood. And that reminds me of me own da, and he a young man. He was not long married, and my mother, God rest her, thought him the gallantest man in the whole parish, and he granted it to her, for all that he had doubts amountin' to certainty, havin' taken his batin' once or twice as all men must. And wan evenin', the bar—a pub they ran same as meself—the bar bein' full, in comes Tim Connors the smith, an' him oiled as a fly in treacle. 'You'll get no drink in this house, Timmy Connors,' says my mother behind the counter. 'Get out!' says she, 'or I'll get John'—that was me father—'I'll get John to pitch you out on your ear,' says she boastin'. 'Let the same man touch a hand on me,' says Timmy, 'and I'll lay him on the flat of his back.' 'I daur you!' says she. 'Aisy, woman—aisy!' says me father, 'an' give Timmy his pint.' 'I will,' says she, 'and a free wan if he puts you on the flat of your back. I daur him!' 'No sooner said than done!' says me bold Timmy, and put his blacksmith's hands on me father, and in two twos me poor father was on the flat of his back, nate as ninepence. Just a friendly fall.

"Me father got up grinnin' like an ould sheep, and Timmy got his pint, and things would have passed off peaceable only for the hurt woman's scathing tongue. 'Wo-wo!' says she, 'and ochone the day! that wan o' the fightin' Kellys is married on a weaklin' of the Sullavans that couldn't lift a herrin' off a tongs. No brother o' mine,' says she, 'would lie down for a Connors the longest day he lived.' And at that minute, there and then, in comes her brother Batt—Batt there is called after him—in he comes, a big, aisy-goin' slob of a lad wouldn't hurt a fly, as well me father knew. 'Woman,' says me father, 'I promised your mother never to lay hands on you, and I won't, but I'll do the nearest thing to it. How are you, Batt?' And he up, and gave Batt the point of his thumb in the navel, and when Batt's head came down me father hit him an unmerciful wallop under wan ear—and Batt didn't take time to get up, but went out the door on his hands and knees. 'Where are you now, Timmy Connors?' screeches me father, his blood up. An', whang! goes the bottle-mallet on top of his head—she had a strong arm on her—and down goes me father again once more for the second time—and there was peace for the rest of the night. Ay, faith! Have a drink, Major?"

"No!" said the Major shortly. He knew many a useful discussion spoiled by the inveterate anecdotist.

Lukey neatly brought back the talk to where Gawain wanted it.

"Who shed your blood this evenin', Sam?" he enquired.

"I did—takin' down barbed wire," Sam said.

"Up at the Old Road?"

"Ay! I put up the wire and took it down again, all in the same day—an' I can tell you we was nearer to more blood than that." He extended his scratched hand.

Gawain took up the questioning. "Did the MacFies make trouble, Thompson?"

"Not what you'd call trouble, sir, but Mr Dukes dom' near did. He was there givin' orders, and in a temper to beat a drum."

"The MacFies did not interfere?"

"No' exactly! but they were about under our feet, fleerin' at us and making fun of the work. And that's how the trouble began—almost. That lad Murrich got in Mr Dukes' way, an' took a root behind that pitched him clean across the road. Dambut! I thought we were for it. But Big Malcolm wasn't for trouble, thanks be! He ran Murrich and twa more down to camp, an' I finished the job quick as I could. That's how I got that hand!"

"The tinkers were fleerin' at you, Sam—what way?" Lukey asked with interest.

"Lots o' ways. About them not wantin' the wire up—nor carin' if it was down again either! How anyone could be shovin' a poor MacFie this way an' that, an' there was nothin' a poor MacFie could do, but if anything aye happened, a MacFie could aye be blamed. And a good thing the MacFies were goin', for the MacFies could not be blamed and they far on the road. Dambut! there was a threat somewhere, but I can't put a finger on it this minute."

"Good man, Thompson!" said Gawain. "You got the turn of a tinker's mind that time. A drink for Sam and myself, Peigi."

"And two up here," said David Keegan.

II

Gawain took a mouthful of his brimming glass, rose to his feet, and stood under the mantel-bar, facing the room.

"Manalive! You've growed up," said Dinny astraddle of a chair. "It looks like yesterday that you couldn't reach that bar with your black poll."

That mantel-bar was the standard of height in the township. It was an inch or two short of six feet from the floor, and a lad felt he was reaching his inches when he could brush it with his hair.

Gawain looked the room over slowly, and smoothed his poll against the mantel-bar.

"As stiff-necked a breed as ever I met!" he said remotely and sadly.

"The warld kens it," said Lukey.

"And your own neck rod-iron," Gawain said. "What do you think, Dave?"

This was David Keegan's cue. He hitched his chair round, stamped a foot, and shook his head.

"Stiff-necked goes, I am sorry to say," he said gloomily. "They have heard Sam Thompson; they heard Big Malcolm;

 they've got hints galore of trouble brewing; and here they sit on their hunkers drinking Dinny Sullavan's hog-wash—"

"Blazes, Major! how can I help it if it is hog-wash?"

"You can't." Keegan thrust his head forward. "Some of you stubborn ones will sit there and let the MacFies do damage in the glen, and you'll take the blame—for blame will surely come your way—and do nothing, because the damage will be within the demesne walls, where a man lives who is as stubborn as yourselves. When did you begin letting outsiders interfere in your own affairs?"

A man here and there moved restlessly, and Keegan went on. "Keep the affairs of the glen in the glen! That was the motto—for how long? No one knows. Iain Torrie, the policeman, down at the harbour, is useful enough to look after sheep-dipping and dog exemptions, and little pin-pricking bureaucratic regulations, but, as a policeman, he has no part in the real life of the township. Neither have the MacFies. The MacFies threaten the Tigh Mhor which is part of the glen indissolubly, and you would do nothing?" He thrust his head forward again. "Would you let them? I am speaking to you, Duncan red-head. Would you let the MacFies do their damndest?"

Duncan Rua twisted his shoulders against a corner of the dresser. Put to him like that he could not show his old resentment, which was only of the surface after all.

"But what can I do?" he half-muttered.

"You wouldn't go down and enlist with the laird?" Keegan said coaxingly.

Duncan Rua flared. "I'm damn'd if I would!"

"Of course you wouldn't. But I warn you—all of you—that you can't be hand-washing Pilates either. Something should be done, and if you won't do it another man must. That man is here."

Keegan had said his piece. He hitched his chair back, picked his glass off the floor, emptied it, and reached it towards Batt Sullavan.

Every eye was turned on Gawain.

III

Gawain took one stride forward. He did not look serious or grim or truculent. He was smiling a little, and the smile had a heart-warming devil-me-care friendliness that

Ardaneigh knew of old.

"You know where I come from; but I am of this glen too—some of my blood came out of it; and this glen taught me most of the things I hold by. Very well! you are my friends; and with the Tigh Mhor I, personally, have no quarrel. Let me tell you, straight off, that I am as much on the laird's side as I am on yours, and that anything I can do is for the glen as a whole. Is that clear? It is."

There were murmurs of assent, and Dinny said: "Begobs! it is."

"You have heard Major Keegan about the MacFies. He is right, of course, but to hell with the MacFies, I say! Listen! What I want is peace in Glen Easan, and I am now taking a hand in the game. Any objection?"

There was complete silence, and not even a head moved.

"No objection," said Gawain. "Good enough! Listen again! I am not telling you the hand I am going to play but it will be completely tough, and I propose to take help where I want it. Any objection?"

Again silence, but a young shoulder here and there moved eagerly.

"No objection—of course not! And listen! What I am going to do may get me into serious trouble, and I warn you that it may get some of you into the same trouble. For the last time, any objection?"

"No—no—no!" the murmur went over the room.

"They are all with you, Bart.," said Dinny, "and we are back to the old days, God be praised!"

Gawain grinned widely.

"Thank you, boys! I knew I could trust you." He lifted his glass. "Slainte!"

"Slainte! Suise!" came the murmurs as they drank with him.

He put his empty glass on a corner of the dresser, and went back to the fireside. The young fellows were whispering among themselves, and, at the same time, watching Gawain eagerly. He lifted a hand for silence, and looked them over slowly.

"I see some of our old shinty team here to-night," he said, and made the slow and tragic gesture of the Gael. "Some of the team we shall not see again, but we will play this game for them. I need not tell you that silence is the rule. Duncan Rua!"

Red Duncan stepped forward, but his face had gone white with excitement—and pride. "Yes, sir!"

"Batt Sullavan!"

"Yes, sir!" And Batt, ignoring the flap, vaulted the counter.

"Japus!" exclaimed his startled father. "The colt is feeling his oats—but why not he?"

Gawain did not call out any more names. He nodded at the two young men.

"I want six, and no more to-night. You two will know whom to pick. If you think any of them is not as tough as a woodbine gad do not pick him. We meet after closing time in Lukey's kitchen—by the back door. Come one by one—scouting order—and if a foot goes wrong to wake a certain young lady, there's a dead duck. That is all!"

He moved to the door, for now was the time to go before any comment or questioning. From the half-open door he turned and whispered confidentially:

"I am thinking that for an occasion like this Dinny Sullavan would have something put by. You can't trust Carnoch with it—nor likewise Keegan. Bring it yourself, Batt."

And he was gone into the night. The Highlandmen could question Lukey and Dave as much as they liked. Lukey did not know. Dave did not know. And Gawain himself was not too sure. But he had done one of the two things that he had told Iosabel he must do.

Chapter XIV
PARLAN GETS MARCHING ORDERS

I

THERE HAD been rain in the night—as some lads knew—and the rain was still sheeting thinly at nine in the morning. The shoulders of Stob Glas were mantled in cloud, and the waters of the loch were whipped greyly by a western breeze.

Lukey and Gawain were going up the road past the

township, and an occasional head appeared in a black doorway, and a friendly hand was waved. Gawain was wearing an old raincoat of David Keegan's, and Lukey's homespun, impregnated with natural oil, was showerproof.

"Blast!" said Gawain. "Is the weather going to be unsettled?"

Lukey turned to face the breeze and sniffed into it like an old hound.

"Na! This is' the last spit o' rain, I'm thinkin'. The wind is shiftin' north, and that's a good sign."

"Fine! I want a dry night."

"You'll mark I'm no' askin' you why?" said Lukey in a grieved tone. "You're keepin' your mind to yourself, but do you think the tinkers will listen to me?"

"That's your pidgin."

"But, man! I'm tongue-tied most times, as well ye ken?"

"And folk listen to you getting the knots out."

"Why wouldn't you do your own talkin'?"

"Because it will be Ardaneigh talking with your voice."

Lukey made his last appeal. "But look, Bart.! You know the way with me: I'd be hot enough inside to boil an egg, but to hear me talkin' you'd think I was shakin' wi' dread."

Gawain patted his friend's lean shoulder. "Yes, Lukey! But when you're done talkin' the other fellow knows exactly what you're thinking of him—the poor auld useless black pugger!"

"Oh, dom'-dom'-dom'!" cursed Lukey.

"And I'll be your witness for the second time."

"But goad be here! I have no law on my side this time?"

"A right going back further than law. Well! here we are!"

They had come to the mouth of the Old Road, with the big sand-pit yawning at the right.

"I'm in the notch now, whatever," said Lukey resignedly, and turned in at the gap at his friend's side.

In the shelter from the breeze Gawain paused to light a cigarette, and Lukey, clasping his hands behind his back, swayed his bent shoulders like a man weighted with years.

The camp looked to be firmly established, though the dead line was only two days off. There was no sign of packing-up anywhere, and the horses and donkeys were still at graze on the edges of the moor. The lurcher dogs, lying back from the cooking fires, merely cocked an ear at the visitors, for no tinker's dog will move to the attack until its master gives the word.

The MacFies had just finished their second breakfast, and the cooking fires were dying down here and there. Usually the tinker rises with the dawn, drinks strong tea, and goes under cover again, unless something is doing—and something often is. No one seemed to notice the two men moving through with studied leisureliness, but no one greeted them, and that was not customary. Ordinarily the two would be regarded as friendly men, and would be greeted pleasantly, and even invited to share what was going; now men and women looked away or looked down, and a silence closed in behind the two. The tinkers knew that this morning visit was not an ordinary one.

In the silence Gawain heard the sough of wind combing through the ragged grass on the crown of the pit, and the twittering of the sand-martins high up on a bluff. The rain had stopped, and the clouds had rifted to let the light pour down into this quiet hollow in the hills.

Old Parlan's van was in its usual place at the back of the camp. A little forward of it, at right-angles on the right, was Malcolm's van, and Malcolm, massive shoulders alean against the tail of it, was drawing carefully on the butt of a cigarette. His wife, that flaming dark woman, was taking the tin dishes round the back of the van. Parlan was sitting at the head of his tail-steps, his heavy bonnet over his ears, and his beardless jaws clamped on the short stem of his black pipe.

"Welcome you are, indeed!" he greeted his visitors. "I will get Sileas to put on the kettle again."

"Not for us, Parlan," said Lukey, almost brightly. "We broke fast or you turned over for a last nap—but I'll ease my legs whatever."

He pulled a hassock round, and sat down, like a closing two-foot rule, to face Parlan. Gawain did not sit down, but moved across to face Malcolm.

"You'll burn the tip of your nose off, you big bear," he said. "Try a fresh one!"

Malcolm put the fresh cigarette behind an ear, and went on drawing on his butt. The smoke-grey eyes never changed, but his massive head gave a small friendly nod. Gawain moved back, set a shoulder against the tail-piece of Parlan's van, hooked an instep round an ankle, and relaxed lazily. He was facing the camp, and could watch every movement; and the men were already on the move.

11

Parlan, after his fashion, waited the first move. Lukey gestured a hand widely, opened his mouth for speech, and cast an eye about him. He shut his mouth again. He had not heard any sound, but all the men and boys in the camp made a half ring about him, and not ten feet away.

Dom'! couldn't he do his own speechifyin'? Lukey said to himself, and looked at Gawain with a reproachful eye, but Gawain was interestedly following the flight of a sand-martin. Lukey tried again, making the same embracing gesture.

"Was it the morrow's morn or the morning after you'd be for breaking camp, Parlan?"

"You heard the news then, Lukey?" said Parlan.

"Ay did I!"

"Out of here, and one night at Cloun Aiternach, and then the long road out of all the lands of the Tigh Mhor."

"Sorry I was to hear it, Parlan," said Lukey.

"Sorry you would be, Lukey, I know." He looked far over Lukey's head. "And, indeed, you might be thinking that it would be the right thing for us not to go?"

"I was thinkin'—" began Lukey.

"And glad am I to hear it," said foxy old Parlan. "You do be speaking for the township we know, and if you would be saying to us: 'Stay ye and outface the tyrant,' staying we would be."

Parlan is carrying too many guns for you, Lukey, said Gawain.

But Lukey carried a long chaser of his own, and tried a sighting shot.

"Indeed I would not be advising you to break camp tomorrow or the day after—"

"That is a fine thing to hear," said Parlan heartily.

"Do you know the advice I would be giving you, Parlan?" said Lukey.

"It will be good advice," said Parlan.

"If I were you, Parlan," said Lukey, "I would break camp today."

Between wind and water, Parlan! said Gawain.

Parlan took the pipe from his teeth, and his mouth opened. "today—this day that's in it?"

"This very day, and any road you like." Lukey's hand gave him freedom of all the hills.

Parlan was giving himself time to think. He said consideringly: "It could be that a day back or fore does not matter—"

"I was thinkin' of this mornin', Parlan," Lukey stopped him, "say in about an hour's time—ah, weel! say two hours—the height o' day—and not a minute more."

You've met your match, Parlan, said Gawain. *That not-a-minute-more is the sting in the tail.*

There was a pause then, and it was broken by the hoot of an owl behind Lukey. There was something mockingly derisive in the note of it, and Gawain saw that it came from young Murrich. Lukey and Parlan took no notice. Parlan was driven almost to the direct question.

"I am not seeing it," he said, "not seeing it at all, but there would be a reason for breaking camp—in two hours' time?"

"It would be a good thing to do, Parlan," said Lukey confidentially.

"I am seeing it at last," cried Parlan, clapping hands together. "It is, that if we go a day before we need go the laird might not be so hard on us in later times."

Lukey might let it go at that, but he had his own rigid code. He was definite now.

"No, Parlan, that was not my meaning. I am speaking for Ardaneigh, and you'll be out of here in twa hours' time."

"Ardaneigh would be harder on us than the laird that walked on Ardaneigh?" said Parlan bitterly.

"No, Parlan! But Ardaneigh would stop a foolish thing being done."

"Far from me to do the foolish thing—if I could help it." Parlan rubbed the bowl of his pipe against his nose and asked cunningly, "You would say it would be a foolish thing not to go in two hours' time?"

"It might be a wee bit troublesome for all of us," Lukey mildly understated.

"What else is there but trouble?" said Parlan. "Ach! now I see it, and blind I was. Ardaneigh is for getting at the soft side of the laird and his factor by chasing the MacFies out of an old camp."

Parlan was trying to insult Lukey into showing more of his hand. But Lukey, having no more hand to show, was quite equable.

"Ah, weel! if that's the way there's no more to be said, and I am leaving it to you, Parlan. But you'll be minding that once, before our time, there was trouble with the Williamson tinkers in Glen Easan—"

"And blood shed, you would say?"

"Far from me to talk of sheddin' blood," said Lukey virtuously. "It was only by way of example, and, maybe, I shouldna have mentioned it." He stirred on his hassock as if about to rise.

Parlan was nonplussed. He had got his ultimatum and a warning to drive it home. He had a good idea why it had been given, but it had come unexpectedly, and the unexpected always disturbs the man of the long road who has constantly to look before and after. He flicked an eye down towards Gawain.

"This tall gent—he has lost his tongue?"

"Dambut! he has," said Lukey warmly.

Parlan rubbed his bald head under his bonnet, and said musingly, "You might be using his tongue for him, Lukey?"

You wise old devil! said Gawain and added aloud, "I'm your witness, Parlan, that this fellow Carnoch has absolutely no right at all to order you out of this camp at any time—much less in two hours' time."

"Someone might have a great right in his own mind," said Parlan wisely.

"Blatherumskite!" said Lukey on his feet. "Moreover, I gave no orders at all—not as much as would keep a child back from the fire—but only a bit of a ree-commendation. All I want is to keep the affairs of the glen in the hands of the glen, and scotch trouble where I see it risin' a head."

"That was three months ago," said Malcolm in his deep rumble.

"I am startin' now, anyway!" said Lukey, and turned as if to go.

Hold on! You've forgotten the important bit, said Gawain.

But Lukey had not forgotten. He stopped, thumped palm with fist, again turned to face Parlan, and gave the important bit as a mere afterthought.

"Hey, man! I was near forgettin'. Anither word of advice, Parlan!" He thrust a thumb back over his shoulder, and his voice lifted. "Some of they young lads might be for a bit of divilment, ye ken! Bent on doin' mischief somewheres and layin' the blame otherwheres! Na, na, Parlan! There'll be no mischief done. The Watch is in the Glen, Parlan, as in the old days." He swung a long arm. "Look you! from dusk to dawn, from there below where the demesne wall strikes the river, along here by wall and wire, an' down the wall to the loch-side again, the watch will be kept and well kept, and all Ardaneigh to keep it. I don't want any lad in trouble, an' that's why I'm tellin' you. Let him who dares try his hand. Let him! And if he's left starin' at the sky wi' sightless eyes don't blame Ardaneigh. The glen is ours, Parlan, and let the MacFies mind themselves."

He turned and went then, and Gawain strode forward to his side.

That was nicely done, Lukey! A guarded wall, and a dare and a warning. Hoy! Are we getting out with a whole skin?

III

The MacFies had no illusions about Lukey's recommendation. Lukey was the mouthpiece of Ardaneigh, and Ardaneigh had ordered them out of the glen in two hours—and they knew they had to go. They would resent that, and with nothing to lose, the resentment might become active and physical. It looked like it.

The tinkers spread apart, indeed, and let the two go through, but gathered again at each side and behind. If there was a straight path to the road the two might have made a quick getaway, but they had to turn this way and that about vans and tents, and that gave the tinkers an opportunity of chivvying them. The only thing to do was to move easily, show no tension, and avoid actual contact. The ringleaders were young Murrich and his two mates, and they were poison, Gawain knew.

Murrich sprang in front of Lukey, faced him, and walked backward with lithe ease, his arms spread.

"Way for Lord Lukey!" he shrilled in mock deference. "Way for the new laird of Glen Easan!"

The other two took up the cry, and circled round in a dancing side-step. Then Murrich swung off his heavy cap, made a saluting gesture, and at the same time swished the cap a foot in front of Lukey's face. The hard peak of a tinker's cap can hurt like a falcon's beak.

Lukey would not jerk or flinch from that swooping cap. Murrich noted that, and set out to make him. He leaped back and forth with his mates, yelled mockingly, "Way for Lord Lukey! Way for the new laird!" and swung his cap within an inch of Lukey's nose.

Gawain walked on the balls of his feet. *Next time I'll*

flatten you, you snake!

A deep voice spoke at Lukey's shoulder. "Murrich is askin' for a slap, Lukey?"

"It wouldn't harm the laddie, I'm thinkin', Malcolm," said Lukey.

"It did me no harm twenty years ago," said Malcolm.

"Very well so! A wee small slappie! I will."

And he did. The cap brushed his nose, and Lukey swung his arm open-handed. Gawain had actually never seen Luke Carnoch in action, and didn't think that a slap like that could be delivered by human hand. Lukey's arm seemed to lengthen by a yard, and become articulated into several links, and it did not seem to be aiming at any object. The loose arm, in sheer abandonment as it were, swung up into the sky, or across leagues of heather, or into the middle of next week. Unfortunately for Murrich, his jowl was somewhere along the course of that mighty curve. There was a smack like a whip-crack; Murrich went up and aside, tangled in his own legs, spun like a teetotum, teetered, sank down on his hams, and with two fumbling hands began refixing his head on his shoulders.

The thing was so easy and astonishing that someone laughed. Then everyone—but Murrich—was laughing. And in that laughter Lukey and Gawain walked safely out of camp. Malcolm walked with them.

"A wee sma' slappie!" said Gawain. "Gosh! and all the times I risked it."

"I learned it out of a cowboy book—I'll show you some time," Lukey volunteered.

Malcolm's voice was a deep musing rumble. "You're having your way, but why? Old Parlan will be out by noon-time—but what good will that do—now?"

"Dom'd if I know, Malcolm!" said Lukey.

"The three of us are in complete agreement," said Gawain.

"I am going today too," said Malcolm, "and I will make my last camp at Aiternach." He stopped and put a hand on Gawain's arm. "Whatever is in your mind, brother, I am a tinker for two days yet—till the MacFies are out of reach—and old Parlan and me will keep the young 'uns out of mischief whether you like it or not."

Malcolm turned back into the gap, and Gawain lifted a valedictory hand.

"Haste ye back, Malcolm!" he gave the Scots salute, and went heavy-footed, heavy-headed down the road. He had done the second of the two things he had to do. And the next twenty-four hours would show whether he had succeeded in putting himself inside the skin of a tinker.

Chapter XV
THIS IS ACT ONE
I

THE LAST weak snap of winter had failed in the month of May, and the night was dark and cool, but not cold. The stars were far and faint and few behind a thin film of mist, but no solid bulk of cloud loomed anywhere. Later in the night there would be the rind of a waning moon. Now and then a fluff of breeze came across from the flanks of Stob Glas, made the waters of the loch lap-lap on the shingle of Cobh Echlan, and rustled in the trees and undergrowth up the slope, not the dry rustle of winter but the meaty, full-lipped whisper of growing things.

These were the only sounds Gawain Micklethwaite heard, and he was listening intently. He was lying prone under a dwarf rhododendron back from the corner of the bathing house, and peering out below a green frond. But he had to depend on his ears mostly. The concrete platform was below him, and he could make out the grey of it, but he could not quite distinguish the steps leading down to the water; nor could he see the water until the breeze, ruffling it, sent faint white lines flowing in from the dark. He knew the tide was about full, for there was no smell of sea tangle. If anything were to happen it must happen soon, for it was only now that a boat could be brought in silently to the foot of the steps, and got away silently again without scraping over gravel.

Nothing happened, nothing seemed likely to happen; sea and shore seemed empty of life, and Gawain was beginning to consider himself not such a good campaigner after all. He had often thought that in more desperate places, so he was not unduly perturbed. And yet he would like to pull this odd chance off. Many men looked to him and trusted him, but they could stand disappointment in the event of failure. His little Alsuin had such an implicit trust that she could not see her knight fail; and Iosabel Mengues, his accomplice, was up at the Big House, subduing her woman's curiosity, and confidently waiting for his signal that the game was on. These two he would like to please. But if he couldn't, well! he couldn't, and that was all. He had diagnosed a tortuous mind, laid a bait, set a trap, and if the trap was not sprung there was nothing more to be done. He would just slip away day-after-tomorrow, his tail between his legs, and that was that. . . .

He went over the whole thing again to see if he had made a mistake anywhere. The MacFies—at least three young ones—had mischief brewing against Sanin Mengues and Oliver Dukes. Granted. Old Parlan, knowing the double edge to trouble, did not want any, and had deviously warned Gawain about it. Again granted. Malcolm, about to give up useless wandering, did not want trouble either, and had been playing herd on the three firebrands. Granted at once. These three things were certain. The rest was assumption based on reason—that fallible thing.

Gawain had assumed that Murrich and his mates would, in spite of Malcolm, remain determined on mischief. The thing, then, that Gawain had set out to do was to precipitate the trouble within certain time limits, direct it in a certain channel, and meet it where it emerged.

The tinkers would never be so foolhardy as to attack from the Sand Pits. They themselves had hinted that they could not be blamed if anything happened while they were twenty miles away. Therefore, order the tinkers out of camp, and set a time limit within which an attack might be made with a good chance of safety.

That had been done. The MacFies had gone that morning, and this night they would be camping at Cloun Aiternach on the Old Road, beyond and amongst wastes of unpeopled heather; and to-morrow night they must be camping twenty miles further on, outside the estate, amongst settled men, and altogether beyond safe strike-and-get-away distance. Therefore the attack, if made at all, must be made from the Aiternach camp, and it must be made this very night.

That is what Gawain had put up to the firebrands. To reach Aiternach from the Sand Pits would take five hours of slow progress. Then, whoever was in the conspiracy would wait for the gloaming to slip out of camp, and take, say, three hours in the tireless tinker lope to make Glen Easan; and, so, the mischief would be done not before midnight—and not much later, in order to give the raiders time to get back to camp in the dark; and, once in camp, every man, woman and child, even Parlan, even Malcolm, would give them an alibi. That was Gawain's reasoning.

But where was the attack to be made? Gawain had worked that out too. It would not come from the landward side. Through Lukey's mouth he had warned the tinkers that the landward side was guarded from shore to shore along the demesne wall. Then the only obvious place, the one safe place that possibly had long been decided on, was from the water, Loch Easan itself. Easy enough to lift a fishing coble in the dark, and the coble would belong to a township fisherman. Then up the other shore and across to a secluded landing place, and the one secluded landing place was here in Cobh Echlan. And right here in Cobh Echlan, on the bathing platform, was the tinkers' opportunity to wreak their bit of vengeance. It would not take a minute. And then up the shore to the river, and along it to the heather, the tinkers' "briar-patch." But the boat would be found, an Ardaneigh boat, showing traces of the purpose for which it had been stolen—an old dry whin root, or an empty paraffin can. . . .

That is what Gawain had reasoned out, but, remembering Murrich of the viperine face, he had reasoned a little further. Murrich would kill. Whom would he want to kill? Oliver Dukes, who had given him a month in jail, and kicked him across the road! And Murrich would kill two birds with one stone: light a fire in the night to hurt the laird, and, from cover, shoot the man that came to it—and get away as before.

Gawain had not told the laird so, but he knew that the MacFies had one communal firearm. It was an ancient, muzzle-loading smooth-bore, five feet long. Loaded with three inches of diamond-grain black powder and four inches of slugs or buckshot it was capable of bringing down a stag at fifty yards—or a man.

Time and time again, as he lay there in the dark under his bush, his mind went over all that, and he gradually recognised it for what it was: a colossal gamble that, in a moment of vanity, he had looked upon sanguinely. Was he a god that, in all this wilderness of loch and moor and hillside, he could draw to his hands at this one minute spot three wild and wily tinkers trained in heather-craft? Bloody nonsense!

And yet—and yet! the attack had been intended. Where else could it be made? Probably Malcolm, as he had proclaimed, had persuaded the firebrands not to make fools of themselves. That was it! But wait! Gawain had imagined himself in the skin of a tinker. Might not a wily tinker outguess him and hoist him with his own petard? Get inside Gawain's mind, and make the attack where an attack was wholly unexpected? Why not attack unguarded Ardaneigh, that had, high-handedly, ordered the MacFies out of the glen? Would it not be a fitting vengeance if Blinkbonny, or the Schoolhouse, or Dinny Sullavan's went up in flames this minute—in ten minutes—in twenty, for it was now past midnight? And he would be wholly to blame! . . .

Gawain's back went cold. He drew in a shivering breath, and was about to lift and turn his head to look up the slope, through the trees, towards the hidden township. And then he stilled, and gooseflesh ran up to his buttocks.

II

A sound had come in off the water. There was no mistaking it. A man, having once heard it, will always recognise it coming off the sounding-board of water: the muted yet resonant little click that a quiet oar makes against the check of a thole-pin. Gawain released his held breath slowly through pursed lips. Where excitement should have come there came, instead, an immense relief.

Pulled it off, dumbbell! Don't spoil it now!

He found the blood pounding in his ears to make them useless for a while. And, then, his eyes sensed a movement on the water. The May night was not so dark after all, or else his sense of sight had sharpened. The water was dark-grey, and pale ripples ran on it, and there, close at hand, a black bulk stood out against the greyness and the running ripple. It was a small boat coming in stern first to the foot of the steps.

There was no click of rowlock now. That first small sound had been made inadvertently as an oar backed water to bring the stern round. Gawain could not see the oars, but he could see the roily gleam of the swirl that the oars made. The boat seemed scarcely to move; there was the silent swirl of the pushed oar, a long pause, and another swirl. That rower was taking no risk. One suspicious sound, and the oars would dig in, and the coble shoot out into the dark. But the only sound was the lisping, fitful hush of the breeze up the slope and away.

And then came the solider little thud as the stern of the boat came to the steps. Another pause, a sibilant whisper, and activity between land and water. Figures bulked big, and crouched, and straightened up; one was definitely on the steps and there was a dry rustle that made Gawain pleased with himself—loosely tied bundles of brushwood and old whins, bulky stuff, but light, and inflammable as touchwood. And yes! that was the half-empty resonance of a can laid on a concrete step! . . .

Three men were on shore now. Three and no more! And there was no more pausing. Things happened with surprising quickness. The three men, under rustling bundles, were up the steps, on the platform, together in a clump at the locked door of the bathing house; and followed the soft thump and rustle of piled burdens.

There was a stir in a bush close behind Gawain. That was Lukey, and he was getting anxious. *Surely to goad! now was the time to jump the rapscallions afore they set the door alight—and once alight what was to save the wooden walls?*

But Gawain clamped his teeth. He knew what he wanted. He wanted the raiders caught in the act beyond any doubt, and he wanted light. He got both quicker than he expected. There was a gurgle of pouring liquid, a match scraped, lit and curved, and flame leaped flaring.

And Gawain leaped too, and his stentorian voice rolled across the water, and up the slope, and across the lawn to the Tigh Mhor itself.

"Suise! Muintir is glinne so! Up! men of the Glen! Hallo-o-o!" That last strident peal was a signal that one was waiting for.

Figures exploded from each side of the bathing house, and in a second the platform was in a turmoil. In the glow of the leaping flames eyes gleamed above the bosses of cheekbones, open yelling mouths showed the white of teeth and the red of tongues, and for a minute the night was alive and savage. And in a minute all was over.

Gawain did not drive in for the MacFies. In three bounds he was at the head of the steps, and in another bound he was down at the stern of the boat. And by heavens! he had been right. The ancient but deadly MacFie gun was there in the stern; the long barrel was cased in brown wood, and copper gleamed where the percussion-cap fitted over the nipple under the half-cocked dog-head.

Gawain did not hesitate. He picked the gun up and heaved it out into the loch. It would be in ten feet of water out there; at low water it would be in three, and might easily be recovered. No one must know about that weapon tonight, but, if things went according to plan, Gawain would never deprive the wanderers of one of their means of eking out life.

Gawain bounded back up the steps, and stopped at the head of them, crouched and ready for action. There was no need. He saw all there was to be seen.

Lukey Carnoch had not gone for the tinkers either. He had made straight for the flaming brushwood, and kicked and stamped it away from door and walls. Now, with his heavy cap he was beating at burning fragments close to the wood—and cursing. The door was smoking a little, but that was from the barely scorched paint. The scattered brushwood, saturated with paraffin, was still burning brightly, but now harmlessly, and lit up the whole scene.

Two of the young tinkers were already securely held. The third, lathy Murrich, had made an active bid to get away. He had dodged under big Sam Thompson's arm, and leaped for the woods, but red-headed Duncan Rua had taken the legs from under him as he landed. The two fell together, rolled, and came to their feet facing each other. Murrich, like a steel spring, his arms slashing, tried to dart this way and that for freedom, but Duncan Rua, solid as oak, drove close in, his hooked arms smashing at the body. The tinker staggered, went on his knees, and came upright again; and big Sam had him firmly at the back of the neck. He sagged, and would have fallen, but for Sam's holding hands.

Gawain saw that all was over. Not all! This was no more than a beginning to the really important things. He strode across the platform, kicked a burning whin root out of his way, and faced the scorched door. He had the key in his hand; Iosabel had given him one that afternoon. The Yale lock yielded silently, and he shoved the door open, felt for the light switch on the right, and the room glowed in yellow and brown woods. He stepped aside, and moved a hand.

"In with them!"

The three captives were bundled through, and six Ardaneigh lads went with them. Lukey looked round for dangerous faggots and followed; and Gawain brought up the rear, shutting the door behind him, and setting his shoulders against it. Long and hard-drawn breaths filled the room.

Lukey Carnoch was boiling inside, and, for once, some of the heat showed in his voice.

"Dom'-dom'-dom'-dom' fools! I wanted this quiet and canny, and ye—every dom' one of ye—made enough noise to waken the dead—an' it was you started it, Bart.!"

Gawain said nothing. If Lukey knew what his friend had in store for him he would go through the roof.

Gawain looked about him. Against the far wall of yellow pine was a teak bench, and a few teak chairs with lathed-seats were scattered about on the coir matting. At each end were curtained alcoves for undressing. There were no windows in the back wall, and the two windows in front were still dark-blue blinded as they had been during the black-out.

"Let them sit, boys—they're safe enough!" Gawain said.

The three were thrust, not roughly, on the bench against the wall, and sat with heads hanging. They had lost the game on their own chosen ground; now they would dumbly take what was coming to them, and surely that would be plenty. The six lads of Ardaneigh moved back to the wall at each side of Gawain. They had won the bout easily, but they were not happy. The excitement was over, and these Highland lads had a sneaking admiration for three young tinkers who had foolishly—but for cause given—attacked their oppressor and run their heads into a noose set by themselves—or by Sir Gawain. If their leader wanted to pull that noose tight that was another matter.

Lukey Carnoch stood at mid-floor and moved his hands impatiently: "We canna stay here all night," he complained. "What's to be done with the young wasters?"

Gawain pretended to consider that, looking up into the varnished cavity of the roof, and eyes were set on him anxiously. He was waiting for the next move, and it was outside his control.

"Deliver them up to the laird, would you say?" he said at last.

Lukey did not hesitate. "And have them jailed by Dukes! Na-na! Keep the trouble in the glen in the hands o' the glen, I always said."

"Well, Lukey?"

"The foolish loons did no damage worth while, an' this'll be a lesson to them. Put them through the gate and let them gang—that's what I would say."

Two of the MacFies lifted heads. Murrich put a hand across and felt his floating ribs. One rib at least had a crack in it. The Ardaneigh lads brightened up, and looked at Gawain hopefully, and Gawain said gloomily:

"It may come to that, indeed," and added with sudden bitterness, "and two roots apiece to set them on the right road."

Is that girl failing me? Gawain had pulled the curtain down on the first act, and could do no more. Everything now depended on Iosabel Mengues, whom he had trusted to raise the curtain on the second act. How that act would go must depend entirely on one man. That was the gamble that Gawain had taken, and it might end disastrously. Well! he had trusted Iosabel, and he would keep on trusting her, and he would wait here grimly for as long as he could—but his heart was sinking into his boots. . . .

A hand brushed the outside of the door behind his shoulders, and a solid thump followed. Without hesitation he turned the small knob and pulled the door open. A head was thrust in through the opening gap, and it was the head of Batt Sullavan, who had been set as outpost-sentinel at the mouth of the track on the main drive. The platform behind him was brightly lit. Batt's eyes were wide with dismay, and so was his mouth, and he was panting through it. He shut it for hasty gasps of speech:

"Goad! the Tigh is stirring—that shouting—two—ay, two people hurrying—on the lawn—this way—and the lights on—everywhere!"

Gawain had him by the collar and inside the door. *My choice one, Iosabel! Who wouldna follow thee?* Gawain's eyes were alight, and his heart again thumping. This was his exit. He lifted a finger, and his voice was a commanding whisper.

"Hush! don't move—don't make a sound! You are safe in here. Hold on till the door opens!"

He went out, and shut the door behind him.

Chapter XVI
A QUIET INTERVAL?
I

IOSABEL was unusually nervous all that evening, and her nervousness grew with the drawing in of the dark, so that she could hardly keep still. Her wise father did not fail to notice, and he frequently turned perplexed and cogitating eyes in her direction. There was no reason within the house for her agitation. Was the reason outside then? She had been meeting this flying officer rather frequently, and a certain intimacy had grown between them. Was she meeting him again to-night—by assignation? Was that girl of his in love at last? He was wise enough and tolerant enough to recognise that he could do nothing about it, but he could keep his eyes open—and not go to his own rooms early as was his custom.

The afternoon had been warm, and the sun-porch too warm; but, with the set of sun, a cool breeze had come off the water, and the hoarded warmth in the sun-porch was very acceptable under the pleasant glow of the hooded lights.

Some of the house-guests had departed that day. After dinner four that were left played bridge in the smaller card-room at the end of the terrace. In the sun-porch itself Iosabel had at last agreed to partner Sammy Veller against Dandy Dinmont and Oliver Dukes. Sanin Mengues did not play bridge. Once he had played a now-defunct game called whist, and thought contract bridge a superficially smart game governed by machine-made conventions. This would be the opinion of a good poker player, and Mengues, in his time, had been as good as any in the foothills of the Cordilleras.

Mengues read for a while, had a drink, smoked a long cheroot, and, a habit of his, walked up and down the long floor, hands behind back.

Iosabel played plain bad bridge to-night. She was a sound player as a rule, though sometimes impishly experimental, but to-night she was reckless and timid in turn. At a quarter to midnight she pushed the cards away, and said: "To hell with it!"

"The Lord be thanket!" said partner Sammy devoutly.

"Four quid you cost me already."

He yawned unashamedly. He had not been to bed until 4 a.m. the previous night, and, of course, nothing had happened. He was beginning to suspect Iosabel of one of her more elaborate joshes.

"Go back to your bed, Samuel!" Iosabel said meaningly, and went across to the glass front of the porch.

Sammy whispered to Dandy: "Come and have a snifter?" Mengues was quite aware that modern young women took snifters as they had never taken mother's milk, but not even modern young women cared to let this austere hidalgo see them imbibe at midnight. So Sammy and Dandy slipped into the house through an open window. They would have a couple of snifters at least; and, probably, some flirtation in the upper hall.

Oliver Dukes spread his muscular hands on the green baize, and looked at them gloomily. In better times he would have got Iosabel into intimate talk, but that young lady was not profitable these days. He was feeling surly, and his temper would flare at a touch; and that dour temper was set against one man: that fellow Micklethwaite who had begun all this, and had some intimate understanding with Iosabel. Dukes felt that he was beginning to lose the dominion that he had acquired over this half-foreign laird. He had begun as accountant-secretary delegated from his father's office in town, had gradually taken control from the laird's slack hands, and hoped to be an accredited Factor in the near future. But of late the laird was beginning to question things, and Dukes, making a false move, might easily find himself back in the town office. He lit a cigarette, rose to his feet, and moved towards the side-door. Iosabel stirred and turned head.

"Going out, Nolly?"

"Care for a breath of fresh air on the lawn?" he suggested.

"Don't think so. Later perhaps."

"I'll be in the Estate Office. Some papers to look over."

That should keep him from under my feet, Iosabel said to herself, and tried to peer through the glass in the direction of Cobh Echlan. All she could see was the reflection of the room behind her, the down-tip of her own nose, and eyes looking anxiously into hers. She wanted a clearer view, and she, too, moved towards the side-door. Her father stopped in his pacing.

"Something troubling you, Iosabel?" he enquired.

She halted, and hesitated before she spoke. Her voice

 was not sure, but she was sincere.

"I am frightened, Father."

"Frightened!" He came to her at once and took her hand. "Frightened, my dear?"

"The tinkers, Father! they mean mischief."

"Oh, the tinkers!" There was relief in his voice. He patted her hand, and looked down at her. "The poor wastrels! I can understand their resentment—but mischief!" He moved a contemptuous hand.

"They've been threatening and plotting," she insisted. "Gawain—Lukey, are sure of that."

"Gawain—Lukey, yes?" he was interested.

"They are afraid an attack will be made on the Tigh from the Aiternach camp. Oh, Dad! All the glen is afraid, and the lads of Ardaneigh are watching the wall to-night."

"My wall—you know?"

"Oh dear—oh dear! Was I disloyal? I knew, and I should have told you—but—but—"

"No, my dear! Things being what they are I am the last—the very last to know." He dropped her hand, and moved his head heavily. "The men of the glen looking after this house! It is a strange thought." He turned his back and resumed his pacing. Ardaneigh had something it would preserve—outside all quarrel—something worth preserving, something that he should help to preserve?

Iosabel slipped out the side-door, and down the steps to the gravel, her back to the lighted porch. Coming from the light, the night was very dark, and it was very quiet too. She could see the metallic green of the lawn where the light splayed, and the dark bulk of the nearer shrubs, but beyond that nothing: just the blackness of the trees fading imperceptibly into the greyness of the sky.

She looked towards Cobh Echlan, beyond the drive and the bracken ridge, but there came no sound from there, and there was no light. She was to look and listen for light and sound, and then she was to act. There was nothing. After a while she went back up the steps, but did not go inside. This was the place from which to watch and listen, until something happened—or nothing happened. She could see her father inside the porch looking outwards through the glass. Poor dad! she had given him something to think about—and she would give him more, God being good! And Gawain playing his part!

She thought she was prepared for any sound or sight, but when the two came almost together, she leaped six inches, gasped her heart down, and loosed a skirl of her own. Sudden light flared at Cobh Echlan, and the trees above it were in an orange glow that wavered and flowed and stayed; and on the flare a clear hallo-o-o cut across the night.

It is come—it is come! Mother o' God, help me now!

She drove the side-door open, and her voice, usually deep-toned, was shrill as a boy's.

"Father—quick. It has happened."

He was already at her side, for he had seen the flare through the glass. She pulled him by the arm.

"Fire—it is fire—at the Cobh! Listen!"

There came shouts from down there, angry and exultant, shouts that stopped short, but the trees were still glowing. Iosabel cried aloud:

"Mother Mary! someone might be hurt!"

She dropped her father's arm, and leaped. He snatched at her and missed, and cried after her: "No, Iosabel! Wait for help." But already she was running across the gravel.

He did not hesitate for long. He leaped and ran too, and he ran quite nimbly for his age, his red-and-white kilt flapping against the backs of his knees. But before starting to run, he put a hand on the jamb of the front door, and pulled down a switch; and, immediately, the whole lawn and drive, and the woods beyond, leaped into light.

II

When Gawain shut the door behind him he was rather dismayed.

Blow it! I should have remembered about those lights! But they had been installed since his time. Above the platform, a hooded arc-lamp sent a widening beam out across the water. That, of course, would be for night bathing in summer hot spells. He dodged away from it round the far corner of the house, but he could not get away from the illumination. An electric bulb grew out of a tree trunk above the track, and another, further on, was on a pole on top of a bracken mound. He kept away from the path and ploughed aslant through the undergrowth to the top of the ridge. There he had one look, and dropped flat.

But, still, he could not get away from the lights. There was a big one, far away, high up on the wall of the Big

House; there was one over the side-gate, another at the mouth of the track to the Cobh, and a fourth, gleaming through the trees, over the South Gate. And all these could be switched on from the hall-door.

But it was not the lights that made Gawain flatten out. Iosabel was coming along at the rate of knots, and her father was not far behind. Already she was across the drive at the opening of the side-track, and in a few seconds passed not twenty feet below him. She slowed down a little then, just keeping ahead of her father, who would overtake her—according to plan—about the time she reached the bathing house.

Only the two of you and no more! I don't know how you managed it, my darling, but you did.

Gawain had always feared a scurry of people from the Tigh: Sammy and his satellite Dandy and Oliver Dukes almost certainly, perhaps others. Mengues was the only man he wanted, and Dukes he would have kept away if he could. Well, here was Mengues, and there was no sign at all of Dukes, and he gave all the credit to Iosabel, instead of to Lady Luck.

He did not follow them to the Cobh. He slid down to the path, and ran for the mouth of it, where he dodged behind a tree and looked across towards the Big House. The clumps of shrubbery bulked black on the lit green of the lawn, and no one moved amongst them—or on the sweep of drive. He was glad of that. Sammy and Dandy he could hold, but could he hold Oliver Dukes? Dukes might easily spoil the gamble that had come off with such amazing success so far, and now was come the critical point. Yes, Dukes must be kept out of it at all costs, and Gawain was here to keep him out.

He turned shoulder to the tree, and looked towards the Cobh where all the trees were brightly lit. He brushed his hands definitely and spoke aloud: "Play it out now, puppets! and ring down your own curtain!"

A scrape of feet on the drive made him jerk and thrust out a head from the tree trunk. Two men were close at hand coming up the drive from the South Gate: a squat, massive man arm-holding a lean and shambling figure: Malcolm and Parlan MacFie, coming in a hurry, and in the open! Gawain's mind was already busy. This was a complication in the game that he had not taken into account, but he must take it into account now—and gamble on it if he could.

The two hesitated in doubt where the drive slanted towards the Tigh. They could see it outlined in the lights, and it looked secure and solid as a fortalice. In Rob Roy's day it would be going up in flames for what it had done to the MacFie.

Gawain stepped out from his tree, and walked across the drive. Here were two new characters, and he would let them play their own parts. What their parts might be he could not tell, but Fate, having introduced them, should be challenged boldly.

"A pleasant night for a ramble, my heroes," said Gawain easily.

The two turned quickly, and Malcolm took a half pace forward, his head hunching dangerously between his bull shoulders.

God help us! Is he in one of his moods?

The mood on old Parlan was plain distress. He was frightened, and threw his palms forward appealingly.

"Oh, sir, sir! are we too late?"

"Late for what?" Gawain said calmly.

Parlan, after his habit, could or would not answer directly. But Malcolm was forthright as ever. His voice rumbled harshly, but it was not strained by savagery.

"You know, and well you know! The lads got away on us. We came down on the ponies—and over the gate—to head them off. They are here?"

"Not far away," Gawain told him.

"Ah! the grip is on them," said Parlan resignedly.

Gawain stepped close to Malcolm, and bent to look into his face. That face was grimly set, but the terrible fighting glaze was not over the eyes. Gawain spoke lowly.

"There was a gun you and I used one November in Aiternach? I have it now."

"You stopped them?"

"So far, but there is a long road to go yet. Can you keep your temper to-night?"

"To-night I can."

"And you will do what I ask you?"

"I did it always."

"Always we trusted each other. Listen! Your three lads are down there in the bathing house." He pointed a finger. "Go ye down and see! Knock at the door and go right in, and do what you can do, using your head. Come on! there is no time to waste."

He turned and strode to the mouth of the by-path,

stepped aside, and let them go by, his arm gesturing them on urgently.

"Hurry! I hold the pass here. Do your best, brother, and it might be a good night's work."

From the side of the tree at the path-side he watched them disappear over the ridge between bracken banks, and Malcolm was again holding Parlan's arm. There would be a crowded stage now, and no other player must be allowed on it. It was then that a high voice hailed him from the side-gate beyond the drive.

"Hey! you fellow! What's all the rumpus about?" Oliver Dukes wanted to play a part too.

III

Gawain turned head, his shoulder hiding the lower part of his face. Oliver Dukes had turned up at last, and Oliver Dukes was in a hurry, like the rest of them. He had not recognised Gawain in the shadow of the tree, but in another second he would, and Gawain did not want that—not yet.

He must stop Dukes going down to the bathing house, but how? He could choose a show-down right here and now. Dukes was a big, muscular, long-armed fellow, in good shape, and might easily take it out of Gawain. That was only an incentive. But no personal urge must interfere with the big gamble. Let the show-down be postponed until the gamble was won or lost. The thing to be done was to keep Dukes off the stage for a matter of fifteen minutes or so, and if that could be done without rough work someone would acquire abounding merit—without wanting it.

Gawain stepped quickly behind the tree, and Dukes barked out:

"Halt there, damn you!"

Gawain dropped in the bracken, rounded another tree, showed himself for a moment, and again disappeared. And Dukes came barging across the road and in amongst the trunks. This was the game that Gawain was master of. He had learned it in a hard and deadly school, and more than once his life had hung on a split second. The thing he did not know was that this game he was now playing was as dangerous as any he had ever played, and that he was carrying a handicap about with him.

He played hide-and-seek with Nolly Dukes for all of fifteen minutes. He played it zig-zag up the slope aslant and away from the bathing house, and again tending down to the loch half-way up the Cobh: disappearing into the bracken at one moment, showing himself in a different spot half-a-minute later, and vanishing again. Sometimes the furious pursuer almost trod on him.

At the end of a quarter of an hour Gawain went finally to earth on the brink of a steep dip falling into a small hollow heavy with sallagh-willows. If necessary he could roll down and shelter in the sallaghs, but here on the edge grew a bush of laurel that suited his purpose, and he flattened out on the inner edge of it. By rolling twice he could go over the lip. He would rest there for a few minutes, get his wind back, and after that—? Well! it was up to Mr Dukes.

As he lay there, no one, not even an expert, could pick him out—or so he thought. He heard Dukes bullocking along the slope, slowing down and halting five yards away, waiting for the next glimpse. He had caught one or two strange glimpses already, and now he caught another. Gawain did not know that. He was lying on his face, and the collar of his old coat was turned up to hide his ears; and he had overlooked the fact that he was wearing Iosabel's plaque under a lapel—her knight's badge of jet and silver, with the spray of larch in emeralds. The very faintest gleams of light came between the trees, but the precious stones gathered every scrap of light into green fire.

And Oliver Dukes saw it, and he knew what it was, and he knew the man who was wearing it. And now that he was concentrating he saw the black bulk at the side of the bush. Very softly he moved his feet, and came nearer, and a little nearer, and yet a little nearer. Yes, that was his quarry lying there, the interloper he wanted to smite. He took one other stride, judged his distance, and leaped. His voice blared.

"Mickle'waite, you dog! I've got you."

Gawain had no time to move a muscle. Two knees hit him low down on the small of the back. An inch higher and they might have broken his spine. As it was a stab of pain shot through him, and his legs went numb. His face was driven savagely into the rough grass. At that moment he was completely at Dukes' mercy, and Dukes had no mercy in him.

It was the intuition—or experience—of the fighting man that warned Gawain. The weight of Dukes' hold was lifted off him for a second, and Gawain threw his head up and back. The savage, chopping blow that was meant for the back of his neck, landed on a hard poll. A spark flashed in his brain, and his face was again driven into the ground. He tasted his own blood. Had that blow landed where it was meant to, Gawain might have died then.

But Gawain's shoulders were free for a second, and he heaved them up, and twisted. He got over on his side, but no further, for Dukes was on him again, and flattened him out. But Gawain was on his back now, and a man on his back, like a fighting dog, is not helpless. Gawain was as nearly helpless as makes no matter. Dukes' muscular body was on top; Dukes' powerful hands were clamping his arms wide; one of Dukes' shoulders was grinding his lips against his teeth. Gawain had been right about Dukes; he knew now that his life was at stake. Dukes would kill him, or he would have to kill Dukes. He had been blazing with anger a moment ago; now he was no longer angry. To a man fighting for his life anger is only a weak emotion, and is replaced by something implacable.

Gawain, the Jungle-fighter, held down helplessly, used the only weapon he had. He had used it once before against a Japanese soldier, wrestler-trained, who had got him under: he had sunk his teeth in the Jap's shoulder, heaved over with him as the Jap tugged, and killed him with his bare hands. He could not sink his teeth into Dukes' shoulder, but he did his best: he got a deep mouthful of homespun with some hide below it, and hung on.

Dukes actually squealed like a vicious horse, jerked his shoulder to get free, and failed. Again, with all his force, he jerked, and Gawain's head and shoulders yielded so quickly, that Dukes went down on his side, and Gawain rolled him over, and was rolled over in his turn. And they went on rolling, clenched together, over and over right down into the heart of the sallaghs.

The sallaghs threshed about as if alive, as if trying to tear themselves up by the roots. Sometimes a head appeared, and was dragged under again; an arm heaved up and fell; a leg kicked into the open, writhed, and disappeared; and once a man yelped in agony and rage. And one man, like a fighting blue terrier, made no sound at all.

The sallaghs kept on threshing, but the threshing was not long-drawn-out. When two strong men are doing all they know to liquidate each other the fight never lasts long. The mechanism of the strongest man is frail in some places, and, at least, one man down there knew the places. In ten minutes, at most, the commotion slackened, stirred, and stopped abruptly.

Everything was still down there amongst the sallaghs.

Chapter XVII

THIS IS ACT TWO

I

WHEN GAWAIN shut the bathing house door behind him he left half-a-score of anxious men in the room. It was like a trap in there.

"Who is comin', you said, Batty?" Lukey half-whispered.

"Miss Iosabel for sure," said Batt pantingly, "and the laird—there was his kilt agen the light."

"My gosh!" exclaimed Sam Thompson, shuffling his feet, "if the laird comes in on us, our goose is cooked—and my name is mud, whatever."

"Dinna be a fool!" said Lukey. "The Bart. would never leave us in a hole-and-corner."

But their leader had left them in just that place, as he had intended from the beginning. He had thrown Lukey to the lion, and Lukey had to prove himself Androcles or bust. Lukey did not know that, or his confidence would have evaporated like snow in summer. That confidence still remained when something—a hand or shoulder—thumped at a corner of the house.

"Hush!" he whispered. "Not a soond, till we're sure 'tis himself."

There was a step on the concrete outside, and then the sound of a key feeling for the lock. And the snowflake of Lukey's confidence was gone. For the firmly-opened door showed Sanin Cejador y Mengues standing there, and his daughter Iosabel at his shoulder.

"What have we here?" Mengues said, sternly calm, and took two strides into the room. Iosabel came behind him, and shut the door behind her. She looked eagerly around. There were the hang-dog young tinkers—poor devils!—and the lads of Ardaneigh—almost as hang-dog—and Lukey Carnoch, dumbfounded! But where was Gawain? Blast him! where was he?

Lukey was asking himself the same question, differently put: *Whaur the bluidy hell is that black devil?* And Lukey was looking reproachfully at Iosabel: *What was the bit girl thinkin' onyway to bring the laird in on us that way—enough to give a man the heart disease?*

Lukey did not know that Iosabel's task had been to bring her father in on them just like that; and here her father was. What neither Iosabel nor Lukey knew was that Gawain, having set the stage, had decided that the men of the glen must play the game out without the intervention of an outsider.

Sanin Mengues, thanks to his daughter, was not taken by surprise. He realised at once that he was master of the situation. He looked sternly around him, but he was not feeling stern. Actually excitement was moving strongly below that cool exterior. There was Luke Carnoch, cap in hands, and trying to tear the cap in two, embarrassment oozing from every pore. There was the chauffeur, Thompson, trying to be inconspicuous behind a smaller man. There were the young men of Ardaneigh, moving feet, looking away from him, but not hanging their heads. The ones hanging their heads were the three glued to the bench: the raiding tinkers probably, but he was not acquaint of tinkers. The three had looked at him furtively as he entered, and then sank back into themselves as if this thing no longer concerned them. And, indeed, they were completely without hope now. They could expect no mercy from this stern laird, whose property they had come to burn, whose person they would have loosed shot at given the chance. And there was the incriminating loaded gun out there in the stern of the boat!

Mengues was also looking round for Sir Gawain Micklethwaite, and was surprised not to see him. But he was not disappointed. He could deal with this business in his own bailiwick, and, as Gawain had diagnosed, wanted no one to interfere between him and his people. Quarrel or no quarrel they were his people, and what was his was theirs too. He was the one confident man in the room. His voice showed it.

"Luke Carnoch, I asked you, what is the meaning of this?"

"Ye ken, laird, ye werna supposed to know anything about it," said Lukey desperately.

"In my own grounds?" said the laird unbelievingly.

"Your ain grounds, sure enough," said Lukey helplessly.

Poor old Lukey! thought Iosabel. *Hang on for your second wind, and that devil Gawain will be in to give you a hand.* She kept her mouth shut, knowing her father.

Mengues moved a hand. "There's burning brushwood out there." He pointed at the bench. "Are these the three—?"

"Och! the door was no more than scaumed," said Lukey hastily.

"Then a fire was lit against it?" the laird came back.

"Barely that, laird! There wasn't a bawbee's worth of harm—"

"There would be, but for—" He stopped and manifested impatience. "Look here, Carnoch! You must have known of this plot beforehand. Why was I not informed?"

He was getting on to Lukey's territory now, and in that territory Lukey was a formidable man.

"Ah weel! we had the notion of keeping it to ourselves in the glen—"

"And would I not keep it in the glen?"

Lukey met the laird's eye steadily. "There's a man in the Tigh Mhor who wouldn't." Lukey was getting his wind back.

"Leave others out of this," said Mengues firmly. "As the—proprietor of this estate I, personally, am dealing with this outrage here and now."

"Vera good, Mr Mengues!" said Lukey. "In your hands it is from now on. The responsibility is yours, and you will be judged all your days by the way you use it."

"Who will judge me?"

"Among others, yourself, the hardest judge of all."

Brave old Lukey! said Iosabel. *You are putting it up to my old fellow!*

And Mengues knew that it had been put up to him by this pliable, tough Highlandman. The responsibility was his. He could carry it off high-handedly by spurning these men of the glen for usurping his authority, by handing over the tinkers to Oliver Dukes for punishment according to a

Law without Mercy. And he would be judged by that all his days. For the men of the glen had saved his property, and his agent Dukes had driven the wanderers to lawbreaking. It was up to him. As regards the tinkers a decision must be come to in this room, and he wanted more time.

Luke Carnoch, you confounded old fox! he thought chagrinedly. *You are the man I want on my side in this infernal business.*

He was saved making a decision there and then. A hand fumbled on the outside of the door, and two sharp firm knocks followed. Iosabel turned quickly and opened the door fully. She expected to see Gawain framed in the light at this opportune moment; so did the relieved Lukey; so did most of the others.

But the light shone on two men outside the threshold: a tall old man and a broad-built younger one: Parlan and Malcolm MacFie, as everyone there, except Mengues, knew. Mengues moved in an orbit far removed from the tinkers.

Thunder and lightning! said Iosabel. *How many more strings is that devil pulling to-night?*

II

The three MacFies on the bench were so deep under in resignation that they had not lifted a head. But now they sensed something in the waiting pause that held the room, and looked up quickly. One look was enough, and their heads dropped as if nerveless. The same shiver went through the three of them, and Murrich alone made a small whimpering moan. They did not fear the laird of the glen or the men of the glen, but Great Malcolm, in the mood, was the father of fear.

Malcolm put a firming hand on his grandfather's arm, and the two came inside the door. Parlan's old eyes blinked in the bright light as he looked dazedly around him. But one dazed look was enough. He loosed his arm from Malcolm's grasp, brought his palms together and threw them wide in the abandoned, tragic gesture of the Gael; and his voice grieved as in a great lament.

"Oh—woe—woe—woe! This is the end now. And my three foolish young ones gone from me!"

He tottered forward, and sat down on the bench by his three young ones, making himself one with them. But he did not hang his head. He threw it up and looked blindly into some far distance. He made no more lament. He made no sound at all, but tears, one after the other, ran down his seamed, strangely still face. They glistened as they ran.

Iosabel felt a stab of anguish. "Oh, no—no, Parlan!" she said huskily. "It is not as bad as that. Oh! my poor Parlan!"

Malcolm did not take notice of anyone but his own, but now he claimed everyone's attention. He walked slowly across the floor, his huge hands on his hips, and his massive head forward. He looked down on his three tinker lads, and they looked down between their knees.

"Well—well—well! Ochone the day!" In the deep resonance of that voice was such a poignant note of regret that the lump, already there, would not leave Iosabel's throat.

He treated them like strayed children. "My poor laddie!" He tugged a black lock. "You foolish loon!" He patted a cheek with broad palm. "You poor dam' rogue!" He flicked Murrich's ear. "I'm not for blaming you now, for this is my fault. I knew the two men who snared you with your own wile, and I should ha' watched you closer. It is done now. Ye are the MacFies, and mind that. Ye will thole what is coming to ye as the MacFies always did—the prood ones."

He turned round slowly and faced Sanin Mengues who was seeing a real man of the broken clan for the first time. He had the dignity of an Indian-Inca chief, the same broad bosses of cheekbone, the same slightly slanted eyes, the same brown sallowness of skin, some far throw-back to Mongol origin—or Pictish. Some of that breed was in Mengues too, and he was not ashamed of it.

Malcolm's smoke-grey eyes hid his thoughts, but he was thinking. A man that was his friend and that he trusted had told him to come down here and do his best. What best could he do? Could he do any good at all at this late hour? And forthwith, Malcolm did his mighty best. The power of language came to him.

"You are laird Mengues of this Glen Easan"—he moved a slow hand—"and that is Parlan, the last chief of the MacFies, sheddin' salt tears. I am Malcolm his grandson, and I am failing him, because to-morrow I leave the road—the long road of the broken men. I will not be hounded by any man ever again. But that old man will keep the road, it is the only thing he has, and he will be hounded all his days." He concentrated all his force on Mengues. "You look a man of parts, laird Mengues, and you are of many acres. Why do you, the settled man, hound Parlan MacFie the wanderin' one?"

"No—no, Malcolm!" protested Iosabel. "My father would hound no one."

He turned to her, his hand up in salute, and his voice softened. "Miss Iosabel! O very heart o' corn! You would hound no one, but that old one is hounded. What harm! Scotland is broad and the roads are long, and he'll lead his bit tail till the end comes." He turned to Mengues again. "The power is with you, sir, and I'm not gainsayin' it. The foolish lads sitting there tried to do you hurt, and I failed to stop them, an' they were herded into your hands by men in this glen. You have the power now to put them to rot in jail away from the sun and the rain and wind on the brae. It is your right, and I have no more to say."

He went to his grandfather, and put a hand under his oxter. "Let us be going, Old One."

"You will not go yet," said Mengues quietly.

Malcolm's shoulders shivered, and the monster in him stirred. But he remembered his word to his friend, and kept a firm hold on himself. He turned slowly.

"At your will, sir," he said. "We are in your power, too, trespassers inside your walls."

Sanin Mengues knew what he must do now. He marshalled his thoughts, and his daughter, Iosabel, was in them. She had a standing in the glen, and she had won it for herself under handicap. She knew what the glen was doing, had a warm sympathy for the poor wastrels, and she was eager for himself to win credit. She would not have him called tyrant. Very well! he must justify her. At the back of his mind was the knowledge that the testing time had come, and that she had helped to face him with the test, having complete trust in him.

He turned about and surveyed the room. The lads of Ardaneigh, against the wall, were looking at him with a live interest. He was important to them at this moment, and that pleased him. Luke Carnoch, who had backed closer to his accomplice, Iosabel, would not leave his cap alone; and Iosabel's heart was in her eyes, and her mother's lovely mouth was trembling a little. Mengues felt a pleasant thrill of satisfaction, but his stern face gave no sign. He pointed a finger at Lukey. He would use Lukey.

"Luke Carnoch! You took the law into your own hands. Towards what end?"

Lukey jerked his head up. "End, sir?" Whatever end that dom' Bart. had in his mind, Lukey only wanted to stop trouble.

Mengues realised that his question was too leading. He must approach another way.

"For instance: you caught these young fools in action—what did *you* intend to do with them?"

Lukey would do some leading up too. He said:

"Ye ken, laird, the damage done wasna worth while."

"Well?"

"And maybe the loons are no' altogether to blame—"

"You are blaming me?"

"Na—na! It was this way I meant: if there was mischief we wanted to know where it would strike, so we—some of us—sort of instigated the puir laddies along a line of our ain, and met them at the end o't."

"And you would hold that as punishment enough?" The laird evinced unbelief.

"I'm no great believer in punishment," said Lukey quietly. "It never served a purpose that I could see. We had it in mind to keep the mischief—and the punishment forbye—to ourselves, in the glen, and not go outside for a cauld verdict." Lukey was doing better that time.

"Then you had punishment in mind?" The laird was inexorable.

A spurt of anger rose in Lukey, not against the persistent laird, but against the absent one who should have borne this heckling. He blurted out:

"Dom' well I know what I'd do my ain self!"

"Well?"

"No chiel has the right to do harm in this glen. Them lads there I'd run to the South Gate, and do you know what I'd do then, laird?"

"That is what I have been asking you," said the laird patiently.

"Twa roots apiece I'd gie them to send them on the road, and two more to warn them to mend their ways, and two more—"

"Oh, the unspeakable old savage!" cried Iosabel.

"Alas! I fear so," agreed her father.

"Who, me?" cried the startled Luke.

"Yes, you, Luke Carnoch," said the laird coldly. "You got rid of your responsibility, and you suggest sadism."

"Sad-sadism!"

"Gratification by the infliction of pain."

"My goad!" cried Lukey, but to himself he said, *Now we ken where our Iosabel got her humour. I'll be puttin' my haunds under this man's feet yet.*

Mengues moved a step closer to Lukey, and the eyes of the two men met understandingly.

"Very well, my friend!" said the laird. "The responsibility is mine. Will you take orders from me to-night?"

"I will, laird," said Lukey simply.

"Thank you. Bring these people along." His hand included them all. "Let them all come with me."

He turned, took Iosabel's arm, and the two went out on to the lit platform, and turned right for the track.

III

The father and daughter went up the side-path without looking round. There was no need; Lukey was obeying orders. Iosabel went quiet as a mouse, not daring to speak a word, fearing to break her father's concentration on his purpose. But inside she was praying over and over again: *God! make me proud of him—God! make me proud of him.*

At the drive the laird, without hesitation, turned left towards the South Gate, and another thrill stirred through Iosabel. The light was on over the gate, and the fresh, polished leafage of the beeches made a shining tunnel. Many steps sounded under that echoing arch, but they all sounded as one, for these men kept time like soldiers on the march.

The laird glanced at the lodge as he passed, but there was no sign of life behind the darkened windows. He halted close to the locked gate, looked up at it, and put a hand aside.

"Thompson! the key."

The wise old bird! and the trouble I had to get it! Sam was already at his laird's shoulder, the big key ready.

But the laird would not let his servant open the gate. He took the key from him, gestured him aside with it, and moved Iosabel back a little. The lock made a thick well-oiled click, and a pony nickered where two of them were tied to the wing-railing.

The laird lifted the ground-sneck and opened one wing of the gate. He opened it wide, and dropped the sneck-rod into its hole in a granite stone. Moving unhurriedly, he opened the other wing and secured it likewise. He heard the long-drawn breaths and stir of interest behind him, but he took no notice. He moved to mid-gate, and reached his right arm towards Iosabel, and she grasped it close with both hands. He looked out into the road through the open gate, and saw it lift and fade and curve into the darkness—the beginning of a long road over the broad of Scotland. He raised a hand above his shoulder.

"Luke Carnoch, I will speak to the old chief and his grandson."

"Here, sir!" called Lukey promptly. Parlan and Malcolm came up from the rear with Lukey, and the laird inclined left towards them. Malcolm was as solid as ever, but Parlan had shed his despondency and would use his tongue if the laird gave him time. The laird did not, and the laird did not beat about the bush.

"That the MacFies have been hounded I regret. It is my duty to undo all that can be undone. The camping grounds at Corran, the Sand Pits and Cloun Aiternach are your camps. Use them as you have used them time out of mind. Go now in peace. But wait!" He flicked a finger as if recalling something. "We must not forget the three for punishment. Luke Carnoch?"

"Here they are, laird!" Lukey had already bustled them forward unceremoniously. They were still shuffling their feet and avoiding eyes, and not at all sure whether they were for hicks or ha'pence. The laird was extraordinarily stern, and no one would have known that he was enjoying himself. He said:

"I hope a certain gentleman will restrain himself." And his daughter snorted softly. He ignored the three lads and addressed himself to Parlan. "Two things I have been told: the affairs of the glen should be kept in the glen, and punishment serves no purpose. The onus is on me, and these two things I will try. Take your three young ones and go, and be not hard on them, for, indeed, they have served a purpose to-night. This affair is now finished."

"It will be remembered for all time, laird Mengues," proclaimed Parlan.

Malcolm brought his hand to brow and cut it away in a military salute.

The laird lifted a finger. "You said you were leaving the road, MacFie?" he enquired.

"To-morrow, sir."

"You might come and see Luke Carnoch and myself," the laird told him.

"I am your man, laird," Malcolm said deeply, and a light came to that sombre face. "Good night, Miss Iosabel! And a good night's work!" He was remembering her man Gawain then.

The men of the glen watched the men of the roads go. Old Parlan was mounted on one pony, his long shanks almost reaching the road; Murrich of the cracked rib rode the other. They were moving in a close clump at the roadman's lope, and disappeared round the curve into the dark.

Iosabel was kneading her father's arm, her shapely mouth trembling, and she was whispering to herself. *Oh, my dear father! Oh, my noble father! I knew—I knew—I knew!*

Sanin Mengues turned round and faced the quiet men of the glen. They had come up in line close behind him and Iosabel, Luke Carnoch on the flank. They were a guard of clansmen at the shoulder of their chief. That thought stirred in him, but his voice remained equable, friendly, subtly confidential.

"Many things happen by chance, my friends, but it is possible that chance played little part to-night." (*And who could fool Sanin Mengues,* thought his daughter.) "I am carrying out my dear daughter's wishes, and my own wishes too. Whatever foolishness may have been we will forget until we can laugh about it. Let us make a fresh beginning. Indeed, you have made yours to-night, and there is mine." He swung a hand across the open road. "The South Gate is open. It will not be closed again, not even one day in the year, so that in time there will be no authority to close it. I am grateful to all who gave me this opportunity, and I welcome your fresh co-operation in Glen Easan. Luke Carnoch, you will come and see me to-morrow?" He finished abruptly.

"To-morrow, sir—and many of them," said Luke softly.

"Then I bid you good-night, my friends!"

They opened a way for father and daughter, and saluted smartly as they went.

Iosabel had every cause to be happy, but, as usual, there was a small cark of care. Where was that fellow Gawain? the man who had planned all this. Kept some things up his sleeve, and then stepped aside to let wandering men and settled men work out their own salvation! Surely he could not be far away at any time—and he could not be far away now. Then where was he?

Luke Carnoch was asking himself the same question; so were the lads of Ardaneigh. And so, indeed, was the laird of Glen Easan, for he felt that Gawain had been moving in the background all the time—from the very beginning.

But where was Gawain Micklethwaite?

Chapter XVIII
THE CURTAIN IS DOWN

I

THE LIGHTS were still on, but they shone faintly on the ridge half-way up Cobh Echlan, and they were barely reflected into the hollow where the sallaghs made a dark-grey patch. A bit of a tornado had shaken that patch not so long ago, but the tough stems of the sallaghs had borne it well.

There was no stir down there for a long time; then a branch swayed, and a black head emerged, low down. Some sort of quadruped moving awkwardly on all fours! And on all fours it essayed the slope to the head of the ridge. There the faint light shone on it, and it proved to be Gawain Micklethwaite. A sorry figure. His nose and mouth had been bleeding, and blood was drying on his chin; one shoulder showed white where a jacket lapel and the neck of his pullover had been torn away; but the other lapel still showed a green gleam where glowed the badge that had betrayed him.

Still on his hands and knees, he shook his head like a hurt Spanish bull, and his voice rumbled indomitably.

Fine! dam' fine! The last thousand feet is always the worst.

On one side, below him, the water of the Cobh shimmered a pale and darker green where the light splayed and failed; and down the shore he saw the glow through a network of branches, where the arc-lamp still burned above the platform. Down there he had set a stage and left it, and he wondered if the play was still going on. But he did not wonder much, for his mind had a dulling cloud over it, and was inclined to wander if he let his grip go.

He was in no hurry. He felt satisfied in a dull sort of way. The night and the field were his; he had vanquished the challenger; and brought his lady's badge off the lists. That is all he wanted at the moment. He turned over, sat down carefully, and moved a hand round to massage the small of his back. His legs were still without pith, but they had sensation again, and in a short time he would move erect under his own steam.

He looked down the slope at the dark bulk of the sallaghs. *I know I didn't kill you—you passed out in time. Would you mind getting a move on—or must I roll down again and see? All right! I'll give you five minutes.*

He waited, and put his head between his knees, for he was feeling sickish. It was nearer ten minutes than five when the sallaghs again stirred, and a figure in black-and-white emerged: black where his tweeds remained, and white to show shirt and hide—and that was most of his torso. That was Oliver Dukes, and he did try not to climb the slope, but moved off waywardly along the hollow towards the drive.

Strong on your props you are, said Gawain, *and good at a night stalk, blast you!*

But Dukes was not so strong on his props, and he was moving rather blindly. Once he stumbled on a root, his shoulder struck a trunk, and he fell and rolled twice; and it was minutes before he regained his feet and went on.

It took Gawain some minutes, too, to get down to the shore, and he did it by inching along on his posterior. The tide was on the turn, and the ripples were barely lapping the bank of shingle. He slid down cautiously until he reached the water. In fact his shoes were well in, and full, but he did not mind that, for the coolness revived him. He felt for the water with a hand, scooped it, and brought it up to his face. A trickle of it stung his lips, and the darkness of his hand, when he brought it away, showed that blood was still oozing. Slowly and fumblingly he laved nose, mouth and chin, shivering a little, and his breath quivering.

Then he hitched back from the water and looked about him. He could see the bathing house further down, and the arc-light blazing out across the platform and glinting on the ripples of the loch. No one moved down there, and the door of the house was shut. There was nothing to tell him that his stage was dark and empty, and the curtain long down. He was not caring a great deal.

After a while he got to his feet, and balanced himself swayingly. His lumbar regions ached, but he could feel the shingles under his soles as he stamped, one foot and then the other. Using his hands for balance he moved shuffle-footed down the beach. The tide still covered the bottom steps, but he moved inwards on the slope, and so reached the corner of the platform.

And at that moment the lights went out—all the lights right up to the Big House.

It is all over, said Gawain tonelessly, *and mice and men are gone abed—and I'll make mine next week or so.* From somewhere a childish sorrow came to him that he was left alone here in the dark—and forgotten. But, indeed, maybe he deserved to be forgotten, for, maybe, he had failed. He would have to thole that as he had tholed worse things, and a poor devil can't do better than his best.

He moved across the platform to the door and felt it over. It was locked, and there was no key in the lock. He had a Yale key in his pocket, but he would not use it. There was no need, for no sound came from inside. There was no burning brushwood now, but there was still a faint odour of paraffin.

It is over—all over! They are gone! I will rest a little and go too. He sat down on the bench close to the door, and drew in long slow breaths. The night, he noted, was not so dark now. The high haze had cleared from the face of the sky, the stars scintillated, and the rind of the moon was over the hills. There was one degree of frost, probably, for the bulk of Stob Glas was outlined strongly against a glow of faintest pearl. And the breeze had died to the faintest breath.

That mauling fight up there in the hollow had been primordially destructive, and Gawain was more spent than he knew. To get down as far as this had taken most of his reserves. There was a sound of many waters in his ears, and darting purple streaks before his eyes. He put a big hand over his diaphragm.

Hell! I'm going to be sick. Hold it, brother—hold it a minute! God! all the times he had been sick in the Jungle—sick, and half-mad, and deadly.

He went across the platform on hands and knees, and felt for the first step. The steps were wide and low, and he sidled down like a crab, until a scouting hand found the water below him. He curled there on the broad step, resting on his forearms, and empty and desperate sounds were wrenched from the recesses of him.

Hang on! If you topple you drown, and that won't be much better.

II

He had heard no sound. He heard no sound now. But a firm hand was over his back and under his oxter, and a second cool hand was supporting his dank brow. And then a soft depth of voice said huskily:

"Oh, my poor boy! my poor boy!"

"Dam' sorry!" said Gawain in a gasp.

Her thigh was against him now, and she was supporting most of his weight, and he felt the extraordinary vitality of her. After a time he said:

"I don't mind if I drown now—but you come too."

"Not that way—yet. You are better now, boy?"

"A king on his throne—pah!" said Gawain, and his lips stung. "Here we come, ma'am!"

He got to his knees and then to his feet, but it was her vigorous young body that bore the brunt, and he abandoned himself to her as they mounted the steps, and swayed across the platform. She put him sitting on the bench with a small clump, and sat down close to him, an arm still around him and her breast against his shoulder. Her heart was hurting her with its beating, so full of anguish and yearning.

"Miss Iosabel Mengues, I presume?" he said politely. "You smell nice."

"My goodness!" she said, holding herself firmly. "Did you fall down somewhere?"

"Oh, curious Eve!" he murmured, and steadied his voice. "Wait! wait now! First I am begging your pardon for doubting you—"

"Forget it! How are you—like this? Just a moment!"

She found a scrap of handkerchief somewhere, and was dabbing his mouth gently.

"Wow!" he exclaimed, and caught her hand, and would not let it go. He knew of old, that he would be wandering in a moment, but he would do his level best to be sensible.

"Your pardon!" he said. "Here I was in the dark, the lights out in my face, and me as lonely as a lost pup! And I thinking you had forsaken me in my need."

"Oh dear!" She steadied, and said quietly: "I came as soon as I could."

"I should have known that. Isn't it a great pity I can't keep my mouth shut? But don't mind me for a bit. Look! if I was lonely for you beyond the mountains o' the world would you come looking for me?"

Her voice vibrated through him. "I would find you at the Well of the World's End."

"Fine—oh, fine! What are you wanting to know, ma'am?"

"You didn't fall down—was it Oliver Dukes?"

"It was, ma'am—"

"Oh, the brute—the big brute—!"

"And me too! Ay, faith! I hurt him." His shoulder snuggled against her, and his free hand came up under her nose. "I'm a prood devil, and your champion, and a rough fighter, and I hurt Oliver—Roland whaur he lives. You did not meet him on the road?"

"No. He's in his room—his light went on." She was going to shake him, but, instead, tightened her arm. "But why—oh, why must you hurt each other so? Why fight him?"

"To stay in life, ma'am, and the invitation was urgent. I thought I had to keep the stage clear for your father and Lukey, and Malcolm—to say nothing of a bit of a dark girl with a grave and generous mouth."

It was strange that at that moment he had no interest in what had taken place inside the bathing house. That was in another dimension. He knew that he was wandering in a world of his own, and opening his mouth too wide, and saying things that he would have kept behind his teeth in a third dimension. He could not help himself.

"A rich and sombre mouth! Many the time I wanted to kiss it. Och! I'm a hurt bairn wantin' to be kissed wi' the kisses of her mouth. No—no!" He pulled himself up and drew his shoulder away. "Forgive me, Iosabel dear! I'm just wanderin'. You'd better take me home to my bed."

Iosabel was not going to loose any of her emotions with her man in this state. Her voice was cool and firm.

"Yes, Gawain, I'll take you home to your bed. Up we go!"

He drew in his breath, and steadied himself on his feet, and the two went off linked together, his arm over her shoulder, and hers round his waist; and her shoulder and hips and long thighs holding and yielding like steel springs. The waywardness of his feet, his weight on her gave her a poignant motherly feeling that suppressed fear.

They went very slowly but unpausingly up the track to the main drive: and Gawain kept telling himself to keep his mind on his feet and not be blethering heart-openly but foolishly. But another self that was a real self kept on talking softly.

"Dinna let anyone mind me! I just keep on haverin'. I had a bad time 'way out yonder east of Suez, and times I was taken bad. That is why I didn't come back before. And that was what was between us two—a wall o' fear—"

"You are all right now, my dear?" said Iosabel softly.

"Och aye! Only to-night I was back in the Jungle for a bit—and I'm not right out of it yet. I sunk my teeth in his shoulder—and blood has a salty taste. No—no! that was a Japanesy wrestler. To-night I got a mouthful of tweed and it tasted like heather. I'm only mixed up in time and place."

"Oh dear!" whispered Iosabel in distress.

"Don't worry, girl! To-morrow I'll be just grand—but sair. There'll be a nightmare or two, but, if I could reach out and find your hand, everything would come right."

"There's my hand then," she whispered, and put her hand across and took his; and he pressed and loosed and pressed hers to get the feel and pulse of it.

Out on the drive he paused, but she turned him towards the South Gate. "Right up to Blinkbonny," she said.

"Of course! Do you think I could let you go? I was only stopping at the place we first met. An intolerant scrap of enzyme, I called you."

"Truculent was my word for you."

"Ho-ho! and look at me now holding on to you. When I hold you like this, and you hold me like that, you are part of me, and we are one in flesh and blood and spirit."

Her breath and her voice fluttered. "You have a nice way of courting me, Gawain."

He jerked. "I'm no' courting—I never courted you—"

"What were you doing then?" she asked coolly.

He turned head down and sniggered into her hair. "Gosh! that's right! I was making love to you from the beginning. I talk too much, Iosabel, and to-morrow I'll be right sorry about it."

"You may not remember?"

"I will, and I'll be ashamed to look you in the face—"

"Not meaning any of the things you are saying to-night?"

"But I do—and more—twice more."

"So long as I know, you can be ashamed to your boot heels," said Iosabel comfortably.

"And I'll be tongue-tied, looking at you, and wondering how every time you are more lovely than my memory of you."

"Now I would call that love-making," said Iosabel.

"I'm dumb from now on," said Gawain, and he did not open his mouth till they got to the South Gate. He was steady-footed now, moving along head down and letting Iosabel do the steering.

"This is the South Gate," she said.

"I doubt if I can crawl over it to-night." He shook his head, and found hers, and smoothed it softly with his.

"It is open," she said. "Look! it is open wide."

He lifted his head and saw the dark gape against the grey slope beyond.

"So it is," he said, but with no great interest.

"My father opened it," she said proudly. "Alsuin's road will never be closed again. We pulled it off, partner."

"Och! that's nothing," he said carelessly. "That was bound to happen some time, and the two of us only gave it a push behind."

He was still smoothing his head against hers as they went up the slope.

"Poor auld Lukey!" he murmured. "And poor Sanin Cejador y Mengues! I am sorry about them."

"You can't be, Gawain!" she cried. "They are meeting to-morrow."

"That's it. There they'll be the two of them, to-morrow and every morrow, patching things up this way and that, and a bit of a girl under their feet, and she—that one—the interferingest young woman I ever met."

"What would you suggest she should do, Gawain?" Her heart was beating against him.

"I know that too," he said cunningly, "but you don't catch me telling you—not to-night, ma'am. Hey! did I tell you that I'm off to-morrow—or the day after?"

"To-morrow—or the day after! No?"

"As ever was! To the Karakoram Mountains—a long road, and I'm no' well off. But I'll manage by travelling tourist and third class, like better men. I have no bluidy pride, and if you were thinking of coming with me you'd have to pay your way fair and square, and no nonsense."

"Are you inviting me?" asked Iosabel, keeping her voice matter-of-fact.

"Gor'llmighty! I have up and told her already. But what harm? Day-dreaming about it I used be. A year in the mountains—or more—and then we'd come home, and I'd be looking for a job—and a job might be agoing in the vicinity, round here, not far off, close at hand as it were. You know? Just to keep an engineer's wife in a frugal way. Nice dream?"

"And a nice word, Gawain: wife—a wife—your wife! Gives one a stir inside. I think I'll consider your proposal."

"Proposal?"

"You've just proposed to me."

"Goad be here! What about Queen Alsuin's consent?"

"We will put it up to her to-morrow."

"Then my goose is cooked," said Gawain hopelessly. "You are her Princess."

"Alsuin and I cooked your goose a week ago, my man—only a week! Poor little Alsuin! And this is her saluting point."

The two pivoted with care, and looked up the slope to where the squat white house glimmered. They each made a saltire cross in the air.

Poor little Alsuin! She will not know jealousy yet—and to-morrow she has her road. That was Iosabel, who could not know how jealous Alsuin was.

"She will be asleep, the little one," whispered Gawain.

"I pray. There's a light in the kitchen window?"

"Two good men in there: Lukey and Dave waiting to give me a long drink. And gosh! I need it."

"So do I," said Lukey, and rose from the side of a bush on the margin of the road. He came across and said: "Thu! thu! thu! You took your time, and my timper is gone."

He did not tell them that he had scouted as far as the Cobh, had heard the murmur of their voices at the bathing house, and come up the drive ahead of them. Luke was another of the loyal ones.

Iosabel released some of the strain. She had been holding in anxiety tinged with fear, and strangely mixed up with agonised happiness. Now she blurted out, her voice lifting:

"Lukey, he's hurt—fighting Oliver Dukes—like bulls! I tell you he's hurt—and wandering!"

"Fair play is a jewel!" protested Gawain, pulling himself up. "Dammit, girl! give a man fair play." He put a hand on Lukey's shoulder. "I'm a plain, journeyman fighter, Luke Carnoch, you would say?"

"You'll do to take along, as the cowboy said." Lukey put a steadying hand under his elbow.

"Fair enough! Yonder Dukes is tough, and he had two points up before I knew. I drawed him away from your storm-in-a-teacup—we'll talk of that again—and I was under a bush when he hopped me, and we rolled down a mile, and brought up in the forest primeval. We fought under the roots of the trees, and kicked mighty trunks flat, and thrust our heads through the branches a hundred feet up, and rolled another mile. And at the end—a week I would say—I was on top, and he was under, and he was as still as a toad after the harrow passes."

"You killed the hound?" said Lukey hopefully.

"No. A year ago I would. I had him under my hands, and I would not kill. The trouble was gone. That's what I have been telling you, Iosabel." He squeezed her shoulder.

"And a lot more," said Iosabel, "and now it's bed-time. Come on!"

The three went up the road together, and Gawain was more under his own steam now. He was feeling strangely light and carefree, and wanted his friends rid of the anxiety that he sensed. He patted Iosabel's shoulder and squeezed Lukey's arm inside his elbow.

"Boys and girls, don't be worrying! I'm all right now, and I'll be better to-morrow. Juist a wee small rifty showing the things I should be keeping to myself, and to-morrow I'll have a patch on it. I wish to glory, young Iosabel, you wouldn't talk so much."

Iosabel gave a small chuckling snort. "To-morrow I do my talking," she said, and moved her head against his torn shoulder.

"You'll let me off a few things, won't you?" he said.

"Not a single thing, Gawain."

"In that case, there's another thing you should know."

"Yes, Gawain?"

He whispered it to her: "I like you, Iosabel."

"I like you, too, Gawain."

"There's love as well, of course! And with love and liking eternity is only a hop-and-a-jump. Hush! not another word out of you, Chatterbox!"

They came round to the front of Blinkbonny, and

 Gawain firmly removed their arms, and stood up steadily on his own feet.

"Hush now!" he warned. "Dinna waken our little one!" He put great dignity in his whisper. "Luke Carnoch, you will convey this my lady to her bower, and—"

"Nonsense!" she stopped him. "In this my own glen—all of it—and I want to be alone."

She was face to face with Gawain. She put a hand on each cheek, and drew his head down. And very softly she kissed his bruised mouth.

And then she was gone.

THE END